Ruthless

Out of the Box, Book 3

Robert J. Crane

Ruthless
Out of the Box, Book 3
Robert J. Crane
Copyright © 2015 Midian Press
All Rights Reserved.

1st Edition

Author's Note: With the exception of the prologue, this book takes place about nine months after the events of *Limitless: Out of the Box #1* and almost three years after *In the Wind: Out of the Box #2*.

Prologue

Fifteen Miles Outside Omsukchan
Magadan Oblast, Russia

The revolution was, in fact, televised, though it was a mercifully short affair. Matfey Krupin had watched it all from the front lines, in Red Square, when the army came marching in to support the people against the tinpot dictator that had held an iron grip on the presidency for more years than a youth like Matfey could even remember. The fires of revolution had burned, brighter and less violent than the one a century earlier, and more justly as well. Matfey had cheered when the word had come through the cold and frigid crowd that the president had fled Russia for good, and the exultations of the populace, the wild enthusiasm for a new and genuine democracy, had carried them through the three months since.

Three months of hard work for Matfey and his colleagues.

Now he was standing here, in the freezing cold outside Omsukchan, this godforsaken corner of the Far Eastern Federal District, in a place everyone outside of Russia would just call Siberia, and looking at a mountain. The mountain stared back, implacable. The roar of the army truck's diesel motor behind him was the only sound in the air as Matfey stood, staring, waiting for his escort to finish his piss break.

"Froze before it even hit the ground," Boris Pasternack called to Matfey, drawing him out of his moment's quiet thought. There were trees lining the road around them, though calling it a road might have been generous. Matfey had been raised in Moscow; to him this had the look of nothing more than a gravel track covered over with some snow. Tire marks were the only indication that it had seen steady use; a most curious thing to see this far out on the frontier, especially when the records indicated that the facility at the end of this road had been closed after the fall of the Soviet Union.

Secrets and lies, Matfey thought, *these are the tools of the trade for the liar-in-chief,* his name for the previous administration's head.

"Come on," Boris said again, trudging toward him over the fresh snow. "It's up here." Pasternack wore the standard army hat, his colonel's rank evident by three stars on his coat and hat. The coat looked somewhat warm, Matfey reflected, but not nearly as much as the coat he had brought. God knew how many hours they had spent on trains to get to this corner of the federation, but they had all been miserably cold.

Now, he stared at the mountain. *Almost there.*

"I haven't asked you yet about your organization's name," Boris said, stepping up into the cab. The heat was roaring, and only a little of the chill followed them into the cab. Matfey hurried up into the tall vehicle and shut the door behind him, rubbing his gloved hands together while glancing at Boris. The army man's cheeks were scratchy, newly grown beard coming into its own now.

"What about it?" Matfey asked, still rubbing his fingers together. They had the ache upon them, down to the bones. Matfey had felt it before, on the coldest days in Moscow. Somehow it felt even worse in this place, this inhospitable hell.

Boris shifted the truck into drive, and the vehicle began to rumble. Matfey fumbled for his seatbelt, numb fingers finding the old lap belt. The truck had been waiting for them in Omsukchan when they had arrived, the local garrison ostensibly glad to part with it for someone of Boris's rank. They had kept their distance, though, Matfey had noticed. Possibly resentful of the change in rank accorded a supporter of the revolution like Colonel Pasternack, Matfey thought. Possibly.

"It is a strange name for an organization such as yours, is it not?" Boris asked, shrugging as though it were nothing but a minor conversation point. "'Limited People'?"

Matfey smiled. Of course, Colonel Pasternack, glorious hero of the revolution, would not have heard of it. He was a tool of the previous state, after all, and possibly even a tool of the one before that. "It's a quote," Matfey said, pulling off his gloves and forcing his chilled fingers up against the hot, blowing air coming out of the ventilation system, "from Solzhenitsyn. 'Unlimited power in the hands of limited people always leads to cruelty.'" Matfey clenched his fingers together experimentally. Even the two minutes spent out in the snow while waiting for Colonel Pasternack to finish his business had been foolish; he should have waited in the warm cab, but he hadn't been able to resist a chance to stretch his legs and look at the sky.

It was a privilege long denied to the people he was about to see, after all.

Boris just shrugged, again, aimless, as though the quote held no more significance for him than a line of English from a brainless Hollywood movie. "If you say so," Boris said. Matfey wondered if the colonel was being deliberately dense in an attempt to avoid discussion of the quote's significance to their present mission, or if he truly was that uncaring. Matfey landed on the latter after only a moment's consideration; he had been traveling with the colonel for many days now, and was well versed in the man's lack of concern for apparent cruelties.

"Up there," Boris said, and Matfey followed his pointing finger to see a tunnel entrance carved into the mountain. Two soldiers waited there, a guardhouse with its ineffectual wooden barrier barely suggesting an impediment. They opened the gate without even stopping the truck, already informed of its imminent arrival.

Matfey watched the guards with a little contempt; trained dogs, that was all these men were. Cruel and not particularly bright, enforcers of an order long gone. These men were a ruble a dozen, expendable and pointless in the new order. Their day was done; they simply did not know it yet. Or perhaps they did, and simply did their jobs from force of habit.

The truck rumbled into the darkened tunnel, the lights casting shadows on the wall as they passed. Boris held his silence as they entered a massive cave, a hollowed-out middle of the mountain. Darkness was not the word; floodlights lit the space, a conical rock chamber big enough to house a small stadium. Here, Boris parked the truck, in a row with two others. Snow from the outside world lay fallen in piles where it had dropped from under the chassis of the transports.

Matfey was the first out; Boris took his sweet time. The colonel seemed less than impressed with the installation, Matfey thought, as though he had been to places like this before. It was an impressive feat of engineering, Matfey supposed, though ultimately useless now that its primary purpose was about to be undone.

Finally.

A man with the bars and stars of a lieutenant colonel hurried up, seemingly out of the nowhere of the darkness. Matfey took his place next to Boris, respecting the traditions of the military ground upon which he stood, though those traditions were about to be rendered pointless.

"Colonel," the lieutenant colonel said, saluting. Pasternack returned the gesture, and Matfey wondered if these idiots ever grew tired of constantly paying homage to one another, kissing each other's corpulent asses. "We have been expecting you." His brass nameplate read "Markovic," and he was in his forties, hair slightly greying at the temples.

"This is my colleague, Matfey Krupin of Limited People," Pasternack said.

Markovic didn't get the reference, either; Matfey could tell by the expression on the Lieutenant Colonel's face. It was the furrowed brow of deep concentration, of a man searching his memory for a hint. "That sounds … a little familiar … I suppose."

It should sound damned familiar, Matfey didn't say, taking a few deliberate steps past the lieutenant colonel to stare into the darkness of the old mine. It was doubtful that the lieutenant colonel would forget the name when he was serving a long prison term thanks to Limited People's efforts. "We're a longstanding organization," Matfey said instead, preferring to speak subtly rather than send Markovic running for the hills like the war criminal he surely was, "but we've only come to prominence with the election of the new administration."

Markovic nodded his head, as though the idiot comprehended anything. "You're here for the tour, then?"

Matfey smiled, feeling a cold, smug superiority. "Of course. As Colonel Pasternack said when he called, this place is something of a … vanished site. We're here to … put it back on the map."

Markovic's expression turned dark, and he shook his head slightly. His movement looked more like a nervous twitch than a deliberate gesture. "That is not a good idea."

Colonel Pasternack's sharp intake of breath was audible and surprisingly cautious given the circumstances, Matfey thought. "Lieutenant Colonel Markovic," Boris said gently, "this comes from the highest authority."

Markovic's shoulders tensed, and when he spoke it was in a cautious whisper. "Do you know what we have here, Colonel?" Matfey felt his cheeks burn with the indignity; it was as though he were not even here.

"You have the last of the damned gulags operating here," Matfey snapped, bringing the Lieutenant Colonel's head around in an instant. "You have the distinction of operating an unauthorized prison that is in violation of basic human rights." He stepped closer, getting right in Markovic's face. He could smell the vodka coming out of the man's pores. "Do you know what sort of penalty that carries under the new government?"

Markovic paled visibly, and a bead of sweat dripped down his temple. "We only have four prisoners," Markovic said, and looked to Colonel Pasternack as if there was some support to be had there.

"Take us to them," Boris said, more gently than Matfey judged necessary.

Markovic snapped off a crisp nod, and turned on his heel in military precision. Boris followed, and Matfey kept his pace even with Colonel Pasternack. "You need not be so accommodating," Matfey said in a hiss of a whisper to Boris.

"You needn't be such a prick," Boris replied. "We are in his mountain, surrounded by his men, and at his mercy." Pasternack's eyes were focused, and they carried a hint of menace. "Don't be an ass, and you'll get what you want."

"I'll get what I mean to however I want," Matfey said hotly. As though these army dicks had the balls to disobey their own chain of command? Orders were all they had, after all.

They followed Lieutenant Colonel Markovic to a set of elevators, steel girders surrounding metal cages at each of the four corners. With a rattle, Markovic unlocked the one on the right, nodding at something above. Matfey looked up to see a booth with more guards. One of them nodded down at the lieutenant colonel and something buzzed; the heavy clink of a metal lock disengaging filled the air.

"Can't be too careful," Markovic said as he slid open the cage and undid the first button of his uniform dress shirt. He fumbled with awkward hands, probably still feeling the hard drink, Matfey thought, and came up with a key. He slipped it into a lock on the elevator console, pressed a button, and the elevator buzzed before moving.

The three of them stood in awkward silence, Boris and Markovic exchanging uncomfortable looks.

"How long have your prisoners been here?" Matfey asked.

"Since 1982," Markovic said.

Matfey blinked at him. "Have they been outside in that

time?"

Markovic frowned. "Of course not."

Matfey could feel the anger, the righteousness burn within him. The prison system of the tinpot tyrant's Russia had been a totalitarian thing, but this was draconian even by his standards. "Are they fed regularly?"

"One meal per day, at varying times," Markovic said. He looked uncomfortable, probably as a result of Matfey's furious expression at this admission, and elaborated: "They were not to be given so much as a detail of the outside world, and no predictable routine was to be established."

Matfey made a scoffing noise and looked at Boris, whose discomfort was apparent at this admission. "You are going to release these prisoners immediately, do you understand?"

Markovic's eyes were wide enough to accommodate the bottom of a vodka bottle each. "Release … them? Do you have any idea who they are? *What* they are?"

"I know they were imprisoned by the old Soviet Union," Matfey snapped back, "and that you are upholding illegal sentences and carrying out practices that violate their basic human rights."

Markovic's face filled with quiet umbrage, lips in a tight line. "I was merely carrying out my orders."

"I'm certain the war crimes tribunal will not have heard that one before," Matfey said with the satisfaction of a man about to watch a heinous leech get scraped off his skin. Markovic's face grew even paler as the elevator rattled to a stop.

"Cooperate, Lieutenant Colonel," Pasternack said quietly, clearly attempting to talk the man down from the ledge Matfey had just pushed him onto, "my young colleague here is a bit … overenthusiastic in his pursuits. He speaks out his ass."

Markovic's paleness dimmed only slightly, and the uncertainty was obvious on his face. "I will do what you ask, Colonel."

They stepped out into a smaller chamber, a mining tunnel

somewhere ahead, cored out of the mountain's hard rock. Lighting was strung all throughout, and the smell was of dirt and must. Matfey waited for Markovic to take the lead, but the man was not moving, his hands shaking mightily.

"Lieutenant Colonel," Boris said, voice low and supportive, "do you need a moment to compose yourself?"

"I need more than a moment to do what you're asking me to do," Markovic said, his head low, staring at a set of jailer's keys in his hand. "I have watched over this prison for over a decade." He looked sideways, from Pasternack to Matfey. "I have been dealing with these prisoners … for longer than that. I ask you again … do you have any idea what you are dealing with here?"

"We are dealing with a legacy of lies some three decades deep and growing," Matfey said.

"You are dealing with the most dangerous prisoners in what was once the Soviet Union," Markovic said in a hushed whisper. "They were locked up for a reason."

"Yes," Matfey said, nodding, "because they were subjects of a tyrannical regime that is now some twenty years gone. They've been imprisoned past the point when all the other political prisoners were set free." He folded his arms across his chest. "Really, Lieutenant Colonel, I would think you'd be eager to rectify this wrong of yours."

Markovic swallowed heavily. "The only thing I could do to rectify this wrong would be to drop the mountain down on them and pave over it with concrete."

Even Colonel Pasternack seemed to think he'd gone too far. "Times have changed, Lieutenant Colonel," Boris said. "You have your orders, and I have them on paper if you require them. All prisoners are to be set free. Do you believe me?"

"I believe you," Markovic said, and started shuffling down the tunnel once more. "But I can only assume that along with our location being missing from the map, the description of these prisoners must also be lost to time."

Boris grunted in acknowledgment of that. Matfey merely kept his peace; this Lieutenant Colonel was a disturbing sort of fatalist.

The chamber widened ahead, and dark, cool air filtered out. They stepped into the center of it and Matfey nearly gasped. The lighting was slightly better in here, but only slightly. "This is …" his eyes took it all in, his outrage spilled out of his heart like vodka slopped into a glass too short for it, "this is … it's criminal!"

"*They* are criminal," Lieutenant Colonel Markovic said with a shake of his head, lips pursed in utter disapproval. "This is merely what we have had to do to contain them."

"You are a despicable sort of cur," Matfey said, poking a finger at the Lieutenant Colonel, "a dog of the lowest kind, to treat prisoners in this manner—"

"I do what I'm told," Markovic said with a surprising amount of calm. "I do what is necessary."

"This seems … excessive," Pasternack said in a quiet voice, eyes looking over the cave.

Matfey's mouth was open in quiet fury. Two bodies were strung to his left and right, bound to the wall by metal restraints of thickest steel, wrapped around the chests of the two men. Their arms were missing from mid-humerus, a slow drip of fresh blood from the recently severed appendages falling to the ground far below. "When did you do this to them?" he asked, when he recovered his power of speech.

"We do it to them every day," Markovic replied. "Every single day, we remove them before they can grow back."

"Barbaric!" Matfey felt the word rush out. His eyes slid across the darkened chamber to the opposite end, where a female figure hung, arms in the air, naked in the middle of a spider web of chains that bound her from each arm and leg, that wound around her waist in thick segments, attached by more thick bands of dark metal. "What have you done to her?" Pale skin and pale eyes looked up from beneath dirty, ragged hair to find his eyes. There was a fierce intelligence there, and he felt immediate pity for her state.

"She is strong enough to break down the door to a prison cell," Markovic said, voice thin and frail as he attempted to explain. "When she was placed here, she was bound in more chains than she could defeat and suspended where she could not—"

"This is disgusting," Matfey said, shaking a finger at Markovic. "How do you even feed them?"

"They are spoon-fed from a distance by soldiers on platforms that slide into place specifically for the feeding," Markovic said. "No one gets within ten feet of them at any time."

"You said there were four prisoners," Matfey said, barely getting his voice under control. "Where's the last?"

Markovic gestured down to the floor far below. "In a cell in the bottom. He is not allowed even within ten feet of another human being."

"And their waste?" Matfey asked. He could feel his eyebrow twitch, and the smell was obvious in the air, nearly enough to gag him.

Markovic shrugged, an empty, uncomfortable gesture.

"This is an affront to basic human dignity," Matfey said, shaking his head. "Get them out of there."

Markovic stared at him. "You have no idea what you are about to release. They are monsters—"

"There is only one monster in this room," Matfey snapped with no small amount of contempt, "and I am looking at him. Are you going to do as I ask or not?"

Markovic hesitated, but caught Pasternack's eye. Finally, the warden acquiesced with a single nod. "It will be as you say," Markovic said, and waved his hand at a booth that hung on the wall opposite them. Soldiers moved around in there, silhouettes in the dark, highlighted by a red glow from a console.

Matfey stood back and watched. A few soldiers appeared, platforms moving into place with a mechanical whirring of old machinery. The steady clack of the machinery was enough to drive a man mad after a long enough interval. Nothing in the room looked new; it all looked like castoffs from seventies-era Soviet space engineering. But the platforms moved, and Matfey watched as the soldiers brought them closer to the prisoners; hesitantly, as though crossing lines they had never imagined they would cross.

The elevator from the bottom of the room rose next to them; a man with a beard down to his belly stood upon it. He was crooked, hunched over, but his eyes gleamed with a bluish intensity that bespoke his intelligence. Two soldiers with AKs stood just behind him, barrels leveled. They were both young and tentative, warily keeping an eye on the man. Matfey figured they both looked about two seconds from running from the room.

"My name is Matfey Krupin," he said, looking at the man as tenderly as possible. He could not imagine that this fellow had had much kind treatment over the last thirty years. "I am here to set you free."

The man stared at him, then turned to look over the proceedings. The rattle of chains being unlocked filled the air. "Are you now?" He licked his lips. "Are you, truly?" His voice was hoarse, as though it had seen little use in years.

"I am," Matfey said, and extended his hand.

"Don't!" Markovic shouted from across the void, where he stood upon the platform by the woman.

Matfey stared at the lieutenant colonel, ready to let fly a contemptuous word, when he felt a gentle pressure upon his hand and turned to find the man had taken it. "Leonid Volkov," the man said, his teeth black around the edges in a smile. He turned his head and bushy beard to look at Markovic. "I can take a hand of a friend without hurting him, Lieutenant Colonel."

Markovic looked as though he wished to say something in reply, but he withheld it. Maybe he was finally getting wise, Matfey thought. One of the two men who had been hung upon the wall was down now, staggering upon the platform with two soldiers, a strange sight with his missing arms.

"Why now?" Volkov asked, his voice rough.

"There has been a revolution," Matfey said with a smile. "Out with the old, in with the new. All political prisoners are to be released."

"'Political prisoners'?" Volkov said with a low laugh as the platform bearing the first freed man eased closer to where they stood. "Well … that's good to hear, isn't it, Miksa?"

The platform that the first armless man was on bumped steel against steel as it docked with their own, and he staggered over to stand next to Volkov. The man named Miksa said nothing, looking up with dazed eyes and a flat, dark face. His hair, too, was long, and his beard also out of control. He did nod, however. The two soldiers with him exchanged furtive glances with the others, idiot dogs in a world beyond their comprehension, Matfey knew.

There was a scrape as the second platform brushed against theirs, and Matfey looked up to see the second armless man stagger forward, using his legs for the first time in decades. "Politics certainly did land us in here," he said, smoother than Volkov. "Of one kind or another, eh, Leonid?" Matfey realized with some surprise that this man had sharp features under the layers of dirt that his imprisonment had left. Matfey silently cursed these soldiers and their reckless cruelty again.

"Indeed, Vitalik," Volkov said with another rough laugh. His eyes turned in silent expectation as the platform began to move with the last member of their quartet. Matfey turned to see the woman standing—still naked, but somehow statuesque now that she was free of the restraints. The marks of imprisonment were still visible on her skin, along with years of dirt and blood. Pale, shriveled flesh showed in clean spots here and there, and the woman stood tall, completely unselfconscious as she looked toward them. The platform carried her steadily along, the clank of gears loud enough to make conversation difficult, but not impossible.

"How are you feeling, Natasya?" Volkov called.

The platform's gears ground slowly, ratcheting her closer to them. She ran thin fingers over her dappled skin, then through her twisted, dirty hair. "I cannot recall an occasion when I have felt better," she said, and her voice was strong. "And you, Leonid?" She waited for his response, which was but a nod. "Fenes?" She glanced at the man Volkov had called Miksa and received a nod of the head in return. "Kuznetsov?" The last was directed at the one Volkov had called Vitalik, and she received a third nod in reply. "Very good," she said.

"What shall we do, Natasya?" Volkov asked as the platform docked, the clang of metal meeting its counterpart nearly striking his question from the air with its violence. "Our new friend here says he is here to free us." Volkov nodded at Matfey.

The woman stood there, straight, next to Lieutenant Colonel Markovic, who looked about fit to shit his pants. She stared at Matfey, her eyes surprisingly blue. Hers bored into his, and he felt a hasty need to say something, as though a weight or pressure was upon him. "It is true. I have come to free you, to bring you back to Moscow if you would like."

"In chains?" she asked, holding up her now free hands.

"No, of course not," Matfey said. "You are free people. You may go anywhere you want."

Her face was inscrutable, and she did not look away from him. "Anywhere?" she allowed at last. The aura of suspicion he had suspected was already evaporated. *Clearly grateful,* Matfey figured.

"Anywhere," Matfey said, and he felt curiously awed by this naked woman, so commanding even in this state. He could feel the other prisoners' deference to her. How impressive, to be so in charge while standing there without a stitch of clothing to give her dignity. Truly, this was a dignity even prison could not deprive her of. "The new government is very eager to make your acquaintance, to make restitution for past wrongs done by the ... previous administration." Matfey looked at Markovic, but the lieutenant colonel did not meet his eyes.

She pondered him with a long gaze, and then finally, nodded her head, passing judgment. "I think we will go with our new friend to Moscow, then, and see what he has to offer." Her eyes narrowed. "Perhaps we will see how things have changed in our long absence from the world."

"I think you'll find the world has gone in quite a different direction since 1982," Matfey said with a weak smile. "Things have … changed. The world has become more closely stitched together."

"And … our people?" This from Leonid, his dark, matted beard blocking sight of his lips.

"The Russians are now free," Matfey said, feeling that smile spring to his lips once more. "Finally, truly—"

"Not the Russians," Natasya asked. "Our people. Metahumans." She blinked her eyes, then shook her head. "You probably have no idea of what I speak."

"No, I know of metahumans," Matfey nodded enthusiastically. "Everyone knows about metahumans now." The heads of the four prisoners came up at that and he could feel their questioning looks. "I will explain in the truck, but let us say that … again … the world has changed in your absence from it."

1.

Three Months Later
Liberty Street
Lower Manhattan

Eric Simmons

"Oooh, baby, baby," Eric Simmons said as he stared at the last half-foot of wall. The drill was quiet, the blades nearly ready for the last push. The winter chill had followed him down into the basement across the street as he'd descended from street level and followed the tunnel they'd been oh-so-quietly working on for the last six months.

"You tip the sensors?" Keith Bailey asked him as he sauntered up. Bailey had on his drilling goggles, looked like a frigging dork between those, the electronic earmuffs, and his grey boiler suit. Like the world's dustiest janitor, dirt dandruff resting on his shoulders from the tunnel's constant settling.

"Yep," Eric said breezily, staring at that last segment of wall between them and the big score. "I hit 'em with a big ass quake over on Wall Street, like 5.5 on the ol' Richter scale, then dropped a smaller one, maybe a 4.2 at the corner of Nassau and Liberty for about ten seconds." He stretched, flexing his arms as he interlaced his fingers above his head. "They are primed, baby. Let's do this."

Keith nodded once, then turned his head toward the drill

panel. He was on his job, which left Eric to watch, running a hand through his long, blond hair. Six months of planning for this. That's what it had taken. Little scores to bankroll things, some bank jobs out of state and in Jersey, enough to fund the drill and the escape route.

And Eric had spent the last six months walking every street in Manhattan and riding the subways constantly, dropping quakes on the entire island. He'd even done a couple in Brooklyn and Queens for coverage. It was a treat, watching people scream and run as the ground started shaking. It wasn't something New Yorkers were used to, after all. Except maybe the ones who came from L.A.

"How long do you need?" Eric asked as the drill throttled up. It wasn't too loud, but it was still a four-foot-across circular drill designed to cut through concrete and rock. The diamond tips hadn't been cheap, either. That had been a whole score from a bank in Yonkers, just to pay for the bits.

"If your girlfriend's right—" Keith started.

"Cassidy is always right," Eric said, good humor gone in a second. He brought back the smile when he noticed Keith almost flinch back. "The sooner you realize that, the smoother your life is gonna go, my friend."

"Yeah, well," Keith said, voice sounding a little hollow, "she told me it'll only take a couple minutes on this last foot, so …"

"So a couple minutes it is," Eric said, settling back to watch. "Crew's ready?"

"They've been ready for months," Keith said, and the drill revved up as he cranked it forward. The ground started to shake, just a little, nothing like what Eric had just laid down up on the surface. This was a little bitty shake, maybe 1.2 on the scale. Eric knew the Richter scale. Knew it like the back of his hand. He'd been raised in L.A., and some things you just absorb in quake country.

"Settle back and we'll be through in a minute!" Keith called to him over the low, muffled rumbling of the drill.

Eric leaned against a dusty wall. The moment was coming. Here they were, eighty feet below Liberty Street in lower Manhattan, six months of planning to lead to this moment. It was gonna be a triumph, the cap on this whole frigging brilliant op. He thought of Cassidy, of how she'd planned this whole thing, and he pulled out his cell phone. One bar of signal, which was probably due to the repeater they'd installed in the basement where the tunnel started. They'd needed communication, after all.

Almost through, babe, he typed into the text message. *See you soon*, he finished and hit send.

Then he settled back to watch Keith Bailey dig the final foot into the vaults of the Federal Reserve Bank of New York, daydreaming about the $200 billion dollars in gold that he'd be laying his hands on in less than a minute's time.

2.

Sienna Nealon

"'Almost through, babe,'" Felix Rocha read aloud in the back of an NYPD panel truck, "'See you soon.'"

"Oh, Mr. Rocha," I said, deadpan, turning his heavily-gelled head around to look at me quizzically, "restrain your romantic side. You can see me right now."

"It's the text message," he said with utter disgust. "Originates from Eric Simmons's phone."

"Suuuuuure," I say, taunting him. I was probably creating a hostile environment, but Rocha did it everywhere he went. The man had the personality of a particularly corrosive acid, so I didn't mind having a little fun with him.

"How the hell did you pull his text message in real time?" asked the NYPD Lieutenant, Allyn Welch, who was sitting to my left.

"This piece of equipment is called a VME Dominator," I said. "It does cool things like that."

"That's classified," Rocha said with great annoyance. Rocha worked for the NSA, with us, and without a hint of politeness, patience or nicety.

I exchanged a look with Welch, who was viewing Rocha with great suspicion—as one might do when someone's being an ass to you. "He can also make it turn on the microphone to listen in on their conversation, but he's being coy about it because you're in the truck." I glanced over at Rocha, and saw his jaw lock tightly, his already puckered lips pressing even closer together. I have that effect on people sometimes.

The back door of the truck opened and closed as a tall guy stepped inside, shivering and shaking his dark coat to drop a few flakes of snow off the shoulder. "It's not exactly Minnesota," Reed said as he entered, "but it's pretty cold out there. Nice wind whipping between the buildings, kinda feels like the prairie."

"Maybe you can use it to float between the buildings like Mary Poppins," I suggested, shooting my brother a smile, which he returned.

"More like Spider-Man," he fired back. "And maybe I will."

"I'm still back on this cell phone thing," Lt. Welch said, running a hand over his thinly combed-over hair. Poor guy was having trouble letting it go with dignity. "So you can use a suspect's own phone against them as a bug?"

"Yep," I said before Rocha could spew the words "IT'S CLASSIFIED!" into the air like an ant bomb. Which he probably needed to do desperately, since he had a bug up his ass the size of a New York taxi.

"How does it work?" Welch asked.

"By violating all your rights to privacy in less time than it takes you to say—" Reed started.

"It mimics a cell phone tower and routes your calls, text and data through it," I said, and then shot an annoyed look at my brother. "And will you lay off already? We're using it to monitor someone who's drilling a tunnel into the biggest gold depository in the world; it's not like we're listening in on Grandma's innocent conversation with her babies or some kinky convo held between a bondage queen and her biggest client." I stared him down for a second, and my confidence wavered. I looked over at Rocha. "Uhm … how many cell phones are we intercepting right now, just out of curiosity?"

Rocha sent me a look of pure loathing. "That's classified,"

he said petulantly.

"Your hairstyle is classified, too, isn't?" I asked. "The amount of gel you use on a daily basis? Number of toilet paper squares consumed per wipe?" He got a look that told me he was pissed and turned back to his screen. I turned to look at Lt. Welch. "As you can tell, we are a highly professional organization."

Welch nodded sympathetically. "We all have our assholes to deal with."

"Hey!" Rocha said, more than a little annoyed.

"I don't even want to know how many squares per wipe it'd take to clean you up," I said. Rocha just grunted, giving up the fight, and turned back to his console without another word. "So, they're about to break through."

"Should we go?" Welch asked me.

I glanced at Reed. "Sure, why not?" I nodded toward the back of the van. My brother opened it and held the door for me as I popped out onto the New York street.

Flakes gently fell from the sky as I stood in the middle of a rush hour the like of which I'd never experienced. People were surging up both sides of the sidewalk in mighty throngs. Reed had told me about this place, about the energy of the crowds, how it's almost a living thing. I stood there on the sidewalk just feeling claustrophobic and wishing for the wide, sprawling view from my office. It looked out over lovely snow-covered fields at the moment, and now that we ran a much smaller organization than when I started on the campus, it was rare that I saw anyone outside my window.

Solitude, thy name is bliss.

I stood on that street, and there was no bliss to be found. A steady line of cars inched by, passing the panel truck at about two miles per hour, with frequent stops as the traffic lights changed. There were a lot of honks, I noticed, more than I thought was reasonable. Of course, I think more than one honk at a time is kind of unreasonable. Either the person knows they're being an ass or they don't, and no matter how many times you honk at an asshole—like Rocha—he's not going to stop being an asshole.

That might just be my life's philosophy: people don't change.

"Come on," Reed said to me, jarring me as he slammed the van door shut. Welch strode ahead of us, right into traffic without a care in the world. I blanched on his behalf and then remembered that a taxicab traveling at two miles per hour couldn't really hurt me. Maybe him, but not me, and I started forward to follow. A cavalcade of horns followed me, and I flipped a bird at the guy, unveiling my inner New Yorker, I suppose.

"Acclimating to the town, I see," Reed said, the perpetual smartass.

"When in Rome," I said, "break everything possible and try and get yourself kicked off the continent." I snapped him a grin. "Oh, wait, that's you."

"You get banned by one massive continental parliamentary government and nobody ever lets you forget it," Reed grumbled.

"Yeah, it's kinda like you and this constant bitching about a surveillance state," I said. "Just submit your emails and your rectum to probing or throw away your cell phone, live like a Luddite and stop griping, will you?"

"Har har," Reed said as we crossed the street, following Lt. Welch into the massive entrance of the Federal Reserve Bank of New York. "You laugh now, but—"

"Just stop," I said, shaking my head. "Put your game face on."

"I've always wondered what a game face looks like," Reed mused. "You know, not being a sports fan."

"Probably not like an O face," I said, deploying something I'd been saving for a special occasion, "though I suppose we'd have to ask Dr. Perugini if the two are similar in your case."

The shocked expression was worth it. "How did you know?" he asked.

21

"That you've been getting far more regular check-ups than our insurance pays for?" I smirked. "It's been, like, years. Does she make you turn your head and cough every time, or—"

"Later," he said, and I knew that was a promise he wasn't going to keep. Not that I really wanted to hear about it, or I would have dropped the fact that I knew a lot earlier.

We breezed into a massive lobby, all marble and granite, opulence and wealth. You could tell the place was money just by looking at the entry. A guy in a suit nervously flapped about near the entrance, fumbling and fidgeting, with a flop sweat on his hair and overlong brow that proclaimed him to be the most nervous nelly in New York at the moment. Of course, he was the head of security at a bank that was about to be robbed, and with a fifth of a trillion dollars in his care, I could imagine being a little nervous if I were in his place.

"Lt. Welch," Corey Fairbine said, about two steps from wringing his hands as he waved us through the metal detectors, "Ms. Nealon, Mr. Treston." He acknowledged each of us in turn, and I imagined his teeth chattering when he stopped speaking. Not from the cold, but from adrenaline. The guy had been a perfect example of a nervous chatterer the day or so I'd known him, and he was not improving as we got closer to zero hour.

Hopefully he'd settle down once this deal was done. "Mr. Fairbine," I said, answering for the three of us, "is everything set?"

"Our security teams are in position with the NYPD SWAT team," Fairbine said, like he was about to go to prom and his fly wouldn't close. "I still want to express my discomfort at this notion. The scheme could have been broken up two days ago, the conspirators arrested—"

"We still don't have the last conspirator," I said. "The biggest, I might add. The brains behind the operation." Whoever was giving Eric Simmons his orders had been pretty shy. We suspected it was a female, but it could have been a boyfriend for all we knew. Simmons had been watched for days, but he was pretty brilliant at disappearing, evading even our surveillance, which was troubling considering he supposedly didn't know he was being watched.

That meant his "brain" was really smart, because everything we knew about Simmons told us he was dumber than a box of rocks.

"Never heard of a shy brain before," Reed said as we followed Fairbine down the stairs toward the vaults. He walked with a hitch in his stride, and I wondered where the man had got it; he didn't look like he'd hold up well in combat, so I discounted the military. "Shy kidneys, but not a shy brain."

"You'd think that'd make it more difficult to produce thoughts while being watched," Welch said, his attempt at a joke. Welch wasn't funny, but he tried.

We worked our way down the stairwell. The building was old, but had been refurbished a lot. Tons of surveillance cameras everywhere. I hadn't been to the ladies' room, but there was probably one in every stall. I suspected the vault was laden with more than its fair share of them as well, which had me wondering what our criminals were planning to do to bring that particular obstacle down. I voiced this thought to Fairbine.

He shook as he answered. "If they're able to create earthquakes all around the island of Manhattan, I don't imagine it'd be terribly difficult to shake our cameras off the wall." Good point, Nelly.

Fairbine opened the first vault door to us with a key card, exposing a half dozen NYPD uniforms in the waiting area outside the main vault. Welch and his boys had called us in on this gig after they'd tracked a string of bank robberies that were just a little too good for an ordinary criminal to have pulled off. His analysis, not mine. I don't deal with normal criminals. The common thread had been seismic events, teeth-rattling earthquakes at the site of each robbery, vibrations that opened vaults and broke through walls like a rock star cracked through the brittle reserve of an excitable groupie.

Which is where my brother and I came into the picture. Man-made earthquakes that were actually made by a man? Sounded like a metahuman at work. Two days on the scene with Rocha and the rest of our crew and we'd narrowed our search to lower Manhattan. Another day and we'd found Eric Simmons and his basement hideaway. A little digging on our part (not literal) and we'd figured out their plan. After all, a group of bank-robbing criminals probably don't rent out the basement suite across from the Federal Reserve Bank of New York because they're genuinely interested in locating their mail-order business there. I mean, we ordered some of the sticky-tack from their website just in case, but I wasn't holding my breath on that order being fulfilled, since J.J. back at headquarters had gotten us access to satellite imaging which had shown us their tunnel pretty clearly.

Fairbine opened the second vault to us, passing through biometrics that scanned his retina and all five fingers. He'd walked us through the security measures when we'd approached him, and I realized pretty quickly that Simmons's approach to the vault was unique, if not ingenious. He'd been setting off seismic sensors around Manhattan for months, forcing even the most hardened, logical of seismologists to question whether there might have been something they'd missed below the bedrock of the island. They all swore up and down that if there was going to be an earthquake on Manhattan, it'd have to be a lot broader based than the small quakes that had been rattling the hell out of the island.

Ergo, someone was messing with them. Someone who could create earthquakes.

The second vault door opened up, and I looked upon a sight of beautiful gold, filling cages as far as I could see. Okay, it wasn't sprawlingly huge, like a warehouse, exactly, but it was pretty big. The gold bars gleamed in the light, too, in a way that they never really did on TV or in the movies. These were actual shiny metals (oooh, shiny!) instead of dull painted bricks, and that gave them a luster that caught this girl's attention. And not just mine.

There should be a diamond storage, Eve Kappler said in my head. *That combined with this would be … glorious.* I'd never taken her for a gold and jewels type. You think you know someone, just because they're living in your head …

Fairbine had told me that each of them weighed twenty-eight pounds, and the workers had to wear special shoes when they moved them. You know, in case someone dropped one on their foot. Because that sort of thing could put a real damper on your weekend games of lacrosse.

I felt a low rumble and looked across the room to the far end, where we were reasonably sure they were going to come in. There were a dozen guys waiting, both nervous security personnel from the bank as well as NYPD SWAT, and while they didn't have their fingers on the trigger, you could tell there was a gameday atmosphere. This was probably going to be the single biggest, gutsiest robbery attempt on the place ever—and certainly the closest to succeeding. I mean, it's probably gonna sound like a humbrag, but they totally would have gotten away with it if not for us meddling kids.

"Everybody ready?" Welch asked, the consummate professional. I hadn't asked him, but I was pretty sure he was so gung-ho because he was getting to ride shotgun on this and get a lot of the glory for it. Most of the crew we were about to take down was human, after all, and they all had the rap sheets of professional criminals. He'd make a nice name for himself on this one, stand out front at the press conference while Reed and I vamoosed back to Minnesota without being heard from at the event.

I was going to get the dregs—Eric Simmons, and maybe his mastermind, if they turned out to be a meta. Simmons was no prize, but the collar would be nice. He wouldn't be able to be imprisoned in a normal place, like Riker's Island, after all. He'd have to go where—well, where metas go.

Once again, that was my department.

My job.

Blocks were moving at the back end of the vault. Fairbine assured us that the place was normally empty at this hour, which was probably why the thieves had chosen this moment to make their entry. Morning rounds had concluded, the next patrol would be a little bit off yet. A subtle rumble ran through the vault again, and the lights flickered.

Showtime, Roberto Bastian said in my mind. Always the tactical thinker, that one.

I strode out in front of Fairbine, who suddenly looked a little weak in the knees. I could feel my brother a little behind me. By unspoken agreement, I always went first. Not only because I was more suited to sponging up bullets, but because I was easily the better person to beat the ass off whoever we faced. Better, faster, stronger. Reed knew it and he didn't make a fuss about it, which was good, because I wouldn't have enjoyed beating him into a pulp just to prove a point. Don't mess with little sister. She will eff you up.

Bricks shifted in the wall ahead of me, high above a stack of gold bars. Fairbine had informed me that the vault wall had been reinforced last year, but that this had gone unmentioned in any public forum. We assumed our criminals would be a little behind schedule because of this fact, but as I heard the rattle of concrete hitting the floor, I knew they'd punched through on time. Taken by itself, it hinted to me that the brains of this operation had known about the reinforcement.

Smart brain. I couldn't wait to knock it senseless.

I could hear the faint noises of jubilation over the high-pitched whine of the drill they were using, the sounds of a bunch of crooks that were about to get a hell of a surprise.

"Clear!" came the shout from within the cage ahead. The drill powered down, whine dying to a whimper in a second. I couldn't see it very well behind a stack of gold bullion that went over my head. I heard guys coming in through the hole in the wall, expressing their low admiration for the stack of bricks that was obscuring their view of what lay beyond.

I glanced back and saw that the SWAT team had taken

cover, along with the security guys, behind the gold stacked around the room. Reed stayed with them, peering out from behind a shiny pile just behind me, reflected light gleaming next to his face. I tiptoed up to the bullion, stacked about seven feet high, and wondered if anyone considered what a safety hazard that was. I considered just shoving it over onto the crooks and calling it a day, but decided that no, that probably wasn't sporting.

"Holy hell, man!" came the clearest voice from behind the pile. It wasn't a thin stack, either, it ran about eight feet long and three feet deep. Just lifting the contents of this one stack would make our criminals a wealthy bunch, and there were a lot more piles than this one, divided out by country. "Look at all this!"

"Cameras," came a calm, clipped voice from nearer by the hole. I had my back to the bullion stack, waiting for my moment and trying to identify by sound how many of them there were. I gently pushed the button on my earpiece that activated my hands-free mike.

"I'm on it, don't get your panties in a twist," came a relaxed voice that I knew came from Eric Simmons. I'd gotten used to the sound of his voice from listening in on his cell phone calls. He had a manner of speaking that was—how do I put it? He sounded like a cross between a surfer dude and a locker-room douchebag. When he was on the phone with his buddies, it was a constant series of profane discussions about the attributes of various women—celebrities, old acquaintances, some woman he just catcalled on the street. For a man with a supposed girlfriend—or boyfriend—he was a pretty dirty boy.

I heard the sound of a single bar being lifted off the top of the pile, and the straining that followed told me that it was a human doing the lifting. "Man ... this alone is worth half a million bucks."

I love it when some assclown sets me up. I slipped out, all demure and sweet (totally an act, obviously) and said, "Then you can afford to buy me a drink." I waited for a moment in the shocked silence that followed and said, lowering my voice to a throaty whisper, "Hello, sailors."

"Aw, shit," one of the guys in back said, "that's Sienna Nealon."

"Got it in one," I said, and I saw a guy in black work clothes pulling a gun, thinking he was covered behind his buddy. I snatched a brick of bullion off the stack and chucked it right at his head. It hit him dead on, and the sounds of skull cracking silenced them all. *Bullseye*, Wolfe said helpfully, glorying in my act of violence. He did that.

"You killed him!" One of the guys said, a dude in a boiler suit that was covered in dirt. I had him pegged as the drill operator.

"Yep," I said, "he's deader than Chester A. Arthur." (What? Too soon?) "Hands in the air, the NYPD is here to collect you boys. The prize for winning in this listening contest is that your brains will remain inside your heads. The loser gets …" I made a faint gesture toward the giant, blood-spattered elephant in the room. "Well, you know."

Hands went into the air, guns were lowered and gently dropped. I watched the whole thing, keeping my eye on the hole the entire time. I could see the faint movement inside it, of course, and knew that Eric Simmons had slipped away like the rat I already knew he was.

Now it was just a matter of waiting, and letting him lead us back to the brains of his operation.

3.

Eric Simmons

Eric slipped through the tunnel, quietly as he could. Did she know he was here? She was still talking, issuing orders to the other guys. He knew her face, of course. Everybody did.

Sienna fricking Nealon. Maybe she knew there was something going on here, that metas were involved somehow, but she couldn't know who he was, could she? Of course not.

He crawled quietly along the tunnel, keeping his head down. He'd seen Ed get the brick, watched his skull smash like an empty soda can as the liquid came spraying out, and he had about zero desire to follow in his footsteps. He kept one hand on the ground at all times, ready to trigger a Richter event if he had to, bring the tunnel down. He kept a listen for that brassy voice. She was a loud one, and that made it all the easier to know that she wasn't following him.

Eric made it out of the tunnel and staggered, almost unconsciously wiping the dirt off his jeans. They knew he and the boys were going to come out of that exact place? Or did they just know they were going to hit the vault now? Could be either, which meant that they could have cops stationed at the building exits. If they didn't already.

But that was okay, because Cassidy had given him a plan for that. She had a plan for almost everything. Except what to do if the Queen of Meta Policing in the entire U.S. suddenly met him on the other end of the vault hole. That had not been covered.

Eric was scrambling, ripping off his jacket and ditching it, leaving the dusty thing behind. His jeans were still a mess; there was nothing to do about that. His beanie was a mess, too, but he needed it if he was going to go outside without his jacket. He tucked his long hair underneath it as he stumbled out the door and up the stairwell, listening for any sign he might be followed, or that someone might be lurking ahead.

Nothing.

He leaped, jumping in a perfectly balanced spring up to the landing above, then leaped again to the one above. He paused there, listened again.

Nothing.

If they were here, they were covering the exits, then. It wasn't a small building, after all; there was a lot to cover. Eric sprinted eight flights, then leapt the last two. He found the door to the roof locked and smashed it. As tenants, they'd been given a key, but he didn't have it on him right now.

The snow was gently falling and the sound of New York was in the air. Traffic below was moving, all background noise. He hurried over to the small chimney and grabbed the backpack he'd left out there on the first day, brushing the snow off as he unzipped it. He changed into the black suit he'd stored inside it. He paused to put his Bluetooth in his ear, then snugged the suit tight, pushing the hood down and putting the glasses over it. He was hitting the button to call Cassidy before he even finished.

4.

Sienna

I was keeping a careful eye on the arrest as the NYPD guys clapped every one of the surviving thieves in durable, meta-proof irons (just in case) when Kelly Harper's voice came in through my earpiece: "We've got a problem."

"Go," I said, aiming for cool. Reed shook his head in my peripheral vision, telling me I did not quite make it. Eager schoolgirl, that's me. I didn't get a chance to do fun things like this nearly often enough. Most of the time we were just training and doing scut work, chasing possible metas that never panned out

"I've got movement on the roof across the way," Harper said. I knew she was watching the scene through her drone's camera at five thousand feet, but it still kind of creeped me out how she could eye in the sky it like that. "Looks like a guy in a wingsuit."

"That's original," I said.

"Not really," Reed said, kind of blasé about the whole thing. "Those are all the rage nowadays in movies and videogames—"

"I'm getting activity on his cell phone," Rocha broke in. "It's data, not a phone call, but I've got his mike active."

"Can you patch us in to listen?" I asked, waving Reed toward the hole that was now empty, since Simmons was now on the roof of the neighboring building.

A heavy crackle pulsed in my ear as Rocha presumably followed my command. He may have been kind of a toxic ass, but he was a pretty efficient one. I felt the dry dirt and dust, the cool air of the tunnel as I hurried through. I reconsidered my approach about ten feet in.

"Gavrikov?" I whispered.

I am at your command, Aleksandr Gavrikov said in my mind, and I felt the power of flight surge through me. My feet lifted off the ground and I hovered in the air in the center of the tunnel and started to fly forward.

"Not fair," Reed grumbled as a click, a buzzing hum and a panicked voice broke into our earpieces.

"Cassidy!" Eric Simmons's voice cried out. Dude was seconds away from soiling-himself levels of panic. "We got a problem!"

That damned buzz-hum answered him, and I felt a swell of annoyance. This was how we'd been receiving this end of Simmons's calls to his mastermind for days. It's really aggravating when the NSA tells you that they have no idea how someone is foiling your attempt to crack their transmissions. It also means your opposition is pretty good.

"I'm on the roof," Simmons's voice came through again once the buzz-hum subsided. "I'm about to jump." There was a clicking noise that signaled end of transmission.

"Rocha," I said, letting my irritation bleed through, "how in the hell is this person spoofing your ability to listen in? It's coming through your damned Dominator!"

"I have no idea." Rocha made a noise in his throat that told me he was as sick of being thwarted as I was. "Some sort of homemade app on Simmons's phone that's decrypting the sender's transmission in real time? I don't know. But at least we're getting the microphone feed from his end."

"If only you possessed the ability to reach into his phone and do stuff," I mumbled under my breath as I flew out of the tunnel into the basement lair of the thieves. Highly technical phrase there, "do stuff." It's a professional term in the NSA, I'm sure.

Their basement office was pretty much filled with nothing at this point except for about five carts. They'd known they were coming through today, and if they'd had anything else here but the stuff they were going to use to execute their heist, they must have cleaned it out long ago.

"I'm not an app developer," Rocha said with some heat, sounding a little like Bones McCoy to me. "I don't know what every single thing on his phone does. Take him into custody and give me the phone and I'll have our people dissect it to figure out the problem, but this is not my area of expertise."

I waited inside the lair for a moment, just listening. A wash of air and dust blew out of the hole a moment later, followed by Reed, who came tumbling awkwardly out and landed on his face. He looked up at me, smudges of dirt on his face, and frowned. "That flying thing is cheating. I declare shenanigans."

"Yeah, you try doing that shenanigans thing with our perp and his wingsuit and see where it gets you," I said, heading out the door of the basement suite in search of the stairs. I found it right outside and launched up through the center of the staircase all the way to the top floor, shenanigans be damned.

"He's leaping off the roof," Harper's terse assessment came to me as I stared at the roof door, which was ajar, cold seeping in. I pushed through as my feet touched the ground, and I got there just in time to see a black-suited guy go off the far end to my right. He dipped out of sight for a second before reappearing, wings stretched between his arms and each leg, like some sort of creepy, black-clad angel. "You might want to get after him," Harper said after a moment's pause.

I strode to the edge of the roof and watched him float up William Street like a leaf on an autumn breeze. "I feel like I should give him a head start to make it sporting," I said.

"How about making it sporting on the rest of us?" Reed gasped, bursting out onto the rooftop, clearly out of breath. My brother's gotten better at doing a little flying himself, but he's not exactly what you'd call good at it yet.

"It's not supposed to be sporting between the two of us," I said as I watched Simmons gradually losing altitude on his way down the man-made canyon, drifting between the two sides perfectly. "Sibling rivalry means I'm supposed to beat your ass in everything I do, without mercy."

"Ugh," Reed said, slumping a little as he tried to catch his breath, "you are ruthless."

"It's probably the most attractive thing about me," I agreed and leapt off the building without so much as a running start before he had a chance to smart off in disagreement. I flew up higher, keeping my eyes on Eric Simmons the whole time, the hawk never taking eyes off her prey.

"Where are you going in such a damned hurry?" Reed asked with a little attitude. I looked back to see him sputtering along on a boosted gust of air, following a slow flight path that looked more like he was gradually drifting along after Simmons. It wasn't pretty, but it'd get him there, albeit slowly.

"I'm going after the Scarecrow, of course," I said, and turned my attention back to the man in the wingsuit, who was about six blocks ahead and ten floors beneath me. "Come to me, my pretty," I said. "And your little dog, too."

"I am never taking you to a Broadway show again," Reed muttered under his breath as he floated along behind me, both of us in pursuit of this earth-shaking jackhole.

5.

Simmons floated along, annoying the hell out of me. I could fly about five thousand times as fast as him, and he just sort of drifted, making me feel like I was performing aerial surveillance on a turtle.

"Harper," I said, "are you still getting this?"

"Yes," she said over the earpiece, voice strong, confident, and betraying not a hint of the boredom I was sure she was feeling. "Looks like you've got a better view than I do, though."

"Reed, how far back are you?" I asked.

"Why don't you just turn your head and look?"

"Because then I might lose sight of the target," I teased.

"Detecting an altitude shift," Harper said, and I noticed she was right. William Street was coming to an end, and I watched Simmons go drifting between a hospital on one side and a towering building on the other. He was definitely coming down, though. I watched him drift lower, and thanks to the perspective of me looking down, I thought he was about to go splat on the side of Pace University. He pulled up in time, though, and cleared the building.

I watched him go lower, heading over a freeway as he made his final descent. I squinted at a building ahead, looking to see if he was going to make it down. "Harper, what the hell is that building he's landing next to?"

"Umm," Harper's voice came back slightly surprised, "I

think maybe that's City Hall?"

"Cheeky of him," Reed said. "What with him being on the lam and all."

He came to a landing in some trees just to the north of the hall, and I lost sight of him as I maintained altitude, feeling a sudden, surprising updraft from below. "Harper, have you got eyes on him?"

"Aye-yup," she said, "he's on thermal still. Looks like he's shedding his suit and trying to disappear."

"There had to be like a thousand spectators that saw him come down," I said. "What is that, like a park or something?"

"Maybe," she said. "But whatever it was, I've got him. He's solid, he's tagged, and he's on the move, heading north-east." I went a little higher, hoping my eagle eyes would allow me to maintain my distance while still keeping watch on him. "Sienna," Harper called to me, "you might want to move closer to a building, give yourself some cover. As it is, you're hovering over the road where he'd just need to look up to see you."

"Who'd look up in New York City?" Reed asked. "That's why they have all those construction scaffolds around town, you know."

I saw Simmons come darting out, moving quick as he crossed the road from city hall. He looked back frantically, and I dodged into the shadow of a municipal building as he started to scan my way. "Reed, he's looking for tails."

"Relax," Reed said, huffing a little. "I'm already on the ground."

"Where?" I asked.

"In the trees, just below you." I saw him moving, with a purpose, looking like a city-dweller on his way to whatever city-dwellers get on their way to. A restaurant, his job, a theater, whatever. Probably not the theater at this time of morning. "I'm on him."

I peeked around the edge of the building, hanging there like ... uh ... well, like a person hanging on the side of a building, sneaking a peak around. It wasn't subtle, but since he was around the corner and a few hundred feet away, what was the likelihood he was going to see me? Simmons was moving away fast too, not looking back any more. "He's heading for the subway station up there," I said, and the consequences of that clicked home. "Aw, hell."

"It's okay," Reed said, "I don't have a famous face like you; I can follow him on the train and he won't recognize me."

That was a persistent problem nowadays, my fame. You save the world one measly time and do one controversial, hostile interview filled with sarcasm afterward and boom, suddenly the world is *Cheers* and everybody knows your name. Most of the people who came up and spoke to me on the rare occasions I dealt with the public were fairly nice. They acted about like I figured they'd act for a celebrity. Selfies with me were a popular request. I heard Madame Tussauds out in Vegas had even commissioned a wax statue of me, which I found decidedly creepy.

"I will not have eyes on you underground," Harper said. She had a tendency to state the obvious.

"Welch got me a backdoor into the city computer, so I can get surveillance footage from the subway," Rocha broke in. "Should be real-time."

"Do that," I said as I watched Simmons disappear down the stairs into the subway station. "Reed, follow him. Keep your distance, and remember that if he makes a move against a civilian, you are authorized to take him down."

"Thanks for reminding me," Reed said with a snort of sarcasm. "Like I didn't know the rules of engagement."

"Just trying to remind you that you've got a gun on your hip for reason," I said, pressing a little. I could not remember a time Reed had used his gun to stop a perp. He hesitated, even though we'd drilled for the last few months until he was brutally efficient with it. I mean, he wasn't as good a marksman as me, but he could put Simmons down from a subway compartment away. In theory.

I say in theory because I had yet to ride a subway, so I didn't really know how big those trains were. Again, people, claustrophobia, blah blah. I rode a train in London; that was enough for me. Now I can fly, so why would I need to take a train?

"Going quiet," Reed said, and I watched him slip down the stairs.

He started to whistle a little tune, and after about thirty seconds I was ready to bite my own hand off to make him stop. "I thought you were going quiet!" I protested about fifteen seconds—and three hundred million years—later.

The whistling cut off, thankfully. For a short duration there, I was finding myself empathizing with Cain. I bet Abel was a whistler.

"I've got eyes on both of them," Rocha said as I floated next to the building waiting for some direction. "Simmons jumped the gate without paying."

"Add that to the list of charges," I muttered. "They take that seriously in New York, I've heard."

"Yeah, I'm sure it'll be a real stiff penalty next to the sentence for grand theft bullion," Harper snarked.

"Every time I hear someone call it bullion," I said, musing aloud, "I wonder whether they're talking about gold or compacted chicken broth." Silence greeted my idle pronouncement. "We ate a lot of ramen in my house growing up, okay?" I said after a few moments of silence. "I know I'm not the only one that was thinking it."

"Train's arriving," Rocha said. "Simmons is getting on the front car. He's got his head down. Reed is a few cars back."

"This is nerve wracking," I said, feeling the nerves part of it. "Is this what it's like listening to play-by-play on a football game that you care about? Because this sucks."

"I'm on the train," Reed said, "two cars away from Simmons, and I've got him in sight."

"Stop touching your ear," Rocha snapped.

"I can't hear you otherwise," Reed replied.

"Nothing to hear except a lot of talk about bouillon cubes and football play-by-play," Harper muttered on the open channel.

"Where are you, Rocha?" I asked.

"In motion," he said, "a couple blocks south of you and moving up fast. The driver is set to follow the path of the six train, which is the one that Reed and Simmons are on."

I felt a shudder as a harsh wind blew past me. It wasn't Minnesota cold, but it was cold. "Mind if I bum a ride?"

"Yeah, sure, float right down off the building and hop in," Rocha said, "I'm sure *that* won't attract any attention."

"Your sarcastic a-hole comment is noted," I said. "I guess I'll just sort of hang around, then."

"They're moving north," Rocha said. "The six train will take him up to the Bronx."

"Marvelous," Reed said, "maybe we can catch a mid-afternoon Yankees game."

"I think you'd need the B train for that," Harper said.

"Simmons is looking around pretty furtively," Rocha said, and he didn't sound too pleased. "But he's not looking carefully, so keep your head down."

I drifted down off the building and hovered for a moment as Reed spoke. "Next stop is Canal Street."

I thought about waiting where I was, but a guy was lingering below, with a cello set up in front of him along with a donations cup. He drew the bow across the strings four or five times, drawing cringe-worthy sounds from the instrument. "Clearly not classically trained," I muttered under my breath.

He did it again, then again, and again, and I realized either he had no freaking idea how to play the instrument or he'd determined that people were more generous when they took pity on him than when he played well. "I'm heading to Canal Street to wait," I said, and shot north, trying to remember the layout of the city, leaving that horrible sound behind.

"Ooh," Reed said, "can you get me a coffee?" He paused, maybe thinking that over, because his next words were more hesitant. "You know, if you have time."

As sour as I felt, I tried to remember that he was my brother, and he was currently riding in a subway car trailing our thieving a-hole of a subject so I didn't have to. "Sure," I said, a little resigned. I caught sight of a coffee shop as I reached Canal, "what do you want?"

6.

I placed my order and sat waiting for the barista to finish it. I neatly avoided the call of the carbs in the bakery display and stood there anticipating my non-fat, non-whip latte. Reed's was not quite so healthy, so I planned to rib him relentlessly later about it, peppermint sprinkles and all. The smell of coffee hung glorious and thick in the air, and there was a modest crowd.

I was still waiting to hear my name when some guy next to me started snapping his fingers. At first I thought he was listening to an iPod, but his ears were clear and he was staring at me, his index finger pointed at me between snaps. He had the look. You know the one I'm talking about. The one that you just want to slap off someone's face when you see it.

"You look so familiar," he said, and I could not keep from rolling my eyes at the great granddaddy of all pick-up lines. I'm pretty sure Zeus used it regularly in ancient Greece. This guy had a half-smile, and he snapped his finger again. I felt a sudden compulsion to snap his finger for him. "Have I seen you on Tinder?"

I just stared at him, my mouth slightly agape. "No. No, you have not seen me on Tinder, that I guarantee."

"Oh, you're not local," he said and snapped his finger again. I felt my eyebrow twitch, and I once more restrained the urge to splinter his digits. Barely. "Where's that accent from?"

"Minnesota," I said, not really sure why I was indulging

him. My excuse was that I was so busy controlling the desire to beat him unconscious that I couldn't keep from answering honestly or generating a sarcastic response. Upon reflection, I decided that was probably accurate.

"So you're not on Tinder?" the guy asked. "Because I would totally swipe right on you."

"What the hell are you doing?" Reed's voice broke into my ear. "I told you to pick up coffee, not fresh jackass."

"He sounds like a real prizewinner," Harper opined. "World's Dumbest—"

"Hush," I said, not taking my eyes off the guy.

He broke into a grin, something he probably thought was dashing or handsome, but which I found obnoxious and wanted to knock all the teeth out of. "It sounds so sexy when you say it like that."

Something came over me, and I suddenly saw a violent shade of red, as though an artery in my brain had ruptured from the act of trying to avoid doing violence to this ass. "Dude, I eat souls when I touch people. So unless you want to spend the rest of your eternal existence formless, trapped as a prisoner in my mind, you should probably get the hell away from me."

The guy blinked at me, face totally blank. "What?"

"Get out of here, moron," I said, and the barista called my name just in time.

"You know, with an attitude like that, I'm not surprised you're single," he said as I walked away.

I froze, almost to the door, and was about to turn around when Rocha's voice blasted into my ear. "Simmons is getting a call from the brain!" I stopped, just listening, waiting to hear what happened next.

It was not good.

"He's looking right at me," Reed said, a trill of unease. "He's not taking his eyes off. I'm made. I need to—"

The next sound was metal screeching, something horrible happening on the other end of the microphone. I dropped the coffee in the middle of the floor and shattered the window of the coffee shop as I flew out, all other idiots but one forgotten.

I needed to get to my brother before Eric Simmons could do whatever it was he was planning to do.

7.

"Rocha, shut down Simmons's phone!" I shouted as I flew down Canal St. toward the subway station. That wasn't likely to do much, but I had to try.

"Done!"

I descended into the station on the fly, went over the turnstiles without a thought, listening to the crash and horror over my earpiece. "Reed!" I shouted, ignoring the startled looks of passersby as I blew through.

I paused above the subway platform, filled from end to end with people, and felt the subtle vibration through my body of so many people in such proximity. It wasn't just an unease born of people-based claustrophobia. There was something else, too, a sense of their souls, all right there, and all I needed to do was reach out and start taking—

Not helpful.

So helpful. So tasty—

Not helpful, Wolfe. Not.

I launched toward the southward tunnel, blackness shrouding it. Sounds were issuing forth, crashing, metal grinding—everything I imagined a train wreck to be and more. The sense of dread that filled my stomach as I flew was pervasive, an acid-tasting horror that crept up my gullet and threatened to overwhelm my mouth and nostrils.

Please let him be okay. That was the thought that filled my head on perpetual loop as I swooped into the darkness.

There was a faint light, emergency lamps showing a subway train on its side. I could see it in the distance, and a low rumble reached my ears. "Rocha, what have you got?" I called as I flew on, seconds from arriving.

"All cameras on the train are out," he said, brusque. He didn't sound like he was having any fun. "I have nothing on the interior."

"Reed?" I asked again, more tentative this time. There was a sound of grunts, of pain, of screams in the background, all bleeding into the microphone.

I was almost to the train when the front windshield shattered, spitting plastic or plexiglass or actual glass out in a shower. A dark object followed, a bundle that did not move as it fell, rolling across the tracks. There was a faint sound of crackling electricity as it hit the third rail, and it—he? I could hardly tell—filled the tunnel with anguished cries as he jerked wildly on the ground.

I struck him purely out of reflexive action, felt the electricity pass through me and scourge my nerves with agony. I'd felt worse, but it was no happy picnic day in Central Park. Not that I'd ever had one of those. The lump of a man flew into the wall, clear of the rail, and thumped down on a ledge next to the tracks, wide enough for a single maintenance worker to walk along it if he were not too large.

"Reed!" I shouted as I shook off the effects of the shock and flew over to the mass. I rolled him face-up, stared down and saw—

Eric Simmons?

"I'm fine, thanks," Reed said, the whoosh of wind filling the tunnel as he coasted out of the hole he'd made in the front of the train windshield and landed next to me. I hit him with a very uncharacteristic and unexpected hug, lifting him clear of the ground before he could protest. I set him back down a moment later, remembering myself. "I can take of myself, you know," he said slyly.

"I know," I said, brushing it off like I hadn't just

overreacted in relief. "I was just … uhm …" I stopped trying to come up with a flimsy excuse. "Whatever. I'm glad you're okay."

"Clearly," he said with a smirk that was visible even in the dark. He made a gesture at the train. "Numbnuts here vibrated us so hard we derailed. I managed to get airborne in order to avoid the worst of the crash, but …" He got a distinctly unhappy look. "It's bad in there, Sienna." I felt my relief at his safety evaporate. "We messed up big time on this one."

8.

Emergency services responded quickly. No fatalities, which was the only bright spot. News trucks showed up even before all the ambulances got there, and they had live reports going out as the first stretchers were being carried out of the Canal Street Station. I got caught on camera, of course, and even though the NYPD had established a cordon, about ten thousand shouted questions hit my ears as I made my way to the nearest squad car and sat in the passenger side, trying to shake off the cold.

"Rocha," I said, "Harper. Status report."

"We're blocks away," Rocha said. "Parked up on Broadway."

"Status? Well, that was a Charlie Foxtrot," Harper opined.

"Not only did we lose the brain," I said, "but Simmons's phone was destroyed and he managed to injure twenty-eight people and wreck a subway train in the process." I did not put my head in my hands, acutely aware that I was being watched by more cameras than I could count. "Reed?"

"Yeah," he said, and he didn't sound happy.

"We need to get out of here," I said. "You got Simmons?"

"Trussed up like he's a roast ham," Reed said. "You think the NYPD is going to happily let him go after this?"

"Not happily, no," I said, "but I doubt they're going to want to put a guy who can cause earthquakes at will into any of their jails or prison units. This is our jurisdiction. I'll talk to

47

Welch and get it cleared." Again I had to fight the urge to hang my head, the despair at how badly this had gone wrong was so thick. "Also, I'm starving."

"I've made arrangements with the plane," Rocha said. "They're waiting at LaGuardia, but they won't be prepped to fly for another two hours. They're still loading the cell to contain Simmons."

I gave that one about a moment's thought. It had come to my attention in the last couple years that the U.S. Government was exceedingly well equipped for transferring metahuman prisoners, considering they had purportedly been out of that business since the 1990s. I'd seen blueprints detailing about thirty different types of meta restraint devices, useful both for short-term prisoner transfer and long-term containment. It was a little disconcerting, but I suppose we hadn't gotten in trillions of dollars of debt just spending $500 per hammer.

"So we've time to kill," I said, and heard a faint rumbling in my stomach. I hadn't gotten my coffee, and worse, now I was hungry. "Suggestions?" I asked, not really sure what would come back.

"Shawarma?" Reed asked, and at first I thought he was joking.

It made me a little angry, no lie. "You ass," I said. Then I thought about it for a minute, and—dammit—the idea held some appeal. When else was I going to get a chance to try shawarma? "Is there a shawarma joint around here?" I asked, a little cautiously.

Reed's answer came back with an obvious smile leaking into his voice. "I know a place."

9.

The shawarma wasn't bad, but it would have been better if Eric Simmons hadn't woken up about halfway through the meal.

The smell of the meat filled the air, wafted through my nose, and every bite was a deeply satisfying antidote to my rumbling stomach. Reed stared at me from across the table. Simmons was next to us, unconscious in the seat at the end of the table, bound hand and foot with meta restraints.

When Simmons opened an eye, I sighed. I had been enjoying myself, even though I'd been watching him like a paranoid person the entire time. As I should have.

"What ... the hell?" he asked, sitting up in his chair. It was pretty obvious when he came to, not just because of the eye-opening, but also because his neck had been drooping back, his body slack, and that changed in a second. He sat up with a start, taking it all in with a confused and befuddled look.

"It's called lunch," I said, taking a bite of my shawarma. "If you're good, you'll get some. If you're not, I'll club you unconscious and leave you drooling blood on the floor while we eat."

He blinked his eyes at me, as though I were a blast of harsh daylight after he'd spent a month in a tunnel. Sorta true, I guess. "Sienna Nealon," he muttered and lowered his head.

"That's me," I said, pausing to take another bite. I spoke as I chewed. Rude, I know, but I was hungry. "You want to make our lives easier and tell us who your girlfriend is and where we can find her?"

"I don't have a girlfriend," Simmons said sullenly, his face going slack and falling. He cased the area around us in seconds, looking for an easy escape route. Not finding one, he drew his eyes back to me.

"Would you like more to drink?" The waitress appeared over Rocha's shoulder, pitcher in hand. She spoke with a slight accent, nothing too heavy.

"Hey," Simmons said and broke into a grin. She looked over at him uncertainly; the place was near empty except for us and the staff. "Would you like a big tip?" His grin got wider. "Or would you like the whole thing—"

I lashed out and kicked his chair out from under him, sending him to the floor. I enjoyed a flood of satisfaction at the panicked look on his face as he hit that moment of weightlessness when he reflexively knew his chair was gone and he was falling but his conscious mind hadn't worked out what had happened quite yet. He hit the ground and all the air rushed out of him. I was on top of him a second later and slammed a fist into his jaw. "Be polite," I cautioned him, menace edging into my voice. "Don't be a pig."

"Damn, girl!" he moaned, cracking his body as he took assessment of what I'd just done to him. He was cringing in pain. I knew he wasn't really injured, but he was making a good show of it. "You are ruthless!"

"Yes," I said, "I am ruthless. And if you make another unpleasant comment to the waitstaff, you're going to be toothless. Ruthless and Toothless, that'll be us. And oh, what a pair we'll make, me beating your ass all over lower Manhattan."

He gave me a seething look. "If you didn't have your power ..." He just let his voice trail off.

"You'd what?" I asked. "Shake me? Bake me? I'm not chicken, jackass. If I didn't have my power, I'd shoot you in the head." I took my index finger and jabbed him in the skull, eliciting an *Ow!* of pain that was probably sincere. "You, on the other hand, are a thief and a chickenshit." I gave him the evil eye. "It comes down to it, you'll always run from someone who gets all up in your face. Coward."

"You should smile more." Simmons turned back to me with a nasty smirk. "You're on camera." I glanced up to see people with cell phones just outside the window, and I felt my heart sink. "How long do you think it'll be before this shows up on YouTube?" Simmons laughed, a low, mean, guttural sound. "Because I'm guessing it's uploading already."

"Doesn't matter," I said, hauling him up by his collar and tipping his chair back up with my foot. I threw him into it and yanked it close. He didn't resist, just sat there grimacing like he was still hurting. "I've got discretion over what to do with metahuman criminals, and as of right now, that means your ass belongs to me." I smiled at him. "I think I could fit that whole chair up inside you without killing you if I was of a mind to. Care to find out?"

"You're violating my rights," he said, and I realized his lip was bloody as a small dribble made its way down his chin.

"I'm all set to violate more than that," I said. "You have the right to remain silent. I suggest you exercise it, you pig." I leaned back in my chair. "Does your girlfriend get mad when you talk to other girls like that?" I waved vaguely in the direction of the waitress, who was now wisely keeping her distance. If she'd thought we were just enthusiastic *50 Shades* cosplayers when we came in, she knew better now.

He looked ready to snap something out, but thought the better of it. "I told you," he said, with a nasty little look, "I don't have a girlfriend."

"Come on," I said, "we know you're not the brains of the operation, Simmons, because you don't have any of your own." I smiled. "Tell us who she is. We'll go easier on you."

He snorted, and I could tell he wasn't buying it. "You have no idea what you've started."

"I've started beating the shit out of you," I said, and stood up, grabbing him by the shoulder and dragging him to his feat. "You better hope I don't finish." I threw a look at the others. "Come on. Let's get out of here." I didn't wait for them to reply, just started dragging Simmons out of the shawarma place while half a dozen cell phones recorded my every move.

10.

The flight back to Minneapolis was blessedly uneventful, and we made our landing at Eden Prairie's Flying Cloud airport shortly before sunset, which was just after five in the afternoon. Stuffing Simmons into a storage tank (literally a tank, filled with gel that negated his vibratory powers) had taken a while, even though he didn't offer anything more than an annoying verbal commentary for resistance. The tank was soundproof, thankfully, and Reed, Harper, Rocha and I rode in the C-130 back to Minnesota almost in silence.

Almost.

"On approach to Flying Cloud airport," the pilot announced, "fifteen minutes to touchdown."

I thanked my lucky stars as I felt the plane bank into a turn. I didn't really love flying on these military C-130's. Not only was the bathroom a curtained-off area at the back of the plane that almost always smelled like it had been used exclusively by men with poor aim, but the pilots also didn't truck with any of that sissy crap that the airlines insisted on for the comfort of their passengers, like gentle turns. Military pilots were authorized to go from point A to point B in a hurry, and they did that. Worries about airsickness were secondary.

On the whole, I'd rather have flown myself, but unfortunately I had to stay on the plane with Simmons to make sure he didn't get up to any trouble. Unlikely, I know, but better safe than allowing a quake-causing dipshit to go free-range again.

Reed looked over at me as we went into a steep turn to the left. "Almost home."

"Yeah," I said, probably a little sourly on account of the not-so-smooth ride. "Maybe you can have a little Italian for dinner tonight," I sniped.

He narrowed his eyes at me. "Gah, you're banging on that drum again." I caught the flinch as he realized what he said a moment too late. "Go on," he said resignedly, "hit me."

"I'd have to bang on it a lot more to catch up with how many times you've ..." I gave it up halfway through, catching the pitying look from him, and changed tacks, "... gone on about surveillance states and indefinite detention." Then I flinched, because I'd set myself up much worse than he'd just done, and just as unintentionally.

He leaned over to me and lowered his voice to a whisper so low that only a metahuman sitting a foot away could have heard it over the engine noise. "Does it not bother you at least a little that we've basically become the judge, jury and executioner for metas?"

We should *execute more of them*, Bjorn said.

I ignored the voice in my head, pondered a smug and snarky answer, which he would promptly batter aside, and tried for something a little more truthful. "I think it would bother me more," I said, "if we didn't presently have in our prison some of the foulest a-holes known to man. I mean, seriously," I said, throwing in a little of the snark that I'd previously withheld, "our little prison is well-named if we call it a penal system, because they are all of them dicks."

He gave me a slightly pained look, and I recognized it as disappointment in my pat answer. "They get no trials to speak of. They have zero recourse. We put them in the ground and don't allow them to see the light of day. What if we have an innocent person in there?"

"We don't," I said, dead certain. "And you know we don't. You're speaking in hypotheticals of what might happen in the future." This much was true; we'd caught every one of our current prisoners in some sort of act of criminality, greater or lesser. There was no doubt in my mind as to any of their guilt, not with as low a population as we were dealing with.

"What about your buddy?" he asked, and he withheld the judgmental satisfaction that I knew was coming. "What about Logan?"

I felt a pained expression work its way onto my face. Timothy Logan was a bit of sore point for me, because he'd been involved in some low-ranging crimes in a rural jurisdiction. He was guilty, no doubt, but he hadn't been violent and he'd expressed a lot of remorse. He was, bar none, our easiest prisoner, and I was of a mind to parole him soon-ish. "I don't have absolute power over these people, okay?" I said. "You know that the DoJ and Homeland Security are just as much in charge of this as I am."

"And that doesn't worry you?" His penetrating gaze was annoying. Really annoying. His accurate points in regards to Timothy Logan were even more so. "They haven't ever interfered with your judgment."

"That's because so far," I said as we started to descend, a lot sharper than a commercial airlincɩ would, "I haven't let anyone go." Passengers? Nah. We were cargo to our pilots. I glanced back at Simmons, up to his neck in gel, and the parallel was not lost on me.

Reed sat back, looking hideously uncomfortable. "It's just not right. It's like those Russians they dug out of that Siberian prison a few months ago." He stared at me. "You know what I'm talking about?"

"It would have been hard to miss," I said. They'd been on pretty much every news broadcast, and I'd gotten email forwards from what seemed like everyone in the government from the White House on down. It was turning into a real human interest story, the tale of four metas locked up by the Soviet Union for mysterious and unremembered crimes, left to rot for thirty years and through multiple regime changes. I had enough requests for comment from reporters that printing them all out would have deforested ten planet Earths.

"Justice systems that take place in the darkness are not typically—" he began.

"Oh, enough already," I snapped at him. "God save me from hapless idealists. What would you prefer we do with him?" I tilted my head to indicate Simmons. "Let him go?"

"No," Reed said, looking like he was about to deliver a punchline of his own, "that's the kind of thinking that causes the death of Uncle Ben." He paused and looked suddenly uncomfortable. "Spider-Man's Uncle Ben, not the rice guy."

"I got it."

"I'm not saying these people aren't guilty as hell," Reed said gently, "and I'm not saying they don't deserve what we're giving them right now and worse."

"Then what are you saying?" I asked, feeling the plane shift directions again. The shawarma was not settling well. Or was it the conversation?

"We have a justice system for a reason," he said. "With penalties civil and criminal—"

"That these guys wouldn't fit into at all," I said. I laughed, but there was zero joy in it. "Try and imagine sticking them in—I dunno, the Stillwater prison. Human guards, meta prisoners. Give them their hour of exercise or whatever every day, under the supervision of normal people, and see how long it takes for Simmons or—" A particularly malicious thought occurred to me, "or your boy Anselmo," I watched him blanch almost imperceptibly, "to break out." I folded my arms in front of me. "The guards don't even carry guns in human prisons, Reed. They'd be completely defenseless against what these guys could unleash. It'd be like taking a prison population and giving them all guns and telling the guards they had to go in with nothing."

"I don't have a solution, okay?" Reed said, and it was not a question. "I'm just suggesting that we're making trade-offs that should be examined. In this case, we're putting people in a black box without—"

"I know what we're doing," I said, in a tone that suggested I was so far done with this conversation that I didn't even want to look back at it.

"Do you?" he asked. "Do you really?"

I tilted my head to look at him. "Unless you've got a better idea?"

He looked like he was going to argue more, but his voice fell. "The guy who got those Russians out? He was part of an organization called 'Limited People.'"

I wanted to roll my eyes, but didn't. "Great name for a human group."

Reed held his silence for a second. "It's from a quote. 'Unlimited power in the hands of limited people always leads to cruelty.'" This time I did roll my eyes. "You don't think it's true?" he asked.

"I think it's a really great piece of fortune-cookie wisdom from someone who's never had to deal with running a prison for people who fall outside the realms of ordinary law and power," I said with a slight growl. "I mean, really, has there ever been a system devised to take into account these extraordinary circumstances?" I shot him a look of fire, feeling like I was burning as I looked at him. "Has there ever been this great a threat to basic security?"

"There's always a threat, Sienna," he said quietly. "So long as there have been people, there have always been others who intend them harm."

"Yeah, well, my job is to stop that harm," I said, looking straight ahead. "Full stop, end of sentence."

I could see him out of the corner of my eye as the plane rattled on final descent. I knew he wanted to argue more, but whether it was because of the roughness of the landing or because he knew my patience was gone, he held his tongue. I sat in silence as we made our way to the ground, thankful for the peace that hung in the air—even if it did not come close to settling inside me.

11.

I led Simmons out of the back of the van, a half dozen guys with submachine guns arrayed around me. We stepped out into the cold, and I felt Simmons gasp as Minnesota kissed him hello. It was January and he was wearing a fairly thin coat. Do the math on that one.

Thanks to long practice dealing with the Minnesota chill, I managed to brace myself. I held tight on his forearm and pushed him forward. "Come on, let's get inside," I said with as much encouragement as I could.

The snow covered the ground in all directions as we stepped out under the portico and walked the half dozen steps toward headquarters front door. Simmons was dripping from the gel still, and I felt it freeze on him as we walked. I've read books where authors talk about the glorious, frigid majesty of winter. Every time I step outside on a day like today I feel the urge to track them down and give them a swift kick to the groin. Or the head. Maybe both. Simmons's steps faltered, and I dragged him along, flanked by our armed guard squad as they opened the glass doors to the agency's headquarters for me.

We passed through the doors into the lobby and a blast of warm air thawed me slightly. Ice had already formed on Simmons's arms and legs, and he walked with a limp, jaw chattering. His lips were slightly blue. "Come on, let's get you locked up, it'll be warmer down there."

I steered him through the security checkpoint with a nod

from the guards and we made our way out of the sweeping lobby with its high ceilings into a metal door that led to a staircase.

"Where are you … taking me?" Simmons asked, shivering.

"The meta equivalent of prison," I said, leading him down the stark staircase. The smell of fresh paint lingered in the air. "Which is also, not coincidentally, called prison."

"I thought that was in Arizona," he said, looking around wildly, taking it all in.

"Used to be," I said. This was a pretty closely guarded secret, since the last prison had been destroyed twice. When we rebuilt it, they—the government—wanted to make sure that it was given every possible security precaution.

Apparently, I was the best security precaution they could come up with, so they stuck it here under the agency headquarters. It was still a secret to the rest of the world—including most of our employees—but since Eric Simmons was about to become a resident, I didn't feel a need to lie to him about it.

I hustled him through the special security checkpoint and into the staircase to the prison entry. There were twelve armed men waiting here with their weapons at the ready, and another dozen waited behind a concrete and metal wall. I put one hand on a biometric sensor while leaving the other on Simmons's arm. "I don't have to tell you what the penalty will be for starting shit right now, do I?"

"I won't get a nice, fluffy cell?" Simmons smarted off.

"I'll kill you instantly by breaking your neck," I said without emotion. "This is a high security area; the guards will shoot to kill, and if they fail, I won't." I pulled a scanner from the wall unit close to one of my eyes, leaving the other free to watch him. I saw him look back, trying to get a read on me. "You escaping custody out in the world is one thing; you causing an earthquake in the middle of my meta prison is a death sentence."

I heard him gulp. I think he believed me. He should have.

The door opened without any fanfare. A firing line of armed guards stood to our right. We left our other escort behind and walked down a long, narrow corridor that looked like it had been shaped out of steel. It wasn't; it was some metal harder than steel, some alloy whose proper name I'd never caught. They made meta handcuffs out of it, and it stretched a hundred yards straight ahead and slightly down, a grim warning that we were entering a place of darkness and seriousness.

Simmons took it all in with an air of uncertainty. His cockiness was all evaporated now, and so was his limp. He was dripping a little on the floor, but I saw his eyes take in the steady succession of men staring out at us from portholes with rifles to our side. The guards called them murder holes, and that was an accurate description. There was one way into the prison and one way only, and anyone unauthorized was to be riddled with bullets until such time as their body was nothing but splatters of tissue and bone.

I didn't take any chances with safety.

We reached the other end of the hallway of death and were buzzed in thanks to the camera above our heads. I pushed open a heavy door and there we were, in the Cube.

I heard Simmons make a gasping noise as he took it in. It was metal all around, too, with inlaid lighting behind bulletproof panels. There was room for eighty modular cells, with an option for another unit further down as maximum security if we ever needed to expand. For now it was just the Cube, though, so named because it was four floors up and down. Only the top floor was presently occupied, though, and not even fully. The rest were reserved for future inmates.

I pulled Simmons along the first row. We passed one of my favorite prisoners, Anselmo Serafini. Reed had run afoul of this particular pig in Italy a couple years earlier. I'd had his cell speaker muted so that he couldn't be heard, and had personally supervised a reconstruction of his cell that allowed only a small window for him to look out of because—I'm not even kidding—every time I or another female guard came past his cell, the bastard would expose himself to us. While I considered neutering a valid option, cooler heads than mine prevailed, and I settled for giving him a two-inch by three-inch mail slot to look out on his limited world.

Speaking from experience, it's a shitty way to go through imprisoned life. When I put him in the new cell, I'd threatened him with covering that last slit up as well. Happily, I'd now gone a year and a half without having to see his genitals. It had been a good year and a half.

I pushed Simmons down to the end where one of the guards was waiting with a cell door already open. "Are you putting me in that gel again?" His voice wavered. I couldn't blame him; I'd tried it once, just for the experience. It feels like being trapped in a Jello mold, unable to move at anything other than a snail's pace, and all the while trying to keep your head above the surface. It burns when you get it in your eyes, too, though I was assured it's non-toxic.

"No," I said, shaking my head. I felt a little pity for him, and he relaxed slightly in my grasp. "Our tech department developed a less invasive version of it for use when prisoners aren't being transported." I brought him up to the door and let him look into his new home.

"Aw, man," he said.

The nullifying gel was still very much a part of the decorating scheme. It was a requirement for all our prisoners who had a certain level of strength or ability to project physical force. In the case of the permanent dwellings, though, we'd found a way to incorporate it into sealed packets that lined the cells. "It's still in there," I said, "ready to stop your quakes if you try and shake the walls. Also, I gotta warn you, if you burst open any of the packets, we will flood the cell up to your neck." I pointed to an itty-bitty vent at the top. "We can get it completely full in less than five seconds, if you can believe it." Anselmo had figured that one out in his first week, the dick.

"Where's my bed?" Simmons asked.

"You sleep on the floor," I said. "The gel packs are pretty comfortable. It's like a waterbed."

"You've tried sleeping on it, then?" Simmons asked, nonplussed.

"I have." He looked at me in sharp disbelief, so I shrugged and elaborated. "I've slept in worse."

"You—" he started, giving me a furious evil eye but apparently thinking the better of whatever he was going to say. I wasn't super petty, but other inmates had occasionally irritated me enough that I pressed the FLOOD button on them as I left.

I sighed. "If you're searching for something to call me that's not going to result in me punching you in the kidney, you could try 'Warden.'" I reached down and started to unlock his hands.

"When do I get out of here?" Simmons asked as he rubbed his wrists. "For exercise or whatever?"

"You don't," I said. "You're in solitary."

"What the hell?" His voice got sharp and high. "When's my trial?"

"You don't get one," I said, drawing up to look him in the face as I pulled the chains free of him. I watched his body for a hint of defiance; I could put him down before he could raise a hand to me, but I'd probably just shove him into his cell and call it good.

"Where's the bathroom?" he asked, peeking in. "Oh."

"Yeah," I said. "And it clogs if we have to flood the cell, so ..." I tried not to make it sound like a threat, but who wanted to float in gel along with their own waste? Other than Anselmo, anyway.

"Man, this isn't right!" Simmons said, looking at me in disbelief. "This isn't fair!"

"I agree," I said, admitting to him something I wouldn't even say to my brother, "but it's what we've got." I shrugged. "It's not like I can stick you in gen pop at the local jail, because you'd just break out." My lips were a grim line as I stared at him. "I wish I had a better solution, but I don't."

"You're gonna regret this." His jaw was set, face was red and eyebrows turned down to show his growing, impotent rage. He believed me now.

"Because your girlfriend is going to make me sorry?" I didn't say it with any spite, just calm resignation.

He didn't bite on the bait, so I pushed him beyond the threshold and sealed the door. It closed with a quiet swish, leaving me staring at his disbelieving face as he stood in the gel-sealed cell, comically distorted by the clear-pack door.

I shook my head and turned away, but I could feel him watching me the whole time. I didn't dare look back as I walked, though. I just kept going to the end of the row.

12.

I stopped near the end, as I always did when I brought a new prisoner down or came for inspection. I paused before a door not that different from Eric Simmons's. It certainly wasn't blacked out like Anselmo Serafini's. I saw the prisoner moving around inside. He'd been watching the entry as I came in—they all had, really—and he stood as I approached. I flipped the switch on the audio microphone and speaker hidden somewhere in his ceiling came to life. "Hey, Timothy," I said.

Timothy Logan walked up to the clear, distorted door and nodded at me through the barrier that separated us. "Howdy, Warden. How's it going?"

"Not bad," I said. That bluster when I closed the door on Eric Simmons? That was the norm around here. It was almost like the prisoners had to posture, had to wave their thingies around to show me that even though I'd stripped their freedom from them, they still had pride. The threats were … graphic, in some cases. Most of them were murderous, and not nearly so subtle and tame as what Eric Simmons had just offered. They were also, between our eighteen prisoners, almost universal.

Except for Timothy Logan.

When I put Timothy in his cell, he didn't fight it, didn't yell, didn't scream or protest. He didn't flail his meta powers around, used to getting his way and knocking down any cop that opposed him. That was the difference, in my view, between Timothy and the rest of them: contrition. That and humility. "How's your time passing in here, Timothy?"

"They've let me have some books," he said, nodding. "One at a time, only, always paperbacks."

"I know," I said with a smile. It had been my idea, and they'd been my paperbacks, from back when I was a prisoner in my own home.

"It fills the hours," he said.

"Three months," I told him, and he blinked at me, trying to process what I'd just said. "Three months and you're out of here." I changed my tone. "If you can handle good behavior for three more months."

He made a slight incline of his head down the line toward Anselmo's cell. "As much fun as it would be to scream and strip naked and generally make an ass of myself until they flood me in, I think I can probably handle that. I just want to do my time and get out, and if I ever see a place like this again even on the news, it'll be too much." His face went slack. "I just want to be ... free."

I felt a curious longing at that last word. "I hear you. Just keep what you're doing and soon enough you will be."

He gave me a slightly wistful look, one filled with more than a little vulnerability. "For real?" I don't think he thought I was lying to him; more like he couldn't quite wrap his mind around the concept.

"You're a good guy, Timothy," I said, thinking back to someone I'd met in a similar situation—Antonio Morales. He'd tried to rob a pawn shop in Las Vegas and it had ended badly. I'd let him go almost four years ago and hadn't heard a peep from him since. He'd shuffled around a little bit and landed in Seattle. I'd kept a watch on him, and not a whisper of trouble had come from anywhere close to him in the intervening time.

I desperately hoped Timothy Logan was going to be my next Antonio Morales story, because none of the other assclowns down here were showing much sign of redemption.

"It means a lot that you think so," he said gently. "I just want to live my life. Make it up to the people I took from, and go on about my business."

"Three months," I said again and slid my bare fingers across his door. "Take care, Timothy."

"You too, Warden Nealon," he said and shuffled back to sit down on the floor of his cell. He bounced slightly as he did, the side-effects of the gel at work.

The walk back up the corridor of death was uncomfortable as always, the guns pointed at me as per my orders. I always thought about flying, but I don't like to give my men a reason to be twitchy with their trigger fingers. They were well trained, but surprising the hell out of them by flying out of here at high speed did not strike me as the brightest move.

I reached the other end, passed the biometric scan, then passed the second checkpoint and stepped into the lobby. Before I even had a chance to draw a breath of relief at being out of that place, Ariadne was upon me. It didn't take me more than a second to realize she'd been waiting in ambush, right outside the door. Her pale cheeks were flushed the color of her red hair, her face looked drawn, and I could tell just by looking at her that something was desperately wrong before she even got a word out. "What?" I asked.

I could see the gears spinning before she answered, my pre-emptive question throwing her off balance. I gave her a moment—felt like an eternity—to gather herself before she finally vomited it out. "We've been replaced as co-directors of the agency," she said, bitterness infusing every word. "The new director just got here from Washington and he's demanding a meeting … right now."

13.

Natasya

The cold of winter had settled in, reminding Natasya Sokolov of every winter passed in the service of the Soviet Union. It had been so long ago, and yet a snap of the fingers in her mind. She stared out the window onto the Moscow street, just as amazed as she had been three months ago, when Limited People—an appropriate name for that band of weasels and lawyers—had brought her and her fellows here.

And ever since, they had been idle save for the occasional chance to play to the capitalist media.

"Another cold day in Russia," Vitalik said from his usual place in their drawing room. Limited People had pursued the new government rather aggressively in legal maneuverings that Natasya neither understood nor cared about. The result had been a stipend as recompense for their long imprisonment. She was left bemused by the situation: a government that proclaimed no responsibility for their predicament throwing money at them to make them go away.

In her day, the government would have disclaimed responsibility, made her and her group disappear, and any reporter who followed up on the subject would have known they'd face the same fate. This wasn't the West, after all.

"'In the midst of winter I find within me the invisible summer … '" Leonid Volkov said from his place by the window. His beard was still long, though now it was more of an affectation. She'd been watching him for the last few months as he interacted with the gluttonous, gross press. He'd studied academics and prisoners, polished his image so that he could better preen for them. She would have viewed it as an affront, but Leonid had done the same thing before the Party meetings, always coming prepared with quotes from Lenin, Stalin and Marx for blandishment at the appropriate moments.

Natasya waited, scanning her eyes over to Miksa Fenes. He was the quiet one, always. He sat in his place, laconic as always, looking almost as though he were asleep. He wouldn't say anything until he had to; for a man who projected energy from his hands, his persona was remarkably lethargic. This was not a precinct that would be heard from.

"What do you say on this fine day, boss lady?" Vitalik asked. He was focused in on her, paid special attention to the honorific.

She stared across the opulent palace of a room, still mildly disgusted by the spectacle. It felt overwhelming, the sort of thing that would get a worker killed in the olden days. The room was almost a monument to the Romanovs and their gross excesses. "I think it's another day we should be looking for an opportunity to escape this garish prison."

"I think we could walk out at any time," Vitalik said, almost hopefully.

"Of course we could walk out at any time, fool," Natasya said. "But then what? Work for the 'new' Russian government? I've seen the names; they're almost the same as the old ones. So then what? Bite our new masters—Limited People—in the hand?"

"You think they want to be our masters?" Leonid asked carefully. He stroked his beard as he spoke; Natasya had known him long enough to be sure that he was doing it to be thought a person of careful consideration. He was nothing of the sort.

"I think they are using us to push their agenda," Natasya said. She looked around the room as though an enemy waited to jump out. In the olden days, there had been no hope of a private conversation, ever. Word always seemed to get out, and always to the wrong ears. After the prison, though, she now found her lips looser than ever they'd been before. It was the disgusting feeling of living in this place, with ideological enemies all around.

This prison was worse; the walls and chains were not visible or obvious. She almost longed for the simplicity of being suspended in the air again. At least then she knew she hung in the middle of a mountain without hope or a future.

"So what should we do?" Vitalik said quietly—so quiet he was almost inaudible.

"We look for … opportunity." She glanced at the window and caught a glimpse of a press car outside. They were out there by the dozens, an encampment. "I, for one, do not trust our new masters nor the supposed demise of the old ones. Whatever situation has come about that has rearranged the government as wildly as it has seems unlikely to result in the forgiving of old grudges forever." At the very least, she was not inclined to forget hers. "I want out of this cold, this uncertainty." She shuddered. "But I don't want to go to the West, or to America. Somewhere warm, somewhere … not a gluttonous pig's paradise, streets paved with oppression of—" She made a throaty sound of disgust. "I want debts settled, revenge, and to leave this frigid ice box of hell." She pulled her arms over her chest. "Find me an opportunity such as that, and I shall leap upon it like a wolf upon a lamb."

There was a knock at the door, the uncertain sound of a man who'd probably never felt the touch of a woman in his life, Natasya thought. It was the knock of Matfey Krupin, the weak-kneed errand boy of Limited People. She glanced at the clock. Time was a thing she was still readjusting to after thirty years of never knowing the hour or minute. Matfey, though, he always came at the same time every day, to conduct his business.

To feed his wolves, Natasya thought, and all the while thinking they were tame sheep.

"Hello," Matfey said in that light warble of his. She wanted to grab him by a nipple and twist it to see if milk came dribbling out. It would certainly not change his voice much.

"Matfey," Leonid said grandly, arms expansively wide. Yes, Leonid could play his role, the eccentric, the comrade academician of old. "It is good to see you this day." He said it every day, and every day it was voltage to Natasya's nerves.

"Today we have six interview requests," Matfey said, straight to business—his business, Natasya thought. She was good at looking at people through half-lidded eyes while smiling politely. It had been a vital skill for a woman in the Kremlin. "A few emails of interest as well."

"Of interest?" Natasya asked. She let her inflection go flat; it was as close to open dissent as she could imagine going. *Of interest to whom?* she left unspoken.

"Yes, several," Matfey said, sitting down on the couch next to her, unasked. She could break his neck right now, but beyond immediate satisfaction, what would be the point? It would be like snapping the neck of a field mouse or a bunny. She wouldn't eat him, so it would simply be good fun. Fun could wait for a more opportune time.

Matfey set up his little laptop computer, his little wonder of Western corruption. She watched with a thinly veiled disgust all the while, him in his little monkey suit, staring at the screen. It made its little boops and beeps while it started up. Natasya watched it all proceed with a studied disinterest. She caught Miksa watching carefully, though. He always watched carefully, though he hid it well.

A harsh trilling filled the air just as Matfey's little device finished its—what did he call it?—boot up? It sounded like something fun to Natasya, the prospect of ramming hers up his soft, bourgeoisie, rich-boy ass, over and over as he screamed in the night. She'd done worse to better men. He reached into his coat pocket—such a lovely, heavy coat. It looked fine and new.

"Yes?" Matfey asked. She could tell by his tone that the caller was important, was deferred to by the little weasel. "Of course. I can be there immediately if it's as important as you say—of course." He was nodding along like a limp-necked thing, like he had no spine of his own. "I was just going to catch them up on their current—it's that urgent?" He stared longingly at his little love, his little computer. She'd seen Miksa and Vitalik, men in prison thirty years, look less amorously at their first woman than this shit looked at his technological marvel. Perhaps it had an attachment to make love to, as well. "I will be there immediately." He stood without preamble, shoving his phone back into his pocket. "I must go," he announced. "I must—" He started to move for his computer, and then his phone trilled again. He glanced at the screen and seemed to make a decision. "I will be back later to attend to our business," he said, and broke into a girlish run toward the door, slamming it behind him.

Natasya stared at the machine in suspicion. She did not trust these things, nor the men who used them. "I thought he'd never leave," she breathed.

"It took some doing," came a calm female voice out of the little box. Natasya had too much self-control to yelp, but she did let out a might exhale of sharp shock at the sudden, disembodied voice.

"What devilry is this?" Volkov said, circling around to look at the screen. Miksa held his place, staring at it from behind the couch upon which Matfey had sat while setting up his little machine. Vitalik merely stared, slightly agape.

The screen rippled and blurred, a dark silhouette appearing in the dots and static. "I needed him out of the room so we could talk," it—she—said, as cool as a fresh spring snow. Natasya just stared at the computer, the little technological evil, and watched it with her half-lidded eyes. This time, there was no smile.

"Who are you?" Leonid asked, "and what do you want to talk about?"

"I want to talk about you," she said. "About what you want. About what you need."

"Aren't you the generous sort?" Natasya asked, never taking her eyes off of it. Leonid had been ready with a reply but he silenced himself as she spoke. "Worrying about us."

"I don't mean to suggest some sort of one-sided arrangement," the voice said, calmly. She sounded … weak. Labored. As though she were having trouble breathing. "I want to hire you to do a job for me. And I will pay you … whatever you want."

"Perhaps you haven't heard," Leonid said with a half-smile, "but we are not that interested in money. Much of it has been offered to us already."

"That's why I asked what you want—and need," the voice came again. "Perhaps it might be … asylum on friendlier shores? Perhaps … Cuba?" Natasya stared hard at the screen. "Don't worry. No one else can hear us right now. I've blotted out the sound on the government's listening devices, diverted it to me. Unsophisticated things, their devices. Limited People's have much more modern ones."

"Meet the new boss," Natasya said under her breath, "same as the old one."

"Maybe you'd like to put a little egg on their face?" The voice was wheedling, searching out motive. "Humiliate your government? Your new friends?"

"Perhaps we'd like both," Leonid said quietly, "and more."

"Name your price," the voice said, soft, smooth, and with a slight gasp. "I can get you almost anything."

Natasya stared at the machine—the box—and wondered if she should even trust it. What would the old KGB do, if this were them at work? Those men always thought the same, worked the same, acted the same. Horned dogs, all the way down to the bottom floor of the subbasement at Dzerzhinsky

Square. "What do you want us to do?" she asked.

The screen changed from its dark and splotchy view to a news program. It was an abrupt intercut, and a face appeared from a distance, a girl—nothing more—with dark hair bound back, a thick coat, hurrying down a city street while the cameras followed her. The scene cut again, and the same girl was shown—this time blurrier, as by a lower quality camera—kicking the chair out from underneath a man who was cuffed hand and foot.

"Do you know who this is?" the voice asked. Now it was filled with cold and loathing.

"Sienna Nealon," Vitalik said, his voice filled with a little interest. Natasya gave him a look and he explained. "She is the head of the United States's metahuman policing unit."

Natasya felt her jaw settle back uneasily. She'd heard the name. "What do you want with this girl?"

The screen froze on the picture of this Sienna Nealon hitting the man in chains. "I want her dead," the voice said coolly.

"So hire an assassin," Natasya said, waving off the voice. "Plenty of those to be had for cheaper than the quartet of us."

"That's not all I want you to do," the voice said, and something spilled out onto the screen, something black and white, with lines straight and curved, and English words all over.

"What the hell is this?" Natasya said, staring at the bizarre picture. It looked like—

"Blueprints," Miksa said, speaking up at last.

"The Hungarian gets it in one," the voice said, almost crowing. "It's a set of blueprints. But not just any blueprints … they're the maps and details for the construction of Sienna Nealon's metahuman prison, where she's keeping almost twenty of our people in restraints day and night, under the ground." There was a pause, and Natasya stared at the computer shrewdly. Now, this was interesting. "I want you to kill the warden." There was a pause, and Natasya could almost hear laughter, faint, digital, over the line, "Then I want you to do for these people what was just done for you.

"I want you to set them all free."

14.

Sienna

I walked into my office to find it really wasn't my office anymore. That was strike one.

My bonsai tree—lovingly cared for by me—was carelessly placed on top of a box of my stuff right by the door. Strike two.

The man sitting in my chair was a little overweight, had sandy blond hair that was combed to one side, and probably the least engaged expression I'd ever seen. His eyes were intelligent but damned cool, and he watched me walk furiously through the door without a hint that he cared.

I'd say that was strike three, but I'm not a bear, so staring me down in the middle of what had been—until hours or minutes ago—my office wasn't a capital offense. Let's call it strike two and a half.

"Sienna Nealon," he said, leaning back in my damned chair. He didn't exude any smugness, which was a lifesaver for him. He was just cool, collected, almost uncaring. I'd never met anyone quite so placid in my presence.

"Well, you've got my name," I said, letting my gaze hang on my box o' stuff. "How about tossing me yours?"

"Andrew Phillips," he said. "I'm the new Director of the—"

"I know the name of the agency I head."

"Well, you don't head it anymore," he said. "You've been given a new post—Head of Operations."

"Well, that's bullshit," I said hotly. Of course. How else did you think I'd respond to an affront like this?

"Interesting way to look at it," he said, readjusting himself to fold one leg across the other knee. He was pretty flexible for a big guy. "Have you watched the news at all today?"

"No," I said, "I've been a little busy stopping a heist at the Federal Reserve and transporting a meta prisoner back here."

"Hrm," he said, and picked up my remote control—*mine*—and turned on *my* TV.

I hate cable news.

The video footage was not good. Someone had snuck a camera into the train tunnel, and they had lots of roll of people being helped out of the subway station at Canal Street on stretchers and hobbling.

Oops.

"Wait," he said, not a trace of amusement. This guy sounded like he was serious about a problem. "It gets worse."

The video flipped to cell phone footage of me abusing poor, helpless Eric Simmons, and I have to admit, I cringed. They showed what almost looked like a mug shot of me—taken from a still frame of that damned Gail Roth interview I did—and then switched to the panel discussion. Thankfully, the TV was muted, but I could tell by the look of the panel that it was like sharks being dropped into a freshly chummed pool.

"Okay," I said as Andrew Phillips flipped off the TV, "this looks bad."

"Oh, yes," he agreed calmly, "it looks bad. It looks bad for you, it looks bad for this agency, and it looks especially bad for the president of the United States, who has backed your actions to this point and is now facing re-election later this year with this eating up the headlines."

"Gosh," I said, "I'm sorry I ate your headlines. I'll go on a diet immediately." He didn't look impressed—he actually didn't react at all to my comment. "Maybe you could spin it as being tough on crime—"

"There's no spinning this," he pronounced. "You're not going to change minds on it. It's just a big, stinking mess that could potentially hang around the president's neck between now and the first Tuesday in November."

"Hm," I muttered, half under my breath, "usually it's an albatross or a millstone around your neck, but a big, stinking mess? That's—"

"I'm sure you're really very funny to a lot of people," Phillips said, folding his arms over his barrel-looking chest. He wasn't fat, just … big. Bulky. Broad. "But I also know you've never had to clean up your own messes." He was lecturing me, I realized at last. That's why it was absent any anger. "Here, in England, wherever you've gone, you've had people behind you motivated to keep secret the things you've done. Well, the era of secrets is over." He let a low breath that expressed disinterest more than exasperation. "The president is tired of trying to cover for you. You are the albatross—see, I can respect your metaphor—around his neck, and I'm here to either make it so you're not, or we cut you free." He shrugged. "Not a threat, by the way."

"It sounded a little like one," I said, feeling the tension in my jaw ratchet.

"Let me clarify," Phillips said. "You're either going to get on board with the new program, or you can find a new job. Either is fine."

I snorted. "You're gonna have a hell of a time running a metahuman policing program without any metahumans to help you."

He didn't even blink. "Not really." He stood, arms still folded. "We'll have to make some changes, though. The capture rate is going to plunge, for sure. We won't be able to guarantee the security of the prison, either, so," he waved a hand at something on the desk and I realized it was a report on the security measures, "at the first sign of an escape attempt we'll flood all the cells to the top. After that, we'll just fill it up with concrete and make sure it stays buried until after November. It'll be easier to explain in a second term."

I felt my mouth fall slightly agape. "You wouldn't."

"Do you think most people care what happens to those with powers that they don't understand?" He stared at me evenly, apparently unconcerned that he'd just outlined a plan for murder that was predicated on political inconvenience. "Let me help you—they don't. They don't mind people like you that they perceive as helpful, but other than a certain vocal segment of the population, the civil rights of your people aren't even in the top ten answers when they commission a poll on 'the single biggest issue facing America today.'" His eyes honed in on mine. "But one meta issue makes the top ten. Care to guess which?"

I felt my eyes fall. I'd heard these poll answers before. "The one where they view us as a threat to ordinary society."

He navigated his way around my—his—desk. "I'm not gonna pretend that killing everyone in the lower levels and giving up on the more humane capture method is our preferred option. But I think you know the president is in for a political fight." He arched an eyebrow. "Against an old friend of yours, probably, if the current polls hold through the primaries. This department is going to stop being the loose cannon on this deck, right now." He looked me in the eye, and I knew he was not bluffing. "You can either be a part of that ... or not. Your choice." He settled back on his heels. "What's your answer?"

I blinked, looking at the floor, and then my eyes came up to find his. "Go fuck yourself," I said. I grabbed my box and headed out the door.

15.

I was halfway across the snowy field to the dormitory when Andrew Phillips caught up to me. "Really?" he asked, and he wasn't all that much more expressive than he'd been in his office. It was cold; I was shivering as I walked. I could have flown, but I think it would have made it worse. He could run, though, give him credit for that. His complexion looked like he was gonna burn up in the sun, though, like a natural-born Minnesotan. I sympathized.

"Really," I said. "In case you didn't read my personnel file, I don't respond well to threats, intimidation, coercion or people who attempt to lean on me."

"I didn't threaten you," he said, his stride keeping up with mine. The bastard wasn't even wearing a coat, and his breath puffed in the air on the sunlight, freezing-ass day. "I didn't try and intimidate you; I can't recall any sort of carrot that would be coercion—"

"You leaned on me," I said.

"I told you how it's going to be," he said. "If you want to take that as leaning, that's on you. Maybe it escaped your notice, but you're twenty-two years old and you've been running this department into the ground for three years without interference—"

I spun on him. "'Running it into the ground'? I haven't even a pulled a 'Man of Steel' and trashed the whole city of Minneapolis yet." I looked skyward. "Though I suppose the day is young. I've minimized casualties where possible—"

"You nuked a resort town in Northern Minnesota," he said, looking at me slightly warily.

"And no civilians died," I said. "I got the job done, against a world-ending group of nutballs who had me grossly outnumbered. What more do you want from me?"

"The job done quietly," he said. "The job done out of the headlines. No high profile failures like this morning, no botched , graceless, disastrous interviews with the press, no ambassadors howling at the president because an agency head assaulted them." He raised an eyebrow at me. "In other words, smooth sailing."

"I can …" I cut myself off, "… be smooth," I finished lamely. No, I probably couldn't.

"No, you can't," he said, not breaking off eye contact. "Not in charge, anyway. You're ruled by your own will to action, by your own sense of … whatever. Justice, lack of impulse control, something."

Kill him, Wolfe suggested. *Wear his skin and keep doing the job.*

Not. Helpful. Also, eww.

"So why not just fire me and be done with it?" I asked. "Why are you chasing me across the lawn?" I was ready to drop my box of stuff in the snow and fly off.

"Because it's not politically expedient to drop you like you've got the plague," he said. "If it were, I would have advised it by now." There was zero remorse in this statement, which I found not at all reassuring. "You're a hero. You're unspent political capital. Sure, the electorate mostly won't care if you resign and walk away, but some will. The question might be raised about our safety, and how the president is conducting metahuman affairs, at least until we get a few high-profile incidents under the new department's belt."

"A few high-profile kills, you mean."

He shrugged almost imperceptibly. "We'll do what we have to in order to deliver the necessary results for—"

"—the election," I finished for him. "You're a one-note

singer. It's all about the politics for you; politics and perception."

"That's all there is in the world," he said. "Perception. See, one of the planks of our platform is trying to reinvigorate that sense of community that people have lost. It's not about actually making things that way again; it's about doing the things that people perceive as pushing us in that direction. And part of that is that they need to feel safe."

"Your opinions are utter bullshit," I said, shaking my head. I focused in on him with fiery eyes. "If I'm gonna have to deal with the misery of listening to them, I feel like I should at least get the joy of extracting them from you with a thousand fearful screams at the end of a chainsaw."

"You can't threaten me," he said, and I could tell he was unmoved.

"I've done worse than threaten to worse people than you," I said, not backing off.

"If you assault me you'll be fired," he said simply, "for cause."

"I just quit, in case you missed it."

"And your file will be leaked to the public," he went on, like it was nothing. "Everything." He leaned toward me. "You have done worse things to worse people than me. What was his name? Rick?" He looked like he was trying to remember. "Beat him to death with his own chair?" He never let up that gaze. "Did that make you feel superior? Did you feel like you showed him the error of his ways?"

I could feel my teeth rattle, whether from cold or anger I couldn't tell. "He was a real bastard. But you should know he leaned on me, too."

"You threatened me, I threatened you," Andrew Phillips said. "Proportional response." He took a small step back. "I won't stop you if you're going to leave. I've got preparations to make if you're truly done, though. Prisoners to … make ready." There was no joy in the way he said it. No emotion at all, really. "I read the report on every one of them. The only one that seems like he's not a waste of oxygen is Timothy Logan."

My head snapped around. Phillips was still looking at me coolly, utterly unflappable. "Now you're threatening him," I said.

"I'm not threatening him," Phillips said simply. "I told you ten minutes ago what the consequences would be if you decided to resign. I'm just reminding you about all the ..." he started to turn, "... aspects of your decision that you might not have considered."

He strolled off across the snowfield, like he wasn't cold, like he had not a care in the world. I watched him go, wondering all the while what the hell I should do.

16.

I started back toward the dormitory building, regretting not taking the underground tunnel. I was usually smarter than this, but apparently in all the fuss surrounding me quitting my job in a fury, I forgot that it was winter and cold, with snow past my ankles. I trudged along, feeling my lips freezing from the chill, my eyes blurring (I wasn't crying, the wind was just hard, dammit), and the tears getting crusty around the corners.

I had the sense I was being followed, and turned to face my pursuer. I nearly did a double take.

It was a dog. I don't know breeds, but it was kinda tan colored, with fur going in a lot of different directions. Not big, and kinda skinny.

I stared at him, he stared at me, his head cocked to the side like he was asking me a question. "What the hell are you doing here?" I asked, like he might answer me. We had a perimeter fence, after all. I blinked, and my freeze-crusted eyes flaked a little ice-dust. "Never mind." I stopped talking right then, because I was pretty out of my mind to be talking to a dog, I thought. I started back toward the dormitory.

I made it about another fifteen feet when I heard a little whimper. I looked back and saw the poor guy shivering. He was up to mid-leg in the hard, crunching snow, and he didn't have anything but that thin coat of fur to protect him. I cursed his master, whoever they were, for letting him out in this, and felt an internal tugging that I didn't care for. "I can't help you,"

I said lamely. "I'm not a pet person." I thought about it. "I'm actually not a people person, either, so don't think I'm discriminating against you."

I turned to leave, and another whimper froze me in my tracks. I turned to see him trotting over to me, the single most pitiful look in his eyes that I have ever seen. "I can't help you," I said, readjusting my box of possessions. My bonsai tree was probably frozen to death already. "Look, I can barely take care of myself. If they didn't feed me in the cafeteria, I would have died of ramen poisoning years ago."

I tried to pull away from those dark eyes, that cute little face, but it was like a black hole that dragged me closer. In fact, I was standing still and he slowly edged toward me, head down, eyes just barely looking up. Like he was … begging. Like some poor, piteous soul looking for a pat on the head.

I adjusted my box of stuff and granted him the pat on the head. He was just sitting there, waiting for it. He rubbed against my hand, and then against my leg. He was panting, and I had a sudden fear his tongue was going to freeze while we were standing there.

"Oh, all right," I said, giving in on that internal tug of war. "Come with me. I'll get you something to eat. But you're going to the Humane Society first thing." He followed me back to the dormitory building walking at my side, the only friend I felt like I had right then.

17.

"What's up with Benji?" Reed asked as he stepped into my quarters. He caught sight of the dog curled up in the corner immediately, of course. I'd given the poor guy a bath, which he seemed okay with, and got him toweled off. He'd chosen a spot on the living room's heating vent for a nap after devouring some bacon I'd had left in the refrigerator and cooked up for him. It was pretty much all I had.

"He was wandering the campus, looking pitiful," I said as I shut the door behind my brother.

"You're taking in strays now?" Reed asked, one eyebrow higher than the other. "For real? You?"

"I have a heart, you know," I said, brushing past him. "It may be buried under a layer of permafrost, but it's there."

"Well, okay then," Reed said, working his way over to my living room to sit on the couch. "What's up with the new boss?"

"You heard about that?" I shouldn't have been surprised. Reed was better connected around here than I was.

"Be hard to miss," he said, glancing at the dog, which was now up and trotting over to him. He stood next to Reed while my brother stroked his head gently, like a natural. "The whole place is in rumorous upheaval." He seemed to reconsider that phrasing for a few seconds, then shrugged. "You know what I mean."

"Yeah," I said. "What's the pulse?"

Reed's face went guarded. "Depends on the branch. Security and Ops are not happy, because they like you and your rampant badassery. Makes them feel safe." He frowned. "Which is surprising, given their casualty numbers. Admin's divided, because Ariadne was tough on them, but she delivered results. Also, they were apparently afraid of you."

I frowned. "What the hell, did you commission a poll? How do you know this?"

"I talk to people," he said with a shrug, still petting the dog. "I'm connected to others."

"You're connected at the crotch to a certain *il dottore*," I said, glaring at him.

"Aghhh," he said, drawing it out. "When will you let it go already?"

"Half a dozen more ill-timed cracks, and I promise I will."

He gave it a moment's consideration. "I can live with that."

I headed to the fridge and opened it to find it rather spare. Still. "I'd offer you something to drink, but you already know where to find the tap." I swung the door wide so he could see. "Would you care to partake of our fine selection of ketchup and mustard?"

"What are you gonna do?" Reed asked, changing the subject.

I shut the fridge door with a little more gusto than it needed. "I don't know. This new boss—Andrew Phillips—he's a tough cookie. Like a steel dough with diamond chips—"

"What did he do?" Reed asked, cutting to the quick.

"He says the government is going to shut down the prison if I leave," I said, folding my arms in front of me. "That they'll dispense with the inmates at the first sign of trouble because they can't provide proper security without meta assistance—my assistance."

"Ouch," Reed said, his jaw slightly open. "You believe him?"

"I don't know him well enough to call a bluff yet."

Reed stared at me shrewdly. "Would it bother you if he wasn't bluffing?"

I let that thought bounce around in my head for a little bit before answering. "It would bother me in Timothy Logan's case. Most of the others … less so. Though I'm not exactly a huge fan of the idea of executing helpless prisoners. Seems …" I searched for a word, but "gauche" seemed wrong.

"Cruel?" Reed asked, still studying my reaction. "Vicious? Over-the-top?"

"All the above and more, probably," I said. "Which is kinda sad for me to admit since I know most of these people would gladly go out into the world and wreak more havoc, kill more people." I shook my head. "I mean, I would have to say that at least seventy percent of them view other human beings as objects at best, with little to no empathy for them as people."

"Which makes them dangerous," Reed said. "Definitely worthy of at least some incarceration."

"Yeah," I said with a sigh. "Anyway, I don't know—"

A hard knocking interrupted me, rattling my door. "Who is it?" I called even as I got up.

"Ariadne," she said, and I hurried to let her in. She was standing there, looking more than a little irritable, and she barged right in without so much as an invite. "Can you believe this?"

"Uh … no?" I watched her come in at a full head of steam, looking significantly more upset than when she'd delivered the news to me only an hour earlier.

"We run the ship all through the war," she said, apparently taking no notice of Reed or my new dog as she paced in, heading straight for the kitchen, "and for over three years after, not a peep from Washington as they kept their distance, but now—one giant screwup later," I blanched at her assessment of my morning, "and this happens." She wheeled on me. "Can you believe it?"

"I can believe it," Reed said, and she snapped her head

around in surprise to finally take notice of him. "You're only as good as your last success—or screwup—after all."

"Ohh," she said, making a kind of cooing noise, "your dog is very cute, Reed."

"That's *my* dog," I said, suddenly irritated. She turned to look at me blankly, like she couldn't understand what I was saying. "And it's a stray that's going to the pound," I finished, feeling my irritation fade with the calm reality that I was not keeping the animal. Back to being predictable me, I guess.

"I'm not sure I want to stick around for this insult," Ariadne said, resuming her pacing in my kitchen. "I mean—it really does feel like an insult, doesn't it?" She swooped past the fridge again and paused, opening it up like she owned the place. She was silent for a moment as she looked into its depths. "How the hell do you not weigh like ninety-eight pounds?"

"We have a cafeteria," I said crossly, "in the freaking building. Also, my figure is naturally like this, okay? I'm stout, my ribcage is a little broader than average—"

"Whoa, sis," Reed said, and I followed his gaze to see my hand was engulfed in flames. "Need me to get a fire extinguisher?"

"Gavrikov!" I snapped, and the fire went out. Sometimes when my emotions got high, the souls I had stored in my brain took the opportunity to bubble to the surface and assert a certain amount of control.

I heard chortling in my head, mostly Eve Kappler and Bjorn. *Shut it*, I told them. My fingers still smoked, but I could still feel Gavrikov's rich satisfaction at the gag. He didn't have much in his non-life, I figured, so I let it go.

I took a breath and counted to five, then shifted my attention to Ariadne. "So, what are you going to do?"

She shut the door to my fridge, but gently, managing to pull off what I apparently couldn't. "I don't know. Probably keep working here, but gripe under my breath the whole time." She shook her head. "It's not like I have anywhere else to go, and the cause is still just, even if management isn't."

I shared a look with Reed, who snarked, "You can say that again."

"What about you?" Ariadne asked, folding her arms and looking at me. I was suddenly consciously aware that my place smelled like soap from the dog bath, and the air felt a little stuffy compared to what I'd been dealing with walking outside.

"I don't know," I said, and felt my brow furrow. Then I sighed because I did know, I really did. "I guess I'm staying for now." She looked at me with a raised eyebrow of her own. "At least until we see how things go."

"Hey," Reed said, "maybe in eleven months, when the election is over, this whole thing will settle out."

"Or in three months I'll parole Timothy Logan and not care enough about the rest of them to give a damn if I walk away," I said. The dog trotted over to me. He stood expectantly, in easy reach of my hand, big dark eyes looking up at me until I relented and reached down, petting him on the head. Maybe I had Ariadne and Reed fooled, but the dog— shrewder than he looked—had me figured out.

18.

I set up in my new office, half the size of the previous one, on my scuffed-up desk. I had taken the bonsai through the tunnel this time, and it seemed none the worse for the wear. I did a little clipping (it's this whole thing; I took a class on proper tree care and everything) and then settled down with a sigh to stare at my walls for a little while. Normally I'd have written an after-action report that would go up the chain to the Department of Homeland Security, but I wasn't feeling very inter-agency cooperative at the moment, so I decided to take a little time to reflect. Which meant I played solitaire for a while on my computer.

Hey, it's probably the least annoying thing I could have been doing. I mean, I could have been browsing porn or something.

I was interrupted by a knock on the door, and shut the solitaire window as abruptly as if I'd been caught doing—uhh, that other thing. "Yes?" I asked as a thin young woman stepped in.

"Ms. Nealon?" she asked, over thin-framed glasses. She had dark skin and curious eyes and was clad in a suit that was a lot more fashion-forward than anything Ariadne wore. "My name is Jackie Underwood, and I'm the new spokesperson."

"Huh," I said, staring at her. "I didn't know we had a press secretary."

"Spokesperson." She smiled, almost apologetically. "Part

of the changes, I'm afraid. Mr. Phillips brought me in to help, uh … address certain deficiencies in the agency." She'd already picked up the slang name in less than a day; most people tried to throw out the mouthful that was our un-acronymable name for at least two weeks.

"Meaning our nightmarish PR faux pas," I said. "Faux pas-es?" Sad that we needed to pluralize that word. Hey, if you're in charge of the supply closet and you screw up, it's not a big deal. If you're in charge of an agency that restrains superpowered murderers and you make a slip on TV, everyone's watching.

Actually, you know what? That supply closet metaphor doesn't work, because if you're in charge there and forget to order toilet paper, people will notice. In the worst way.

"To say the least," she said, drawing me back on point. "I'm here to facilitate a better image for the agency, and to make it possible for us to communicate with the national and local press without … missteps like we've seen in the past."

I cocked an eyebrow at her. "I like how you managed to say that without casting blame."

"The press is a tricky beast," she said knowingly. "Dealing with them is more art than science. So many different personalities."

"Okay," I said. I already liked her approach, which was a lot more delicate than Andrew Phillips's. That tool. I figured I might as well cooperate. "What do you want from me, Jackie?"

"First, I'd like you to direct any press inquiries to me," she said.

"Done," I said. I got probably ten a day via email, and presently they all went straight to the spam folder. It might have been quicker to just trash them, but I got a certain satisfaction in marking emails from famous talking heads and their assistants as spam. Because I'm petty, that's why.

"I would also like you to consider letting me prep you and schedule some interviews with the major networks." She watched my reaction, and it must have been good, because she immediately backpedaled. "Or maybe just one to start."

"Urgh …" I made a kind of growling noise. "Maybe I'll just make a YouTube video."

"Don't you think there are enough of those floating around at the moment?" Ouch. She looked apologetic again, but I sensed she enjoyed her own riposte. But credit to her—that was a choice shot, and it landed dead on target.

"I will definitely think about it," I said, "but do you really think that's a good idea after the Gail Roth thing?"

"I think you got awfully defensive, awfully fast," she said, and I knew she'd prepped this answer. "In return, Gail got more adversarial, and you entered a downward spiral until you crashed and burned."

"Hey, it wasn't that bad." It wasn't, really. I mean, it was bad, no doubt, but not plane-crash worthy.

Without even speaking, Jackie handed me a sheet of paper. I skimmed it, instantly recognizing it as a transcript from the interview.

GAIL: You shredded him. Chewed him up and shredded him to death.

SIENNA: (pause) Yeah? And?

GAIL: Did that … I mean, did you … isn't that kind of like state-sanctioned cannibalism?

SIENNA: Well, I did spit him out afterward.

GAIL: But there had to be pieces—

SIENNA: And I flossed like there was no tomorrow when I got back home, gargled with mouthwash for, like, hours—

GAIL: Cameras and videos all over Minneapolis recorded your showdown in minute detail. It's been aired on every channel, had millions and millions of hits on the internet. You're kind of a celebrity for that fight. What was it like, in that moment?

SIENNA: He kinda tasted like chicken. Maybe that was the dragon tastebuds at work, I dunno. But it was—

I closed my eyes. "Okay, I get the point. It was bad." I had walked out for a reason, after all. This was actually one of the high points, I thought.

"I think we can avoid this sort of thing next time with a little preparation," Jackie said sympathetically.

"Yeah," I said, balling up the transcript and tossing it into the recycling can. "Because now it'll be questions about why I attacked a defenseless prisoner who was already in custody."

She let that linger before she spoke, carefully. "Why did you attack him?"

I sighed. "Because he made a nasty, piggish comment to the waitress."

She lifted a small notepad up. "'Do you want a big tip? Or do you want the whole—'"

"Yeah, that was it," I cut her off.

She stared at me seriously. "This I can work with."

I looked at her through one open eye. "Seriously?"

"I'm already spinning it," she said, with a twinkle in her eye. "We got the waitress to talk, and she's giving a detailed account of how you upheld the dignity of all women or something. It's playing well with some of the audience anyway, and it's a better explanation than letting the assumption you beat prisoners for no reason linger out there unchallenged."

"All right," I said. "Let me think about the interview, but … probably. If you think you can prepare me for it."

"I can work wonders if given the chance," she said, and stood. "We pick the right interviewer, we give 'em some other things to work with, like this reception—"

Something about that caught in my head. "What reception?"

"Oh, Andrew didn't tell you?" she asked. I bit back a bitter reply about how Andrew and I were not fast friends yet, and she went on. "Directive from above. We're having a meet and greet; a reception here on campus with press, local politicians, some national names, and those Russian metas that just got out of prison. It'll be a nice little opportunity to mingle with the latest media darlings and let their current fame rub off on you a little."

I stared at her blankly. I had been in charge of this agency yesterday, and it'd have to be a lot colder day in hell than this one to prompt me to hold a reception. We're talking absolute zero, no particle motion. "What ... the ... actual ... eff?" I asked.

"It'll be fine," Jackie said, smiling. "You'll talk, you'll eat from the buffet table, you'll smile for pictures, and maybe at the end of the night, if you're ready, you'll do an interview. The Russians are PR gold right now, and if you can make nice with them, maybe they'll throw a little associative fairy dust on us, and we'll be through this scandal in less than a news cycle."

I just blinked at her as she started to leave. "When is this happening?" I asked, still stunned.

"This Friday," she said with a smile, and headed for the door. "You'll do fine. Just be a normal, civilized person, like you have been with me, and you'll come out of it covered in rose petals." She gave me another reassuring smile as she headed out the door, closing it quietly behind her.

"Well, shit," I said, utterly heartfelt, as I stared at the door. Meeting with a bunch of newly freed prisoners in a formal setting with buffet tables, booze and—dammit, me probably having to wear a dress or something.

I let out a low, self-pitying moan that I was thankful no one else could hear. How could this possibly get any worse?

19.

I found out at five o'clock the next morning when I got awakened by a scratching in my quarters. I was out of my room in seconds, my Sig Sauer pistol in hand. Nothing was going on outside the sliding glass door on the balcony, so I slid around the corner and pointed my gun at the front door, where I found my houseguest scratching to be let out, a pitifully sad look on his face.

"Dammit," I muttered and went looking for a bathrobe some idiot had gotten me as a gift. I didn't even have a leash for this dog, which I was determined to take to the pound today. I might have been somewhat irritable from being awoken at five in the morning.

I stood just outside the dormitory building, my breath frosting in the air, my lungs hurting in the chill of the dark night that showed not a hint of morning yet. There were stars in a blanket overhead, the few campus lights failing to do much to dim their shine. I wrapped my arms close around me and the wind picked up like an icy sheet of water had been thrown on me.

You take this insult too easily, Sienna, Wolfe said to me. He didn't say much anymore, which was surprising. There had been a time when he'd talk non-stop, whether I wanted him to or not.

"I know this must shock and astound you," I said, not bothering to just speak inside my own head since no one was

95

around, "but I live in a civilized world. There are rules we have to follow here, and killing people who annoy me isn't part of the game."

Bad game, Wolfe said. *Play a different one. Play your own. Make your own rules. That's what Wolfe did.*

"Not when you worked for Omega," I said, and felt him bristle within. "Pretty sure Alastor and the ministers had you on their leash then."

He's just trying to tell you not to take any crap from these politicians, Zack said, in a much more sympathetic tone. *You're better than them.*

"I'm not better than anybody," I mumbled, "but nobody's better than me."

A charmingly egalitarian statement, Gavrikov said. *But it reeks of naivety. Someone is always in charge, whether you want them to be or not. Someone always has the power, and right now they have it over you—unless you walk away.*

"I'm not ready to walk away yet," I whispered, shivering in my robe. I was wishing I'd thrown my coat on over it. I watched the dog scratch and paw at a snow mound before lifting his leg to—finally, thank the heavens—do his business. He came trotting back to me a few minutes later, looking marginally less piteous.

A hesitant voice emerged. *Tell Ariadne that she should not be willing to accept this turn of events lightly*, Eve Kappler said with quiet certainty. *Tell her ... she's better than this.*

I raised an eyebrow at the invisible person talking to me. "And I'm not?" She didn't answer, and I sighed, watching my breath frost into pure, white clouds in front of me.

The dog whined, and I ushered him inside in a hurry, catching a look from the night security guard, who was reading a book at the podium in the dormitory lobby. He smiled at the dog, though.

When I got back inside, I collapsed in my bed, pulling the covers over me even as I tossed the robe. I was sleeping in a tank top and pajama bottoms, and the warmth of the comforter felt oh-so-good. I felt a heavy thump as the dog landed on the bed, and I might maybe have shrieked just a little in surprise.

"No!" I said sternly as he circled round to the empty space next to me. Up to now, he'd apparently been quite comfortable on the vent in the living room. Now he was encroaching on my personal space. I put a hand on his head. "If I keep touching you, you're going to lose your soul," I said, then paused to wonder if it was true. I'd never really been in close contact with an animal before that I could recall.

The dog got that piteous look again and shuffled back a half an inch, and it almost felt like he was begging me to stay.

"Argh!" I said (it's mostly consonant sounds, all dripping with frustration, in case you were wondering how to pronounce that). "Fine," I said in the voice I reserved for things that were pretty much not fine at all. "But if you lose your soul, it's on you." I wondered what having a dog in my head would be like. Probably not all that much different than Wolfe. Maybe a little more genteel.

Not nice, Little D—

Shut it, Wolfe.

I fell back asleep to the sounds of steady breathing next to me, a kind of snuffling noise, a muted breathing through the nose that was surprisingly relaxing, reassuring, telling me I was not alone.

20.

Natasya

Natasya broke the neck of the soldier with a smile on her face. She wore the black, the warpaint, with some digital-scrambled camouflage pattern like the voice in the computer had told her. She followed the orders. It was what she did.

"Candy from a baby," Leonid said as they strolled out the door. He carried the canisters on his broad shoulders, his bearded face smudged with the dark paint. "I think that's how the expression goes."

"Easy, easy," Vitalik said. The depot which they were leaving was quiet; it was early morning, an hour from shift change. The air was cold, crisp, not unlike the air outside the prison when they'd gotten out. Frost covered the grass, like spring in Russia. Winter here was mild.

For this, Natasya smiled, letting the corpse fall from her grasp. It made a *thunking* noise as it hit the concrete below. "Capitalist pig," she said, almost an afterthought. She'd trained to kill American soldiers for years beyond counting. When she got out of prison and learned that the war was not only over, but that her side had lost, it had been a disappointment, to say the least. This was like a rekindling of the fire, a fond remembrance that maybe—just maybe—their war was not over yet.

"The truck will be there in thirty seconds," the voice came over her earpiece. It was hard to believe she could so trust a voice on the other end of an earpiece, but here she was, and the voice had not failed her yet. "Prep for extraction."

"Any other soldiers?" Natasya asked. She looked through the dark, pre-dawn disposal facility. There was nary a hint of movement, which was good for the plan. She couldn't help but feel a hint of disappointment, though, at the lack of targets.

"No other patrols, no alarms," the voice replied, a little out of breath. Natasya listened for weakness, and whoever this woman was, she sounded like she had a breathing problem. It was worth noting. "You are clear."

Natasya felt the mild disappointment, but buried it under the feeling of a job well done. "Gate guards?"

"The mercenaries have already taken them out."

The truck rumbled up to them, and Natasya lifted the canvas back. It was like any other military truck, not all that different from the diesel models that they rode in the Russian army back in the days of old. Leonid got in first, aided by a man in a soldier's uniform. She watched them handle the canisters on the big man's shoulders with care, watched them strap them down carefully, carefully, to the decking as Miksa and Vitalik got in the back of the truck.

This was not her first operation on U.S. soil. But, Natasya thought, as she climbed up and the truck started to move, it was perhaps the beginning of her greatest. "Next stop, airport," Vitalik said, leaning back in that easy manner of his. "And then ... what is the name of the place we're going again?"

"Minnesota," Natasya said as she sat down on the bench, suddenly uneasy, staring out the back of the truck. She looked once more at the sky and let the flap drop, sealing them in darkness. The truck rumbled on, undisturbed, into the night.

21.

Sienna

I missed the morning briefing. I was a little surprised, because we'd never had a morning briefing before, so naturally, I didn't think to check my calendar to see if I was missing something until after Harper dropped by my new office, looked around with a low, unimpressed whistle and said, "Missed you at the meeting this morning."

Son of a gun.

I'd kinda of spent a few minutes cursing the name of Andrew Philips after that. Not that I really enjoyed going to meetings, but I tried very hard not to be an unprofessional idiot. Call it the unfortunate side effect of running a government agency at the ripe old age of twenty-one, but I had to work pretty hard to command respect, and that meant I didn't do boneheaded things like miss meetings.

Until today.

It irritated me so much that I just left, walked out of my office and headed back to my quarters. I walked across the snowy campus, burning aggravation and frustration and a sense of HOW THE HELL COULD THEY DO THIS TO ME? coursing through me with every freezing breath.

Note to self: take the tunnel from now on.

And before you ask, no, I had not dropped the dog off at the pound yet. Because I was busy. Busy missing meetings.

And playing solitaire and brooding in my office. (Reed would say sulking, or maybe even pouting, but he can go screw a rude Italian doctor.)

I'd just made it back to my quarters and greeted Rover (I'm not a pet person, and I'm worse with names, clearly) when the knock at my door jarred me out of a solid reverie, and it opened before I could grant permission to whoever was knocking to enter. Of course it was Andrew Phillips.

"You missed the briefing this morning," he said, like opening the door to my quarters was just a normal thing to do.

"Thanks, Lumbergh," I said, and he didn't even raise an eyebrow. Maybe he thought I'd genuinely forgotten his name. I backburnered his invasion of privacy and failure to respect a door and launched right to petulance. "Maybe if I'd known about that briefing, I would have been there. Whose bright idea was it to drop that one on the calendar without mentioning it to me?"

"Mine," he said, unimpressed with my withering sarcasm. His arms were still folded, his tone as flat as Iowa. "We're getting more cooperation from Homeland Security now, as we're further integrated into the department, so regular briefings are going to be held to keep our people up to date with all the normal intel, law enforcement happenings—anything that might be useful."

I withheld more sarcasm because … that actually might be kinda cool. "Okay. I'll be there from now on. Now that I know about it." Couldn't hold back that little dig, though.

"I'm having the condensed version of today's report forwarded to you," he said. "I'm assuming you're in, since your stuff is in your new office."

"I'm in," I said, grudgingly, like every syllable was parting with a tooth. "For now." The dog wagged his tail hard enough to strike my leg.

"The reception is tonight," he said. The dude still hadn't spontaneously sprouted an expression of his own. "Jackie talked to you." This wasn't a question.

"I will be on my bestest behavior," I said and mock saluted him. "Trying to regain some public relations yardage."

"She'll be by your office to coach you later," he said, "after you've had a chance to read your security briefing. Assuming you're going to be there? Otherwise I'll just have her stop here."

"I'll be in my office," I said. "Where are we holding this reception?"

"Third floor," Phillips said. "I'm having some of that extra cube space cleared."

I felt a frown crease my face. "What about the people who work there? That's finance, isn't it?"

He didn't even tilt an eyebrow. "A lot of them are being let go. The finance department isn't needed like it used to be. We've got a lot of dead weight down there."

"So you're not just here to make us politically attractive," I said, shaking my head.

"No," he said, "I'm here to make this agency run. In case you missed it, there's no one left in Congress agitating to give us more funding, and your old methods are dried up. Welcome to the new world."

I doubt my expression fully conveyed my feelings, so I reached for words. "I don't know if I like your new world all that much."

"I don't really care." He truly sounded like he didn't. "I've got a platform to work with, and the job is minimizing the nuisance and threat of metas, smoothing the public relations gaffes so people can forget about you and the vital job you do. President Harmon is running on his 'Great Community' platform, and national security threats distract from that."

"Sorry to interfere with the campaign strategy," I murmured, not really all that sorry. Not that I was gonna vote for the ass for re-election anyway. "Surely even someone with the blinders on as heavy as you must realize that threats like Simmons are always going to be out there, waiting for their chance to strike."

He looked at me like I was stupid. "Yes, there will always be criminals out there, regular and meta. But it doesn't have to be front page news when you take one of them down."

"Don't you think people deserve to be at least made aware of the threat?" I asked. "I mean, I'm not talking a full-fledged cable news-style fear campaign, but … something. A little vigilance? There are metas out there who don't fit into ordinary criminal activity, who—"

"A normal human being has a lot higher likelihood of dying of cancer, heart disease, car accidents—" Phillips's lips twisted at the side and he looked like he was displaying emotion for the first time—loathing, "any of the top list of causes of death. There are fewer than one thousand and probably more like five hundred of your people still left walking this earth. The entire planet. Yes, most of the remainder are in the United States, but thanks to Sovereign, metahumans are less of a threat than ever." He stood with folded arms. "No, I don't think people need to worry about metas. I think there are other priorities."

I stared at him in numb disbelief. "You might feel differently if you'd ever met Sovereign face to face."

"But I'll never have to, because he's dead."

"Because of me," I said, snapping slightly. "Because I was—"

"Because you killed him," Phillips said, and I felt the dog at my leg, panting. "Well done. You got a medal for that, right?"

"Or something." I stared him down. "Some people don't want to be part of your 'community,' great or otherwise. They want to douse it and everything in it with gasoline and watch the flesh sear off bones while they try to figure out if they feel anything one way or another about it."

"Are you one of those people?" Phillips asked.

"In the world of metas," I said, skipping barely over calling him 'dipshit' to start the sentence, "I'm the only one left standing between you and them, and if you ever looked one of them in the eye, you wouldn't even need to ask me that."

Phillips stared straight at me. "Really? Were you that sort of line for Glen Parks, standing between him and the 'forces of evil'?" He let no amusement creep into his voice, just hard steel, and I flinched. "Eve Kappler? Clyde Clary? Roberto Bastian?" I knew he sensed my horror, but he showed as little care for it as he had for anything else I'd said. "Because you killed all of them too, didn't you? And you weren't protecting anybody, it wasn't even heat of the moment like with Rick, it was careful stalking and cold-blooded murder—"

"You don't know what you're talking about," I said, but I didn't believe it.

"You killed them," he said. "It's in your file. Revenge. Agent Li wrote a long, extensive report on it. So you're the … wolfhound, I guess? The protector? But you're also a wolf. If the people of the United States have a meta threat to worry about, don't you think it might be you? Because it's seems like you're the most likely cause of death—"

"I am not—" I'd had to deal with this before, the past rising up to choke me. "It was a long time ago. I did my part, my penance, to make up for it—"

"Can you really make up for it?" Phillips stared at me. "Because if I went by the arguments you've made for the prisoners we're keeping … you'd be in a cell right next to them. Forever." There was no threat there, but he'd doused me with a fair amount of verbal cold water. Or possibly gasoline.

"I'm not the same person I was back then."

He leaned in a little, eyeing my dog. "Without powers … you're just a criminal. With them, you're worse. You have the potential to be the biggest active threat this agency could face." He didn't even blink. "Just so we know where each other stands."

"Where do you stand, Mr. Phillips?" I asked, feeling more than a little sick.

"I have a job to do," he said. "It sounds like you've chosen one for yourself. I'm not threatening you—"

"If you have to keep saying that, you're probably being threatening."

"—but if you're going to work here, I'm not going to hold you up or cover for you," he said. "Play by the rules, do your job, keep things quiet. On a tight leash." He looked down at my dog. "The election will be over in less than a year, and I'm sure I'll be out of your hair before you know it." He frowned. "Speaking of which, you should go have something professionally done to your hair. For the reception." He turned his back and started to walk away from me.

"You just called me a criminal," I said to his receding back. "You know I'm dangerous. But you keep going out of your way to rub it in my face, if not threatening me then at least inflaming me. Why in the hell would you do that if you think I'm no better than anyone locked up in the cages below?"

He didn't even glance back as he hit the button for the elevator and it dinged. "That's the difference between us, Miss Nealon. I know who you are, and you're still trying to figure me out. One way or another, I don't have to worry about you anymore." He stepped into the elevator and disappeared, leaving me wondering exactly what he meant by that.

22.

I was more or less dressed when Reed knocked at the door a few hours later. I'd had an angry rallying of my souls, desirous of slitting Andrew Phillips's throat for that last snub (I told them no). I'd also had my meeting with Jackie, I'd read my security briefing, I'd sat around fretting for a while, thinking about how much things had gone to suck—yeah, actually I'd spent most of my time thinking that. My souls, randomly agitating for violence as they were, weren't helping. Wolfe kept floating images of Phillips in various states of disembowelment up to me, presumably for my entertainment. It didn't help.

I was taking a break from it when Reed knocked, though, and I answered the door to find him standing out in the hall in a tuxedo. "Very 007," I said as he came in.

"You look nice," he said to me as he entered. The dog was back on the heating vent, and Reed's gaze caught him immediately. "You've kept the mutt, I see."

"I didn't even have time to get my hair done," I said, self-consciously fiddling with the chop-sticked style I'd put it into. Of all the things Phillips had said to me, I had to admit that the petty crack about my hair was in the running for most aggravating. What did that say about me? "I'll get to the pound."

"Sure you will," Reed said, giving the good boy a rub on the belly where he lay. "How you holding up?"

"Other than feeling pretty damned powerless?" I asked, heading back to the bedroom to take a look at myself in the mirror. I was actually wearing a dress this time. A real, legit dress. Hold the shock.

"You're like the most powerful meta in the world," he said, voice muffled where he stood out in the living room. "How is it you're feeling powerless?"

"Because the ability to destroy everything is kinda meaningless unless you're willing to employ it, duh." I put in my earrings. I don't wear earrings often. Because I heal rapidly, I basically have to pierce them myself anytime I do. I'd formed some scar tissue on my body once upon a time, before I gained Wolfe's healing powers, but it had long since dissolved. This is why I don't do formal occasions, reason #85,764,938. It stung a little as I pushed them in, then I dabbed away the blood as it welled and then stopped in seconds. "So, while I could level entire cities with my amazing powers, imprison countless people in nets of light, heal from numerous bullet wounds or even turn into a dragon and start devouring people like the miniature quiches that I'm hoping they'll be serving tonight … that's not really me." I stared at myself in the mirror, looking at the drops of blood on my fingers. It certainly wasn't the first that had rested there. "Is it?" I whispered.

"No, it's not," he said, leaning in the doorway. I hadn't meant for him to hear that.

"For all our conversations about how brutal and uncaring I am about our prisoners," I said, building a brick wall inside to keep these overwhelming, hot-running feelings from running over me, "I would think by now I'd have come to a point where I'm just … numb to it." I looked up at him. "I've killed enough people I ought to be numb. I shouldn't feel … like this."

He stared at me. "Like you want to kill Phillips?"

"I don't want to kill Phillips," I said. "Don't get me wrong, I don't like him. I wouldn't mind bopping him on the head and watching him pitch into unconsciousness in a snow bank—in formal wear, just for fun." Even that image didn't do much to make me smile. "I'm not Wolfe. I'm a smartass, and I can be violent, but … I don't want to kill everybody. I don't want to kill anybody." I looked up at myself. "I'll do it when necessary, but it isn't a joy for me." I looked sideways at him. "Not even when I killed that turd in England a few months ago."

"Getting soft in your old age, huh?" Reed cracked a grin. "Or am I just starting to influence you?"

"No," I said. "No. I guess it's hard to explain."

"You use your powers for good," he said. "You don't want to use them on the basically defenseless. You're not a murderer, Sienna." He stood up in the doorway, my tall brother. "You're a—"

"Don't say 'protector,'" I said, looking away. I stared at the few little tins of makeup and stuff in front of me. "Or anything similarly sappy. I just do my job. Whatever it takes."

"But you do make the world a safer place, right?" he asked. "I mean, I know you do. But is that how you see yourself?"

I stared at myself in the mirror. "I'm having a little trouble at the moment separating the flagellated ego from the drive to do what I'm supposed to."

Reed stood there in silence. "Wha … what?"

I took a breath. "Phillips … he hurts my ego. My sense of self—"

"Have you been reading psych textbooks or something?" Reed asked, glancing toward my bookshelf in the corner. "Is this New Age mumbo jumbo?" He looked at me seriously. "Have you been doing affirmations?"

"No," I said, annoyed. "Listen. I've got this sense of duty, all right? That I'm supposed to do things with my power that can help people. Because of the—" I waved a hand. "The thing. With Wolfe."

The time he massacred hundreds of people while I hid.

Reed gave me an eyebrow. "I would say that debt was paid when you saved the whole city of Minneapolis."

"That debt is never paid," I said. "Anyway ... my purpose, my duty ... is the reason I have this job rather than something else, like running security for the Hope Diamond or working for a private military contractor, something that would pay better. People who cross my purpose—like that dipshit in England, like Sovereign—get scratched off the list of still-breathing persons. That's easy. But Andrew Phillips hasn't—I mean, he's threatening to interfere with that by messing with the agency, but I've known all along that this place belongs to the government, that it's not mine." I looked over at Reed, who was studying me all through this diatribe. "He's not in danger of life and limb, or taking all his meals through a feeding tube for months or years to come, okay? He's just an ass. As much as I'd like to smack him, I won't. Because he's not like Simmons, who had already crossed the line on the purpose thing. Get it?"

Reed frowned, his whole face screwing up. "People who personally offend you live, people who are threats and also personally offend you either die or get the hell beaten out of them? Is that how it works? Roughly?"

I sighed because that was the closest approximation I could come up with to express how I felt. Exasperated and not really understood by the only person left who might stand a chance of understanding me. "Roughly."

"Well then, I guess I'll work not to be a threat to the balance of civilized society," he said, and I could hear his smirk, "while quipping merrily about you all the while."

"And I will happily fire back with endless witticisms," I said, picking up the mascara ... uh ... doodad. When was the last time I wore this stuff? A thought occurred to me. "You ever have that time in your life you wish you could go back to?" I felt him rustle in his tux as he stood there. "When things just felt ... right?"

"Sure," he said. "Lots of people feel that way about high school, or college." He paused. "Why, what was it for you?"

I dropped the mascara in frustration without even touching

it to my lashes. Screw it, they were full and hearty enough. "Believe it or not … when we were still in the Directorate, and Omega was dogging my footsteps every day."

I could tell I stunned him because his answer was slow to come. "Um, okay."

"I'm fully aware of how crazy that sounds," I said. "But I never had a high school, and my life before the Directorate was … well, you know …" I sighed, and stared at my pale face in the mirror. At least I hadn't been crying. I'd born my suffering in silence. I stared at this black dress in the mirror and had a revelation. "Crap. This is kinda like the prom I never wanted."

Reed laughed, and shook his head. "The ball approaches, Cinderella. Are you done trying to figure out how to apply makeup?"

"This is as good as it gets," I said, running a hand over myself. The self-consciousness leaked out. "How do I look?"

He smiled. "You'll do just fine." He offered me his elbow. "Shall we?"

I took it. "Yeah." I tugged at my dress, which ended just below the knees. I was feeling self-conscious about everything, including my calves. "Are you sure it looks okay?"

"It's wonderful," he said as we started out. "I mean, unless you start a fight in it. Then it'll probably inhibit your movement or something. Plus I'm guessing it will inhibit your ability to carry."

"Ass," I said as we headed out the door. "I've got a Glock in my purse and one of those new Smith and Wesson Bodyguard .380s at the small of my back." I checked for the dog, but he was still asleep on the vent. I left the light on for him because I was still new at this dog thing. "Besides, what makes you think I'd be the one starting the fight?"

He just chuckled, and I punched him in the arm as I closed the door quietly behind me, trying not to wake my little pet.

23.

Natasya

She sat in the back of the limousine with the others, listening to the voice over the phone. The heat was roaring, the snow was piled up outside the car windows. Natasya listened to the hollow tones, that faint rasp in the voice that hinted at a struggle for breath every few sentences. She was developing an opinion of the voice at the other end of the line; it was based on respect and a search for weakness.

Unfortunately, a breathing ailment was no consolation given what she was up against. No consolation at all.

"You'll remain in character, innocent party guests until you receive the signal," the voice said, with a faint wheeze in the middle of the sentence. There was a hollow, echoing quality to the acoustics, as though the call was being made from inside a confined chamber. "At that point, your task will be to corral the other guests, keeping them in place as hostages in case of a swifter government response than we've anticipated, at which point you'll switch to Contingency Plan A."

Vitalik spoke up with his characteristic suaveness, as though he were trying to flirt with the disconnected voice. "So we just have to be ourselves?" He grinned. "Except Miksa." He glanced at the Hungarian. "He should be anyone but himself." The quiet Hungarian made a lazy, profane gesture at Vitalik.

"There shouldn't be a problem," the voice continued. Natasya had noted that the woman on the other end of the line had seemed to take the personalities in the call into account, but she never allowed so much as a hint of familiarity to creep in. She kept her distance, commanded their respect, never let the ice between them thaw. She was sharp, professional.

Natasya would not have wanted to be playing on the opposite side of the table from this one. In her considered opinion, whoever the voice was, she was the most dangerous strategic planner ever. She understood the value of planning, and her plans had yet to run across a contingency unplanned for. The voice knew all, saw all, like some sort of god of old, the sort of thing to make the weak-minded fear a vengeful hand landing upon them in the night, unseen.

"Give the caterers time to do their part," the voice went on. "Once they've completed their assignment, you'll have no resistance to worry about. Once the hostages are secure and the ports are open, I'll be able to unlock the prison. Less than an hour, and you'll be extracted before anyone even has a chance to hear about it, let alone prepare a government response of any sort."

Natasya hesitated before she spoke, trying to consider how to phrase her question without offending the voice. "The … caterers?" *The mercenaries*, she thought. "Who will they answer to should we be forced into a contingency plan?"

"They'll answer to you on site," the voice said without a hint of indecision. "I've already directed them to take orders from you if things go awry. Until I have access to the network, I'll be blind. They'll listen to you."

That was a soothing feeling. The voice knew when to do that, it seemed. "Good," Natasya said, feeling a little hollow. It was a relief knowing that the voice—whoever she was—had little ego about the whole endeavor. It was also disconcerting, because the woman knew what she did not know. The worst sort of enemy was the self-aware enemy, one who was thoroughly aware of their weaknesses.

Yes, that was concerning.

"The signal should go off approximately twenty minutes after your arrival to the party," the voice said. "You'll know when it happens." She paused. "Now's the time to take your injections."

This was another moment of concern, as Natasya took the little case that had come with them from Kentucky and opened it, offering the syringe pens to Leonid, who was strangely quiet, then Miksa, and finally Vitalik before taking one for herself. She stared at it, a little blunt object that looked like an elongated capsule, before she finally pressed the needle into her arm and depressed the button. It was a tiny little pinprick, an annoyance and no more. She held out the box wordlessly. Each of them put their emptied pens back into it, and Natasya snapped the lid.

"Any questions?" the voice asked.

"No," Natasya said after looking around the limousine one last time. The seats were leather, and there was a full bar with countless bottles at the far end under the window that led to the driver's compartment.

"Then this is where we say goodbye until you're in control," she said. "If I need you urgently, I'll call." Natasya felt a self-conscious itch where the thin plastic of the cellular phone rested in her coat pocket. "Remember … remain cool until the signal. You're party guests. Have fun, but not too much fun." There was a pause, and the voice's tension increased. "No more drinking, Leonid." Natasya's head whipped around and she caught Leonid with a glass in his hand that she hadn't noticed before. Clear liquid, full to the brim. Vodka, straight up, of course. He looked mildly contrite and nodded.

"And one last thing," she said, her voice filling the small chamber. "Do not let Sienna Nealon out of your sight. She's canny. She's dangerous. Keep an eye on her, and don't let her get away." There was a pause, and the cold, emotionless voice crackled with something that sounded like distant fury. "And as soon as you get the chance, kill her."

24.

Sienna

"You really would have dug that briefing this morning," Reed said to me as we made our way through the tunnel from the dormitory to the headquarters building. It was a relief not to have to carry a coat, not to have to trudge over snow-covered walkways and get my shoes—flats, but way less comfortable than what I was used to—all slick and dirty.

"I read the report," I said as we walked down the fluorescent-lit hallway. The walls were solid concrete, functional but not beautiful, a channel cut into the ground between the buildings that was even more cold and sterile than the tunnel of death that led to the prison. I could tell after a moment that Reed was waiting for my reaction. "It was cool," I conceded. Because it had been.

"Did you see that thing about the chemical weapons depot in Kentucky?" he asked, arching his eyebrows. Usually it was me that got all excited, like a kid, about the idea of details being shared. There hadn't been a ton of them in the report, just a mention that a depot had been hit.

"Yeah," I said. There hadn't been any info on the perps, just a basic description of the event. "They didn't mention what was taken, though."

"That place held Sarin, VX gas, all sorts of nastiness." Now Reed's voice had gone solemn, which was probably more appropriate given the subject matter. Someone had made off with the kind of weapons of mass destruction that could turn New York City into a ghost town. "If they didn't say what was taken, it's probably because it was something inconceivably bad."

I frowned. "You mean like something we haven't even heard of?"

He shrugged. "That's kinda how the government works, right? Secrets upon secrets. If it was just VX, they'd have mentioned it in the report." He talked about these things like he knew what they were.

"You know anything about those gases?" I asked. A chemist I'm not.

"You see that movie *The Rock*?" he asked, kind of cringing. "That stuff they used was VX. Sarin is pretty bad too, as I understand it from reading Wikipedia."

"Ugh," I said, shaking my head. Part of me was glad that this particular assignment was not mine to deal with. "I hope stuff like this doesn't happen all the time."

"If it does, I guess we'll know about it now." He shook his head. That was a dreadful thought.

We emerged from the tunnel into the basement of the headquarters building and climbed the stairs to the lobby. A guy was just hanging out there, on a chair in the stairwell, loitering with his back against the wall, laptop computer spread across his legs. I frowned and looked at Reed, who shrugged like this was perfectly normal.

"J.J.?" I called out, experimentally. The guy looked up at me through glasses with thick black frames. Hipster.

"Oh, hey, Sienna," he said, cool as a January morning. He nodded at Reed. "What's up, Reed-with-a-screed?"

Reed chuckled. "That one's not bad." He looked at me, almost guiltily. "It's this thing we do."

"I know," I said, shaking my head. I'd seen it before. "Geeks. I'm surrounded by geeks."

"Don't dis the geek," J.J. said, turning his attention back to his laptop. "Diamonds are overrated; *we* are actually a girl's best friend."

I started to respond to that utter nonsense with an appropriate verbal slapdown, but Reed grabbed me by the elbow and pulled me toward the door past J.J. "Come on, we've got a public embarrassment to attend."

The lobby was buzzing with anticipation. Security was there, and a flotilla of white-suited waitstaff was making their way through the room with trays of canapés and stuff, feeding our personnel. Our guys were on the guard, but taking a few bites here and there. I couldn't blame them. It smelled great.

Ariadne was waiting for us there, a glimmering silvery gown highlighting how pale she was. Her red hair was hanging loose today, styled nicer than mine. Wait, no, that's not a good comparison. Hers looked really nice. Jackie was standing next to her, also dressed to the nines.

"Is this it?" I asked as Reed and I made our way over. "Are we the welcoming committee?"

"Director Phillips will be here momentarily," Jackie said with a relaxed smile. It wavered a little as she looked at me, like she realized that using his title was like salt in the wound. Her gaze flicked to Ariadne, and I could see the comment had found its mark with her, too; there was a little flush on her cheeks, more subtle than her flaming hair. To Jackie's credit, she looked like she wanted to apologize, but didn't. She shouldn't have to apologize for stating a fact, I thought. But it still stung.

The metal detectors trilled as I walked through them to lead the way out toward the doors. I could see a limo parked just outside. I glanced at the security guy manning the detector, and he shrugged at me. I always set them off; I was never unarmed. He glanced out at the limo. "Been here about ten minutes," he said.

"Trying to be fashionably late?" I asked, looking back at Jackie.

"Probably downing a few bottles of vodka before they get

out," Reed said. "They are Russian, after all."

"Best behavior," Jackie said under her breath.

"It's a formal occasion," I said. "We've got an open bar, right?"

"Yes," Jackie said with a hint of hesitation. "But may I suggest …" she said it lightly, and the inference was not lost on me.

"I'm not much of a drinker," I said in reply, heading her off.

The limo door opened and a woman got out first. I had the immediate impression that she was the sort who wanted to set foot on the battlefield before her compatriots. She loomed when she stood, a tall figure, scanning the glass front of the building as she took it all in. She caught sight of me lit up by the lobby lights and did not hesitate, offering a thin smile, the sort I expected was regularly employed in these situations. I knew their names, and I knew she was the leader. Natasya Sokolov. Tall, blond, regal, austere … she just radiated toughness and seriousness. I could identify with that.

The next guy out of the limo was a charmer. He had that smile, the dark hair, the cool eyes, and he fiddled with his cuffs like he was Bond, James Bond, as he straightened up. He was average height, way above average in the looks department. I had a file photo of him taken from Russian news media, and he'd looked handsome in it. His charisma was even more apparent here, even with thirty feet and a series of glass partitions between us. Vitalik Kuznetsov. That was his name.

The next one out was another man, this one below average height, with a look like he was about to fall asleep. His eyes drooped, but he took it all in like there was nothing here that he hadn't seen before. The light dossier hinted he was Hungarian-born, and ended up recruited by the Russians solely because he was a meta. Miksa Fenes. He gave not one hint that he had ever smiled in his life.

The last guy was a bear, fitting for a Russian. He got out of the limo with a hint of a stagger, like his balance wasn't all there. He had a long beard that had been somewhat groomed but still looked kind of wild. Leonid Volkov was his name. I didn't know exactly how to pronounce it, but I suspected it was like Leonard, maybe.

They stood out in the subzero weather like it was nothing, cold frosting their breath. It misted in the lights, clouds swirling across their faces. I stared at each of them in turn, and felt a presence next to me.

"Try to smile?" Jackie suggested. She hadn't set off the metal detector.

"Where's Phillips?" I asked as I did what she'd told me to, pressing my lips into a tight line. I went for friendly and welcoming. Or maybe like when you're passing a coworker in the hall and nod to them. Something in that vein.

"You look like you're about to dive into their midst and kill them all with your teeth," Phillips said as he passed through the metal detector. No beep for him, either. "Do you not know how to smile?" He was still expressionless, which I thought was ironic, considering.

I kept from throwing the obvious reply right into his blank face. "I'm working on it," I said instead, and tried to think of something that would give me cause to genuinely smile. I had trouble with it.

"The bathroom scene in *Dumb and Dumber*," Reed said from behind the security post, like he could read my mind. I knew he didn't want to walk through the detector because it'd be sure to go off.

"Heh," I said. "Hehe." I felt my lips stretch into a broad grin, and I barely restrained a giggle. I looked back at the entry in time to see that the Russians were coming. *One if by land*, I thought.

Phillips and Jackie flanked me, while Reed and Ariadne hung back behind the security checkpoint. Ariadne looked hesitant, and I wondered what was up with that.

Natasya Sokolov entered the lobby, Vitalik holding the door for her. She surveyed everything warily while trying not to look like she was. She had a smile on, too, but it reminded me of a wolf trying to convince you that she wasn't about to eat your flock.

It probably wasn't that far off what I'd been displaying a few moments earlier, actually.

"Ms. Sokolov," Jackie said, taking the lead. "I'm Jacqueline Underwood. It's a pleasure to meet you." She offered a hand, which Natasya Sokolov looked at for a moment before she took it, shaking it awkwardly.

"A pleasure indeed," Sokolov said, without a trace of Russian accent. That caused me to raise an eyebrow. It also caused my mind to race; where would she have learned flawless English? We had the public version of her file that had been compiled over the last month or two by PR hacks like Jackie. I suspected there was a government version of her file somewhere else, maybe in a CIA or FBI vault, something in the intelligence or counterintelligence sections. I gathered that this was not her first visit to the United States, though that was total speculation on my part. Her eyes flicked to me. "And you must be Sienna Nealon." She offered me a hand and waited to see if I'd take it.

I faked a smile, thoughts of scenes from comedies gone in an instant. "I must be," I said and hastily took her hand, giving it a quick shake before letting it go. It was two seconds contact, max, but she didn't pull away first; I did. She studied me all the while, waiting to see what I'd do, how I'd handle the contact. It was in her interest not to touch me any more than she had to, but she was fearless in the way she did this; she was measuring me in her own way and giving me a little insight in the process.

This was not a woman I would happily choose to mess with.

"How do you do, Ms. Nealon?" Vitalik Kuznetsov asked, sliding up to me. I had a sudden vision of a shark gliding through the water, nothing but a fin cutting gently above the surface to warn its prey.

"I'm doing just fine, Mr. Kuznetsov," I replied, noting the unmistakable pleasure in his eyes that I'd gotten his name right. "How was your trip?"

"A little bumpy in the middle," he said smoothly, "but it's looking oh-so-much better now." His English was flawless, too, and this once again made me uneasy. There were a lot of classified files in government keeping that I had no access to, but I had this sick feeling that I was missing a whole lot of stuff that I should have been privy to. There was a story here, somewhere. These people were not just prisoners for the last thirty years because of some whim of the post-Soviet government. I had a whiff of something here, and I did not like the smell of it. And it wasn't Phillips, either, though he did have a distinctive and unpleasant cologne.

"Sienna Nealon," Leonid Volkov said to me, and I caught the faintest hint of a slur to his words. "The face of American metahumans." He broke into a grin. "And a pretty face at that; no wonder Vitalik dotes on you."

"I have an affinity for beauty," Vitalik said, and he offered me his hand. When I gave him mine he took it with both hands, clasping it warmly. I could feel a slight tingle as he rubbed against the back of my hand for a few seconds, then, almost reluctantly, let it slip away. It felt like he'd been counting the seconds and released it only with the greatest regret. Beneath my mind's whirling curiosity and discomfort at their English-language skills and all the little implications that came with them, I had to admit that Vitalik was … charming. Handsome.

He smiled at me, warmly.

Dangerous.

"This is Miksa Fenes," Vitalik said, still smiling, introducing me to the silent Hungarian, who gave me a subtle nod. "But you probably already knew that."

"Well, you are all pretty famous at this point," I said, my eyes flitting to Sokolov, who was now in conversation with Phillips and Jackie, listening to them with stiff politeness.

The first flashbulb reminded me that this wasn't just a

chance to meet new people and worry about their pasts. I froze, Vitalik staring straight at me, almost warmly. Almost. "Ah, the press. A curious Western sort of tradition."

"I'm pretty sure they have reporters in Russia now," I said.

"They had them before, too," Vitalik said with a wide grin, "but they used to be so much more manageable." Was that regret in his voice? He placed a hand on my elbow and gently steered me to face a half dozen people with cameras. "Now, smile," he said quietly. I looked to the side to see Jackie making a similar suggestion with both fingers pointing to the corners of her mouth, which were twitching madly.

So, I smiled. On command. Like a trained dog. Certainly better trained than my dog.

The photos lasted about a minute, and then one of Jackie's people funneled the reporters away from us, back toward the elevators. "Well, that's a relief," Vitalik said.

"They'll be upstairs at the party," I said, grudgingly, and watched him steel himself.

"In the days of old," Leonid said, words still slurring just slightly, "these people would have been in the—"

"Leonid, recall your manners," Vitalik said gently, still smiling at me. "We are guests here, at this party." He leaned in closer to me. "And what a party I am sure it will be." He offered me his elbow. "Care to lead the way?"

"Sure," I said, feeling just a smidgen of unease as I guided him through the metal detector. It honked once, for me, and I smiled apologetically and pushed my free hand toward the metal chopsticks in my hair, just to reassure him. Turns out people get antsy when they know you're armed. Vitalik nodded, and we walked arm in arm toward the elevators, that same nagging feeling tugging at the back of my mind, like it was trying to tell me that some disastrous social faux pas was soon to follow.

25.

There was a round of applause from the guests as we entered the reception room. Most people don't applaud when I enter a room. Leave it, maybe, but not when I enter it. Vitalik refused to detach from my arm, not that I demanded it of him or anything. He smelled nice, not drenched in anything offensive to the nose, and he seemed genuinely glad to be here. I felt like my mind was playing shadow games with me; the cold war was long over, after all. Russia had changed, the new administration over there had been pretty docile, and their human rights record was pretty glasnost-ic.

I still felt a nervous murmur in my stomach.

Phillips announced each of the Russians like royalty, as I looked around the room. I didn't recognize half the people here, and I suspected it was because they were either from the press or from Washington. You don't throw a shindig like this without making sure some of the right people are in proximity for political purposes, and I suspected there were more than a few figureheads to spare. I recognized at least one big-mouthed senator from the president's party as well as a couple other familiar faces that looked like members of the House. I'm no political junkie, but these were some fairly big names. Everyone wanted a piece of the action on this one, I guess, and getting a handshake photo with recently released political prisoners was probably a golden ticket to somewhere. Not sure where. Re-election, maybe. It all felt like image-work to me, attempts to look concerned without actually being concerned. That sense of nerves was now coupled with a disgusted sense that I was part of this theatrical display, and I was suddenly glad that I wasn't wearing makeup. Maybe it'd keep me off the front page.

"You look so uncomfortable right now," Reed muttered into my ear. I turned to see him standing there with Dr. Perugini on his arm. She was in a dress that was tight and black and wouldn't have looked out of place on a hooker. A classy, high-priced one, but still. He looked fairly relaxed for a guy who was standing in a stiff tux in the middle of a party like this, and I suddenly realized he was playing cool in front of his girlfriend.

"I'm fine," I said, in the tone of voice that women reserve for occasions when we are most definitely *not fine, but don't ask me about it.* Perugini got it. She looked sour as ever, but I could see she got it.

"What is it?" he asked, and she smacked him on the shoulder. He blinked in befuddlement.

"Nerves," I lied. Or was I telling the truth?

"It'll all be over soon," he said. "Want a drink?"

"N—yes. Yes, I do."

"Martini?" he asked.

"Ugh, yuck, no," I said. "Something sweet. I've had enough bitter for a while."

"Jagerbomb?" he asked, and I gave him a look. "Err, I'll see what I can do. Something sweet." He wandered off toward the bar that had been set up in the corner, a white-jacketed caterer moving around behind it. Dr. Perugini followed, still on his arm. She hadn't said a word to me, and I think we were both happier that way.

"You look nervous," Vitalik said, sliding back up to me. I hadn't noticed, but apparently Phillips had finished with his little speech. Day two of knowing him, and I could already tune him out. There was mingling going on now, and I felt a sudden desire to entirely down a drink I didn't even have. The room was crowded, packed full of people in fancy clothes. This was not my jam. I could feel the souls moving around here in this confined space, the cocktail party from hell. Volkov circled nearby, watching, and then wandered into a circle of reporters who proceeded to ask him a question, which he began to answer loudly, trying to make himself sound profound.

"I'm not really a party person," I said to Vitalik, trying to focus on him and ignore the noise of the party and the thoughts rattling in the back of my brain.

"I understand completely," he said, and his hand landed on my shoulder, keeping his fingers on the strap rather than letting them touch me on the flesh. I looked at it, but withheld the usual ire that would have left him with the impression that he could lose the hand or *lose* the hand. I'd get no points for that, not with reporters present. "I've recently spent a great deal of time with almost no company at all. To be thrust into circumstances such as these, with so many people in a confined space … it's an adjustment." His eyes bored into mine. "I've known succubi and incubi before. Do you … feel the presence of all the people here?"

I couldn't tell whether he was genuinely curious or pressing for something more. "I can sense the people around us, yeah," I said. Of course, I didn't know if that was normal or not, since I'd never really had much in the way of a mentor for my powers. I think my mom had expected me to just figure it out on my own, because even in the months when we worked together she hadn't exactly been free-flowing with the advice.

"I hear it's worse in crowds," Vitalik said with a slow nod. "Almost like you can feel the souls without a touch."

"I felt that in New York," I said. "I don't get out much."

I was trying to find my way to extricate myself from the conversation with Vitalik when the quiet guy, Miksa, came wandering up. He moved slowly, just drifting along like the wind was carrying him gently on a current. When he parked himself next to us, I felt Vitalik's hand fall off my shoulder.

"Did you know Liliana Negrescu?" Miksa asked, his voice low and polite.

I blinked at him in surprise, an action I saw mirrored on Vitalik's face. I got the sense that Miksa didn't talk much. "Uhm …" I started to answer, and honesty popped out. "Briefly." Where the hell did that question come from?

Miksa nodded, slowly. "Did you kill her?"

That froze me right in place. I'd run across Liliana Negrescu almost a year ago, in London. She'd been working as a hench … woman? Person? Whatever. She'd been the knife hand for a guy named Philip Delsim, who was a real piece of work. Liliana had been his aide, his trained killer, and I'd left her splattered against a wall in a basement in central London.

But I didn't think anybody knew that. I hadn't even mentioned it to law enforcement over there because they'd already been pretty cross with me over my breaking Philip Delsim's neck.

"Uhh," I said, searching for an answer. Behind Miksa's dull stare was an energy, and he was wholly focusing it on me. I didn't get the sense he was emotionally invested in the answer at all, but appearances could be deceiving. My lies were almost always transparent in any case, so I went with the truth. "Yeah," I said. "She fought me, and I killed her."

Miksa nodded absently, like this was just some minor detail he'd filed away. "Okay," he said and wandered off before I could recover my wits and ask him a question. Which would have been, "What was Liliana Negrescu to you?" Stranger? Lover? Friend? Enemy? Based on his reaction, I wouldn't have guessed any of those.

I glanced at Vitalik, who still looked … shocked, really. "I've never heard him speak so quickly to someone he didn't know," Vitalik said.

"Clearly a pressing question on his mind," I said. "Were they friends?"

Vitalik shrugged, a blanket falling over his face. "I have no idea. I can't say I'm familiar with this Liliana. It's not as though he talks about himself."

A waiter came by bearing a tray of canapés, and I snatched one off and tossed it in my mouth to keep. I was hungry, and I had yet to see a buffet table. I frowned as it hit my tongue. It tasted awful. I searched the room for a trash can, for a stray napkin, for anything, catching the amusement from Vitalik all the while. I finally caught sight of someone's discarded drink sitting on a table, and a cocktail napkin was left behind underneath. I made for it at just below meta speed, pushing the glass aside and raising the napkin to my lips. It wasn't ladylike, but it had to be done.

I looked up to see that Vitalik had followed me through the crowd. "I take it the catering is sub-par?"

I ran my tongue all over the inside of my mouth. "I wouldn't hire them again. I think that chicken was raw." It had been slick and slimy, and not in the good way, like sushi.

Vitalik nodded. "I guess I'll avoid that, then."

"I would," I said. "It's not good."

"Probably still better than what we were spoon-fed in prison," he said with a little amusement. I looked past him to see Volkov detach himself from the group of reporters he'd been holding court with and start to stagger our way. That made me just a little uneasy.

I looked for an avenue of escape and found the place pretty well and truly blocked. We were beyond capacity, a surprising number of people in here considering how few of them worked here. Caterers made their way through the crowds awkwardly, their trays held high. I caught a glimpse of someone else making a face as they took a bite of something, then remembered I was looking for an exit route. Two sides of the room were glass, windows that looked out on the snowy campus. Darkness had swept in early, as per usual in January, and only the faint light of some lamps in the distance gave hints of what lay outside in the night.

"You," Volkov said, plainly tipsy. The guy didn't even have a drink in his hand. He came at me without any sort of hesitation. If I had to guess, I would have thought he'd mainlined a couple shots in the interval between his arrival and now.

I withheld any scathing rebuttal to that somewhat accusatory calling and smiled politely. It was something I hoped I was getting better at, but from the way Vitalik flinched, I guessed I'd have a ways to go. "Hi," I said.

"'O for a muse of fire,'" Volkov said, leveling his eyes on me.

I frowned. "Why are you quoting Shakespeare at me?"

He looked a little surprised. "You ... recognize that?" He was damned tipsy.

"*Henry V*," I said, still a little baffled. "Not really sure what setting the stage for sweeping drama to follow has to do with me, but ..."

"A muse of fire," he said weakly. How drunk was this guy? "That would scorch us all."

I cocked an eyebrow at him, and looked toward Vitalik, whose face was curtained off from expression. "You think I'm going to ... scorch you?" I certainly had that power, but was this the rambling of a drunk man?

What the hell was going on here?

"He quotes from literature constantly," Vitalik said under his breath, face still shrouded. "It's what he does."

I blinked at that. The context was just ... strange. But drunk people do weird things, I suppose. "Okay."

"You," Volkov said, stumbling closer. The group of press he'd been standing with earlier stood there, watching our exchange. If I acted the fool, this would definitely meet the objective definition for failure for the evening. I held my tongue and let him come closer.

"Still me," I said, smiling politely. Or wolfishly. Something.

"'The apparel oft proclaims the man,'" Volkov said, now only a few feet away.

I racked my brain. It was a short search. "*Hamlet*," I said. "Polonius's goodbye to Laertes." Mom made me memorize scads of Shakespeare, quizzed me on it at the end of each day with punishments for failure and no reward for success. It kept me occupied when she locked me in my house for a decade. Whiled away the dull hours.

Volkov seemed surprised, again. "Clothes make the man," he said, like I needed a translation.

"I like to think that skin and bone make the man," I said, my patience with whatever game he was playing dwindling fast. "His clothes just keep him from showing his ass." I eyed Volkov, as though I could transmit by thought the obvious follow-up: *Though they're not doing a great job of keeping you from showing yours, drunkard.*

Volkov stood up straight, adjusting his tie, which was loose around his collar. "'And this above all else … to thine own self be true.'"

I stared at him, still not sure why he was spitting these random quotations at me. "I'm not sure what you're going for here."

"You must forgive my friend," Vitalik said, stepping between Volkov and I. He had the solicitous look of a man who was trying hard to stave off some embarrassment. "He's clearly … impaired."

"I see clearly," Volkov said, wobbling closer. "I see who you are."

"Who I am?" I asked. I saw movement in the crowd; Natasya Sokolov herself was threading her way through a knot of reporters, her eyes fixed on me. I glanced back at Volkov. "Who am I?"

"You …" He broke into a grin. "You're ruthless. Vicious. Unrelenting."

"You are insulting our hostess," Vitalik said, suddenly urgent, like he had to get this mess cleaned up before Sokolov came over. I doubted he'd be able to finish in time, because Volkov looked like he was about two steps from drooling and toppling onto the floor. "This is unlike you, Leonid. Don't be *nekulturny.*"

Volkov's head snapped back at that, like Vitalik had punched him in the face. "You call me that? You're sitting here speaking to an oppressor of the people like she's a comrade you want to lay."

I felt my face burn. "Hey! I don't hear anyone crying out, *'elp, 'elp, I'm being oppressed!* while I'm walking around town."

Volkov stared at me, utterly without comprehension. "What?"

"It's a movie," I said. "Probably came after you went into the gulag. Which, BTW, I'm starting to see why they stuck you there."

Volkov just stared. "What is … 'BTW'?" He stared at me with watery eyes, still seemingly unsteady on his feet.

"It's called English," I said, annoyed enough to start being a jerk. Then I rethought what I'd said. "Sort of."

Sokolov was still threading her way forward, stopped by a reporter with a camera. That same damned senator put an arm around her shoulder and I saw the flash, the hint of loathing, the desire to break that arm off and hand it back to him. It looked familiar. But she just stood there and posed, stiffly, as a waiter strolled by with his tray tilted at an angle on his shoulder

What the hell?

I watched the waiter striding off, and it occurred to me for the first time that there were legitimate reasons why this was all damned wrong. The waiters were moving like they'd never carried a tray before. It was awkward, and I would have been prepared to accept it from one of them. Training a new guy, right?

Not one of them moved like they had a clue what they were doing.

My eyes locked on Volkov as he staggered to within inches of me. I didn't like having him this close, but it was the last worry on a pile that was about to catch fire. "I heard you can fly." He reeked of vodka, like he'd spilled it on himself. He probably had, come to think of it. "If God had meant for man to fly, he'd have given him wings."

I stared at him in utter disbelief. Vitalik did much the same just over his shoulder, and I could see he was very close to intervening on my behalf. Or maybe on his drunk friend's behalf. "I'm not a man," I said curtly, "so I figured it out for myself, no wings required."

Volkov let out a low grunt of amusement at my reply. "I like you. But I don't." His face changed in an instant, from the drunken smile to a look of something darker. More angry.

Savage.

It wasn't the first time I'd been face to face with someone who meant to kill me, but it came as a surprise how quickly it occurred to me that this was what was about to happen.

And then something exploded in a rush of air near the elevator bank, and blue smoke hit me in the face, setting me to coughing immediately. My nose registered something like rotting flowers, sweet and yet foul, and it crept up my nostrils and stayed there. I coughed twice, looking into the face of Volkov, who reached out and grabbed hold of my throat in his fingers.

I returned the favor and wrapped my fingers around his neck, meeting his gaze with a furious one of my own. So this was how he wanted to play it. All thought of the blue smoke and playing nice for the press vanished the instant he laid a hand on me.

He pushed, hard, and I felt myself lose my footing. He ripped me from the ground and carried me forward like the bear of a man he was. I felt the window shatter behind me as he carried me out into the night, the stinging of glass mingling with the first sharp shock of the winter air as we plummeted three stories toward the ground.

"Gavrikov," I murmured to myself as we fell, expecting the lightness of gravity peeling away from my body to follow. It was natural to me by now, this feeling of flight. I waited a second, two. Three.

There was no answer.

26.

I twisted my body as I fell out of the building, but I felt sluggish, slow, and barely got around in time to land with my knee in Volkov's gut. He grunted as the air rushed out of him, and I felt pain lance down my knee and into my leg as I slammed into him and the ground. It hurt a lot.

I felt the disorientation, though it took me a few minutes to realize what it was. I blinked, slowly, felt the Russian stir beneath me.

It wasn't like Gavrikov not to answer me. He could be as childish as any of us, sure, but I hadn't had an argument with him, and he had no reason to ditch me now.

"Wolfe!" I said aloud, rolling off Volkov onto the ground. Hard-packed snow greeted the back of my neck, my legs, and I felt the rush of chill across my back even through the dress. My breaths were coming hard, the frigid air rushing into my lungs and adding to the aches of my body.

Wolfe didn't respond, either, but I felt a faint touch in the back of my mind, like a voice too distant to hear. I looked down at my leg, and I saw blood falling into the snow from my lips. My head must have hit him on the landing, and I was dazed. I hurt.

I saw movement to my side, and realized that Volkov was coming to as well. Security would be here in a moment, with guns, and—

No. No, something was wrong. Why the hell had this

Russian attacked me?

A memory made its way up. The caterers, awkwardly moving their trays around like newbs, offering food to the security personnel in the entry—

Aw, hell.

I staggered to my feet, my thin shoes tainted by snow as I felt the frigid wind whip over me. I cradled myself with frozen fingers, running my fingertips over icy flesh, already starting to feel the freezing air do its work on my unprotected skin. "Wolfe," I said again, seeking protection. I felt my leg get slightly better, the pain recede, but I couldn't tell if it was because of Wolfe or because I was going numb.

"You won't ... be able to use him," Volkov said. He was looking up at me, drooling into the snow. He laughed, a husky sound that echoed in the night air. "Or any of your powers."

I stared at my fingers, remembered the blue smoke that had blown through the reception just before Volkov had seized me by the neck. "What the hell did you do to me?" I managed to get out through chattering teeth.

"You like it?" Volkov laughed, and blood ran out of his open mouth. "It's called ... Suppressex. Or that's what your government calls it."

"I'm assuming it doesn't just lower your sex drive." I felt a chill unrelated to the weather. "The chemical weapons stolen from Kentucky."

Volkov looked at me with glazed eyes. "You're not stupid, that's for sure." He propped himself up on an elbow, but only with some struggle. "You're weak now, you know. Essentially human. Your strength is gone." His beard dripped with red and white, like some perverse image of Santa. "We've drugged your security personnel. You and your brother are powerless." I watched him getting stronger by the minute. I may have turned the tables on him by forcing him to accept most of the impact, but it wasn't going to keep him down for long. "Every one of the caterers is a mercenary that works for our employer. Your little agency is ours, and nobody outside of here even knows it yet." He laughed, and the blood had stopped flowing. "So what are you going to do?"

I reached my hand behind me, lifting up my dress. "Whatever I have to."

I watched his eyes widen in amusement, and I realized what he thought I was doing. It made me feel more than a little disgusted. "That's not going to save you," he said. "Even if I didn't want to rip your skin off, the person who hired us wants you to die."

My hand found what it was looking for, the Smith and Wesson at the small of my back, and I unsafetied it as I drew. I fired.

And found out that without my meta strength, my aim was way off.

A small circle of red spread across his belly, and I steadied myself for a second shot as Volkov looked up at me in surprise. "It was a reception," he said, like he couldn't comprehend the gun in my hand, like it had materialized from thin air. "A diplomatic—"

I shot him again, and this time I was ready for the recoil. The hollow point caught him in the forehead and I saw pink mist paint the snow behind him. "Never trust a Russian," I said as I looked around for my purse. I'd had it in my hand before Volkov had grabbed me, and I had hope that it'd be nearby—

I froze as the first sounds of voices hit me. I shuddered again from the cold, which was settling in on me like I was standing there naked. I had way too much exposed flesh to just sit here. It had to be below zero, and the air burned me from the cold. I looked up at the window we'd fallen from and saw faces looking down at me. I wondered if they could see me out here.

A burst of automatic weapons fire answered that question, and the snow at my feet exploded from the impact.

I ran, losing first one shoe, then the other, racing for the nearest tree and barely finding shelter behind it before another burst of weapons fire slammed into the bark behind me.

I stood there, freezing, and now fully realizing just how bad my predicament was.

My agency had been taken over by unknown forces, leaving a hundred hostages under their control.

There were countless mercenary soldiers in the building just behind me, armed to teeth and looking to kill me.

And I was hiding behind a tree, as another burst of weapons fire filled the night. As it faded I could hear more voices, these on the ground, snow crunching beneath booted feet as they headed in my direction.

Without my powers, I couldn't fly away, couldn't throw flames at them, or shoot nets, or even heal myself from the nagging injuries that were already causing my body to ache. Their bullets could kill me, injure me, cripple me. And all I had was a little bitty .380 with five shots remaining.

The voices got closer, and I huddled there behind the tree as the rifles in the building fired again, my feet frozen against the snow, bark ripping in the night as I stood there, shivering, skin hurting from the chill, without a clue of what to do next.

27.

I listened to the bullets sing around me, peppering the tree trunk I was hiding behind, and felt strangely vacant of fear. I should have been scared witless; this was the most vulnerable I'd been in years.

Instead I felt strangely alive. And cold, though that was fading fast into numbness.

The wind blistered around me, howling like a primal force. My ears felt like they were encased in ice, and I shifted against the tree and felt fabric tear; I'd partially frozen to the wood in mere seconds.

I needed to get the hell out of here.

I looked into the distance, searching for an answer, and the only probability was right there in front of me.

When we'd rebuilt the campus, we'd done so using funds that Ariadne had pulled together using some complicated strategies that basically boiled down to insider trading. Okay, so it wasn't that complicated. Before its destruction, back when the agency operated independent of government oversight as a plausibly deniable cat's paw for the United States, we'd had a full scientific research staff. So when we rebuilt the place, we rebuilt the science building, not really counting on the fact we'd be back under full government scrutiny and operating under a federal budget that viewed us as a liability. So the science building had sat, unfunded and unloved, pretty much abandoned, for the last couple years.

And it did that sitting right in front of me.

I checked the angle quickly; if I kept the tree between us, I could make it most of the way to the science building without exposing myself to the broken window where the gunfire was coming from. It wasn't my best plan ever, but it was better than sitting there and waiting to freeze to death or for searchers to come put me out of my frigid misery.

I started off at a run, and was amazed at how slow I was going. The cold air hurt my lungs. My knees were aching. My skin burned from the wind, hurting in a dull way, like someone pressing pins into it. I stumbled after a half dozen paces, my feet numb. I clutched my gun close in my fingers and kept going.

It was slow, painfully so. I was used to being able to spring ten feet in the air at a jog. I could leap short buildings in a single bound without using my powers of flight.

Now I was running like a normal person, and it felt like I was already frozen.

I had to choose my steps carefully, acutely aware that my life was on the line here. I glanced back to see flashlight beams dancing over the ground behind me, trying to find me in the darkness. They were a ways back, but that was irrelevant; with the snow, they'd be able to follow my footsteps right to me.

This was not a good day. Not a good night. Not a good anything.

The building was ahead a hundred feet by this point, but it felt like it was two miles away. I felt like I was swimming toward it, bobbing in syrupy solution. I was dimly aware that frostbite had to be taking hold, that I was a mess, that I needed to be warm—

Oh, dear heavens, to be warm.

I almost fell and realized it was because my body was shivering so hard I could barely stand straight. I raised my gun hand and found my finger frozen to the trigger. Even if they caught me now, I'd have a hell of a time firing a defensive shot. Or maybe not, since my finger was stuck to the trigger.

I could see the single light of the science building ahead, like a lighthouse in the middle of a cold, empty ocean. My jaw was full-on chattering by now; I was going to lose some teeth if it got any worse. I couldn't feel my toes, or the bottom of my feet. I stepped on the slippery sidewalk and up to the entry and slipped in. The science building opened into a small foyer with a biometric scanner just inside. Back when we didn't have a budgetary crisis, we could do things like biometric locks.

I shoved my hand against the scanner and pushed the damned button. It buzzed at me and glowed an angry red, denying me entry. I swore under my breath and rubbed my hand against the material of my dress. I couldn't feel it, but I tried for friction, tried to warm up my extremity. I pressed it against the glass again, hoping that Andrew Phillips hadn't suddenly changed my authorization to go anywhere on campus. If he had, this was going to be a messy end for me.

The light glowed green and I heard a lock click.

I fumbled for the door handle, frozen fingers failing to grasp hold the first time. I heard the lock click back into place—time expired—before I could get a grip on it, and I wanted to cry from exasperation.

I looked behind me, out the glass entry door, and the flashlights were drawing ever nearer.

I slammed my hand against the scanner again, got the green, and ripped at the handle with fumbling fingers. I got it open and squeezed into the dark, empty hallway, pulling the door closed behind me. I sighed, but not in relief.

Now I was in a science building that hadn't ever seen a single worker use it, still powerless. I had five bullets and a frozen/impaired trigger finger, and a host of what I presumed were mercenaries on my trail.

This is why I don't do formal occasions.

28.

I figured I had something on the order of sixty seconds to search the building for useful things before my enemies had me dead to rights. I couldn't outrun them, and my lead was vanishing with every second I spent trying to elude them. I damned sure couldn't outfight them, especially not with five .380 bullets, strength absent to steady my aim and my hand still shaking and numb.

I took a deep breath of the stale air in the science building and pondered the layout. It was all labs on the first floor—chemistry, and ... uh ... other stuff. The medical staff was originally supposed to move over here at some point, but since the building had been mothballed, that idea had been scrapped.

On the plus side, while the air was hardly warm, it was certainly warmer than it was outside.

I stood there for a ten count in the hallway, trying to think of something I could do. I took a few tentative steps forward, and realized that—once again—I was leaving a trail behind me. This time it was wet footprints.

Crap.

I hurried forward and looked into the room to my left. It was a chemistry lab with a sweeping view of the snowy terrain outside, complete with large black islands in the middle of the room, independent sinks with an eyewash and a shower in the corner, silver fixtures with gas taps to run experiments with

RUTHLESS

fire—

Hrmm.

Hmmmmmmmmmm.

Hehehehe.

I darted into the science lab and out of it less than thirty seconds later, skedaddling along the central hallway and around the corner. I ran for the back exit, hoping that I could pull this one off. It was a long shot, but if I could make it happen it would solve a couple of my problems.

The science building was a square with four exits, one at each corner. I'd entered at the bottom left of the square and now I was sitting at the top left, with the chemistry lab taking up all the space between the two. I listened, waiting to hear—

There it was. Tinkling glass. My pursuers were on my trail like the dogs they were.

I could hear them breaking through the glass and forcing entry into the science building to pursue me, and I hoped they were feeling overconfident. I suspected they weren't, since I'd already left Volkov dead behind me, and they'd surely found him. But maybe there was still room for some arrogance. There were a half-dozen of them and one of me, and I couldn't have been carrying much in the way of guns, right? If they were smart, they'd pursue with care, but still speedily.

So far, so good.

As soon as I heard them enter, I ran out the back door and angled my path to take me straight across the wide glass windows of the chemistry lab. They stretched roughly waist-high to ceiling, black glass that I could barely see through from outside.

As far as schemes went, this was probably one of the more harebrained I'd come up with. After all, I was placing myself directly in the line of fire with these guys and essentially saying, "Here I am! Shoot me!" Given my prior experience, they, being bad guys with guns, probably would oblige.

Hopefully quickly and without giving it much thought. Or smell.

I glanced back through the chemistry lab's windows as I took off across the snow. I was moving at the speed reserved for a grandma whilst napping, struggling across the vacant snowfield as the freezing chill dropped down on my exposed flesh. Why hadn't I worn something more formal to this party, like a bearskin rug? Or a Gore-tex jacket? You know, on the off chance I'd be thrown out a window and hunted through the winter night, as they do at most formal events.

No, they don't? I'm just special, I guess.

I hoped, hoped, hoped that the mercenaries pursuing me wouldn't do something smart, like make for the exits and run me down. They could definitely do it. The only thing ahead of me was the training building, and it was a long ways off. If they were even in average shape, they could catch my tragically limping ass with ease.

But whoever had hired them hadn't paid them to capture me alive.

I saw the movement when I looked back, the shadow in the hallway beyond the chemistry lab. It was a man with a rifle, raising it to his shoulder in preparation to fire. I threw myself down into the snow and waited as I heard the first shot crack over my head. I waited and hoped for another.

I didn't have to wait long, though I didn't end up hearing it.

The first shot broke the window from the hallway into the chemistry lab, where I'd run through and slapped the valves for every single gas line in the place on full blast a couple minutes earlier. They were designed for heavy-duty flame experiments with Bunsen burners, and I'd left them wide open. I doubted the lab had completely filled up, but it had filled up enough. One shot broke the glass dividing the mercenaries from the gas.

The second shot exposed the propane—or butane—or whatever-ane—to a lit flame in the form of muzzle flash.

Mom wasn't big on chemistry when she home-schooled me, but she did teach me what happens when you expose an explosive gas to an open flame.

Kaboom.

The lab exploded and propelled flame and glass over my head. My ears echoed from the force of the blast, even though I'd covered them with my hands as best I could. After they stopped ringing, I rolled over and looked at what I'd wrought.

Destruction of government property. Whoo-ee.

Lots of destruction of government property.

Flames blazed out of the wrecked windows and billowed up the side of the building to light up the night. I could feel the heat like it was reaching out for me, even though I was a good hundred feet away by this point. It was warm, felt kinda nice for a second. Then it started to get way too hot for my taste. It spread too, and I realized that the explosion had ripped through the structure to leave a lot of the guts of it exposed.

That ought to get someone's attention. Hopefully local PD, then the FBI, because I could use some help.

I looked toward the entrance to the science lab on both sides, but all I could see was flame, crackling within. I'd blown my pursuers up but good.

I sighed into the wretchedly cold air, staring straight ahead, my eyeballs feeling like they were going to freeze, and then I stumbled to my feet and off into the night, the fire guiding me toward the training building.

And the armory within.

Don't fuck with me, people. Powers or no, I will hunt your sorry ass down.

29.

Natasya

Natasya stared at the billowing flame in the distance, at the building that had exploded in the night. She stared, mouth slightly agape, and listened. The detonation had broken windows all along the side of the headquarters building, filling the air with the freezing temperatures of outside, causing the sheep that they were overseeing to gasp and cry out.

It was enough to make her even more livid.

If she hadn't had to keep her calm while speaking on the phone with the voice.

"Where's my network access?" the voice demanded. Apparently this contingency had not been planned for.

"I plugged the drive you gave me into their computers," Natasya said. She was not used to missions going this awry, either. Except for that last one before the gulag, of course. "I have done all I can."

There was a pause before the voice spoke again, and Natasya could tell the voice was suddenly alarmed. "What … the hell is going on there? There's a thermal imaging bloom on your location—on the science building."

"Nealon escaped," Natasya said bluntly. She'd sent six men after the little bitch, and she had a suspicion that they'd been in that building when it had gone up. Damn it all.

"Escaped how?" the voice asked coldly.

"Volkov picked a fight with her," Natasya said. "Just before we took control. The suppressant went off just before they tumbled out a window."

There was a pause, and the voice came back as frosted as the ground. "Where is she now?"

"I don't know for certain," Natasya said. "But I suspect she either died in the explosion or used it to cover her escape."

"Where is Volkov?"

"Dead," Natasya said. "She shot him in the head. Apparently she had a gun, which was something you failed to mention—"

The voice came laughing back. "I thought four of you with a small army to back you up could handle one de-powered twenty-something. Apparently, I was wrong."

"This isn't over yet," Natasya said, cold determination racing through her. "We're getting you your link into their network. Until then, I have Vitalik working on the first contingency for the prison."

"And their security force?"

"Neutralized," Natasya said. "They took the bait, the laden food. We had to kill three or four, but the rest are tied up."

"Find the girl," the voice came back again. "Get me into the network. Open the prison."

Natasya fought back a bitter desire to say something untoward. "As you wish," she said instead and pushed the red button that terminated the call. "Miksa!" she called, sweeping her gaze over the hostages, mewling like frightened kittens. The Hungarian snapped to, hurrying up to her from where he'd stood, staring lazily into the distance. "Do you want to hunt Sienna Nealon or would you rather I go?"

The Hungarians eyes gleamed. "I would revel in the chance to burn her alive. Slowly, of course."

Natasya showed no reaction his proposition; inflicting pain was not something that interested her, not even for the capitalists she so despised. Removing them was a satisfaction, a tiny step forward for the cause, but the act itself? It was a means, not an end. She shrugged. "Of course. Take a few men with you and hunt her down." She waved a hand at the burning remains of the building in the distance. "I suspect you should start there and see if you can find some tracks."

Miksa nodded and jumped out the window without another word. Not that he had much to say in any case, but this was notable even for him. His reaction had been … not entirely unpredictable. Metas recruited from the satellite states behind the iron curtain had had it rough when they'd been brought into the KGB program. Russians were insular, preferred to keep to themselves. The outsiders forged their own connections, found their own friends. It was a tie that was difficult to break, Natasya knew.

She'd worked with Liliana Negrescu and Miksa before. He had spoken almost normally during those missions. Almost. It was a good sign for how he felt about her, Natasya figured.

And she wouldn't have wanted to be Sienna Nealon when Miksa caught up with the girl. She'd been wandering outside for quite some time now. Frigid cold. Perhaps wounded. Already a long day, and she'd fought with Volkov … no, it was best if she'd died in the explosion. Best for her, best for them.

But if she hadn't … Miksa was sure to slowly roast the skin off her bones. Of that, Natasya was certain.

30.

Sienna

They'd come to kill me.

That was my conclusion as I ran across the snowfield, barefoot, toward the training building. They'd attacked the agency, taken hostages, and chemically castrated the metas, which was just my brother and me. Volkov said that they were here to kill me before I shot him in the face. Four Russian metas and who knows how many hired guns, here to kill little ol' me.

Well, three Russian metas and six or so fewer hired guns, now. Still, numerically, the odds were not in my favor.

But I'd beaten worse odds.

I struggled through the field, the cold burning my nostrils inside, forcing the air into my lungs with each hard, ragged breath. My body was numb through and through, and I was pretty sure nerve damage was already setting in. I wanted to lie down in the snow and die, but I struggled on, in my flimsy damned dress, on bare feet that I couldn't really feel anymore. It was like I was walking on stumps at this point, each step a labor of a thousand years.

I made it to the training building's entrance and into the lobby, a ten-foot by ten-foot cube, tops. It was a little warmer there, and I breathed the air that was probably less than normal room temperature like I had been submerged under the water for ten minutes. I gulped hungry breaths, felt a hint of warmth on my skin, and then slapped my hand to the scanner and prayed for a green light.

It beeped and I struggled with the door again, shoving myself into the tiny crack I was able to force open with my hands refusing to operate normally. I fell to the ground and started to crawl. I wanted to rub my hands together, but the .380 was still clenched tight in my right. I needed clothing. I needed warmth. I needed something to eat, because I was supposed to be devouring miniature quiches right now, dammit. Not crawling through snow and ice with bare hands and feet, powerless and being stalked by a bunch of assholes with a grudge I couldn't even begin to comprehend.

Okay, well, I might be able to sort of comprehend it. I do have a tendency to—shall we say—inflame the emotions of people who cross me. But I used to just kill them, so problem solved. Like that guy in the bank vault with the bar of bullion. Splat, done, no more issues.

Clearly, someone had a grudge, though. Well, probably. My logical mind ran through the possibilities. Assassinating the head of the United States's metahuman policing unit? Not a terrible idea, not when the supply of replacements is low. I mean, Reed was good, but—

Aw, hell.

Reed.

I'd totally forgotten him in all the hubbub and fleeing for my life. I'd left Reed behind in the party, fetching me a social lubricant to help me make it through the party. Now he was there with the terrorists—

Or dead. He could well have been dead.

My stomach sank as I considered that possibility. The idea of my brother dead because these Russians came to kill me ... it didn't sit well with me.

It made me sick.

I struggled on, working my way forward into the training building. It had a lobby beyond the glass security one, and I crawled through it at a turtle's pace. Even the thought that men were coming to kill me couldn't spur me to move any faster. I just wanted to lie down and sleep, which was probably a sign of hypothermia. This was what you get for going out in a thin dress at negative ten degrees with a wind chill even higher than that.

If I got out of this alive, I vowed to move somewhere sunnier. Like Mercury.

I made it down the hall and looked back only to realize that I was trailing blood behind me. Great. Another problem to deal with. Because I didn't already have enough of those. I looked down and saw that my legs were red, frozen crimson ice smeared along the length of my knees and shins, blanketing the pale flesh. I looked down and saw similar marks on my hands, but I couldn't find the wound. Blood loss probably wasn't helping with the hypothermia, though.

I vowed never to go to a party again. This is why I'm a hermit in my off-time. Another decade of self-imposed isolation was starting to sound like a damned good idea.

I made it to the armory and slapped a bloodied hand on the biometric sensor. It dinged for me and opened the door, but I had to force my fingers into the gap to pry it open. This door was heavier, and I struggled with it for a while before it opened. I managed to crawl inside and shut it, and then I pondered what the hell to do next.

My dilemma was getting worse by the minute, and my logical mind whirling with the possibilities and inevitabilities. They were here to kill me. They were armed and in force. I'd just left a trail of blood, footprints and crawl marks from the scene of my last encounter with them to here, and for certain there were more of them out there, just waiting to get me. I was bleeding, weak, tired, hypothermic, frostbitten and without my usual powers. Or spunk.

But I was also pissed off, hurting, backed into a corner and afraid for my life. Not a good place to find me.

I pushed myself back into the work, crawling through the

armory and taking inventory of what I'd need. First aid kit? Yep. Rifle? Yessir, please. With extra magazines. Weight was going to be a limiting factor here, so I went with an M-16 variant. It had quad rails, with some fancy doohickeys on the side. I ditched the laser and kept the flashlight and red dot sight. We didn't have a quartermaster, per se, and this armory was exclusively for the use of our meta personnel—i.e. Reed and myself—and since Reed only practiced with these weapons when I made him, I knew where everything was. I found an M209 grenade launcher and latched it to the picatinny rail on the bottom of my rifle. That took some doing, what with my hands being in the state they were. The next time I ran into one of these clowns, I wanted them to ask themselves, "Where does she get these wonderful toys?"

You know, as they were being blown into itty-bitty smithereens.

The extra weight made the rifle kinda heavy, especially without my meta strength, but I didn't feel able to walk at the moment, so I wasn't tremendously concerned yet. One insurmountable problem at a time.

I was trying to figure out what pistol I should carry when my eyes traced the ceiling. I saw the security camera, one of a million stationed all over the campus. A little light clicked on in my head, and I went from zero to shit-a-brick in 1.8 seconds. They could have been watching me. They could have been watching my every move, playing with me like Kat used to play with her hair.

Damn, damn, damn.

If they had access to the network, I was fried. They'd have to be closing in on me right this very moment, because I'd been parading—also known as crawling—around in front of the camera for at least five minutes.

On the other hand, I was deeply impaired and needed at least first aid, not to mention a change of clothes. Which, fortunately, we had on hand, in the form of the sort of tactical clothing a SWAT team would wear. Oh, how I wished we had a SWAT team at that moment. We even had winter camo, kind of an army surplus thing.

I grabbed a smaller Glock 19, the type of gun Kat used to carry, with her effeminate little hands, and I cursed these bastards for stealing my power. I hoped like hell it was temporary. It had to be temporary. It had to.

Right?

Later.

With my pistol picked out and a few spare mags ready, I dragged everything I had so far over to a space in the far corner where the surplus crates sat. I dug and dug before I finally found a package of emergency signaling mirrors. With the mirror at hand, I sat on the cold metal floor and inspected both legs, up and down, then tore open a cleansing wipe from the first aid kit and gave them a quick clean. The flesh was dirty, was scuffed, nearly-blue in a few places like my knees, but there were no wounds there. As bad as they looked, my legs were not the source of the bleeding. Neither were my arms, I determined after a thorough inspection. I did this all hurriedly and pulled on some thick, white-digital camouflage pants as soon as I was done. Because I didn't want to get caught with my pants down. (Har har.)

Next were my feet. I had never been particularly enamored with how my feet looked; they were kind rough and misshapen, though thankfully not huge or anything. My second toe jutted out above the big toe, which I always thought was kind of weird, and it made me self-conscious enough that I didn't wear sandals. Were everyone's feet like that? I dunno, but I still felt weird about it.

The soles were bluish but not black, giving me a quick sense of relief. I poked at myself and realized I could feel the touch, although it seemed muted somehow. I sighed and dried my feet off, then hurried to pull on socks. One less thing to worry about, because while I had certainly gotten cold as hell, I wasn't suffering from frostbite thanks to my five-minute journey between buildings.

I had my dress pulled up over my camo pants and finally just pulled it over my head so I could get the rest of my camo outfit on. It was here that I discovered where the blood was coming from. The back of my dress was shredded, and as I pulled it off I felt something tug loose, then hit the floor with the tinkle of broken glass.

I had broken glass in my back. Sonofagun. It must have come from my tumble out the window with Volkov, that drunken idiot.

That drunken idiot who saved my life. If I hadn't gone out the window, I would have been stuck in the reception, powerless against all those people who wanted to kill me. I felt a moment of grateful thanks to the bearded jackass, but not an ounce of remorse for putting a bullet through his head. Cold, I know. I didn't care. Clearly, I was a product of my environment.

This was rapidly becoming a time sink that could cost me my life. I used the mirror to look at my back, and it was messy. The good news was that it was one laceration that appeared superficial, not a deep and penetrating wound that hit bone or anything. The bad news was that I was not exactly a trauma surgeon, and the thought of trying to stitch myself up with weak and shaking fingers while looking into a mirror over my shoulder was unappealing, at best.

Fortunately, I had butterfly bandages in the first aid kit, and if I ended up with a scar, so be it. I was more worried about survival than having an immaculate, scar-free back. Besides, I was never going to wear an effing dress again.

I haphazardly placed the butterflies, about six or so along a four-inch laceration, and then ran tape around a big ol' gauze bandage and slapped it on. Then I reflected on how much it hurt to slap a gauze bandage on an open wound, and decided—while screaming a bevy of curses into the armory's cool, dry air—that I would try to make better choices in the future. If I ended up having one.

But now I was armed, with my M-16 and my pistol. I

strapped on boots, lacing them tightly around my still-numb feet. I tried to take it easy on my back by not making sudden movements. I slipped the first aid kit in a backpack with extra mags (so thankful I didn't have to load them myself with numb fingers), along with a bandolier with a half-dozen grenades for the underslung M209. The M-16 felt heavy, but manageable. I put the stock against my shoulder, hoping the recoil wouldn't be too much for my newly weakened self to handle.

I tried to ignore the nagging doubts inherent in going from the most well-known, superpowered person on the plane to just another ordinary human.

I was John McClane in *Die Hard*. I was Steven Seagal in *Under Siege*. I was Shia LeBoeuf in every day of his delusional life.

Crap. Didn't Reed accuse me of doing affirmations earlier? Well, whatever, I was doing affirmations because I needed them. My everything hurt, and people were trying to kill me. I was a long way from the top of my game, and I needed all the help I could get. I adjusted my pack and realized just how heavy everything felt. Then I took off the pack and put on a heavy jacket, because I'd need it if I was going to be out in the cold. A ski cap and balaclava went on after that, and I tucked my hair up, suddenly glad I hadn't wasted time or money on the professional styling that Phillips had suggested. I finished the ensemble off with a holster for the Glock and a Gerber knife on the other hip, just in front of the spare mags for the M-16. Then I put the backpack back on and stood there for a minute, just feeling the weight of it all. It was heavy.

Crap. This was going to suck. But still, I was dressed a lot more comfortably than I had been for the reception.

I stowed a couple extra surprises as I prepared to exit the room, and stopped at the door when I heard a strange buzzing sound. I frowned, trying to figure out where it was coming from. It sounded like it was in the ceiling, and then I traced it back to the camera in the corner, the little black dome that was watching over me. It was making a frantic noise, like something inside it was moving constantly, back and forth.

I wanted to stand on something and reach up to touch it, take the dome off, maybe see what it was doing under there, but I realized in a second that the lens had to be shifting back and forth rapidly enough to make noise. Someone was clearly controlling it. Someone was watching me.

But why would someone watching me give away the fact they were doing so? It made no sense at all, unless they wanted me to know it and come to the conclusion that I was being watched—

Aw, hell squared.

I felt a cold worry shiver my whole body as I came to two possible conclusions. Either one of the bad guys was working the camera in order to make me question my decision to walk out the armory door, which was—well, a flimsy possibility compared to the other, which was …

… that someone—some fellow member of the agency— was watching me through the security camera. Watching me, and warning me not to go out the door because something— *someone*—was waiting for me on the other side.

31.

When backed into an impossible situation, most people tend to despair. They think about what's happened, how it could have been prevented, what they'd do if they had a chance to try again, to make different decisions. It's the paralysis of analysis, and we've all done at various points in our lives. Being in a life-or-death situation is a shitty time to re-examine prior decisions and reflect, though. And the worst time to get in a feedback loop of "Should I have done this?" or "Should I have done that?" is when armed and superpowered enemies are standing right outside the door of your military armory, waiting to ambush you the moment you set foot outside.

But it was me in that armory and not most people, and that door was locked with biometrics and had zero glass for someone to break their way through. I was vaulted in, and it'd take an army to drag my ass out of that safety zone. They may have had fifty or a hundred mercenaries (I doubted it was that many, my guess was on twenty to thirty—minus six), but …

I was locked in an armory.

Me.

In an armory.

Teehee.

I opened the door long enough to see faces, surprised at my sudden exodus. I didn't actually do much more than peek out, though. Well, that and throw eight grenades out in a scatter before slamming the door shut again. They were a mixture of pineapples—that's fragmentary grenades—as well as a flash, and two WP. WP stands for "Willie Pete," which is what soldiers in Vietnam called white phosphorus. It's a really nasty bit of business.

My mentor, Glen Parks, once showed me what one did. He took a fifty-five gallon drum, filled it to the top with water, pulled the grenade pin, and dropped it in. Then he took a whole lot of steps back and we watched the magic. It evaporated every drop of the water and melted the drum to slag, leaving a rather large, black scar on the ground.

Ah, memories. Things like that are why I thought of that time of my life as the best.

I hit the deck out of habit, even though none of the grenades were likely to penetrate the armory walls. I pulled up a gas mask and secured it on my face as I heard screams from the other side of the door. No sounds of shots fired at random, though, so that was a positive sign. For me, not them.

I opened the door again, this time in a squat, peering out through the literal fog of war. Men were screaming, fire was blazing, I was pretty sure someone was in the middle of the flames, and I cared about none of it. The smoke was thick, heavy, and a perfect cover for someone who knew this building like it was her own home. Hell, it pretty much was.

I crept along the corridor, thankful that my aim with the grenades had worked out like I planned it. I'd chucked the Willie Pete to the right, intending to go left in the chaotic aftermath. I stayed close to the wall as a guy ran by, billowing flames. He flapped his arms like a chicken. Like a big, roasting chicken. I think he was screaming, but it was hard to tell. He collapsed after a few feet, and I didn't take the time to mourn him.

However many men they sent after me, I'd blinded them, but I was under no illusions that it was anything other than temporary. I kept my hands firmly on my M-16, which I had attached to me via sling, in case of emergency. I had lost one gun tonight already, and I aimed to not lose any more. If I made it out of this alive, it was going to be due to my grit and daring, and while those were very fine things, they wouldn't stop a bullet from splattering my brain into a nearby snow bank. Ask Leonid Volkov if you don't believe me. Take his silence for the answer.

I kept as quiet as I could, even in spite of the screaming still coming from behind me. I had to assume that not all the enemies were down, and whoever was left could end me with a stray, blind-fired bullet just as easily as a carefully aimed one. The smoke may have been my friend and ally, but it was hardly a protective blanket from everything my pursuers could throw at me.

Plus, there very well could have been an active meta back there. Vitalik, Natasya or Miksa. I had no idea what any of their powers were, so they were just giant question marks for me at this point.

I dodged into a training room quietly, slipping behind the metal doorframe and using it as cover while I peered out into the smoke-filled hall. The air was choking, a heavy cloud hanging on the ceiling and thinning closer to the ground. I had a suspicion that the force of the grenades exploding had probably blown out some windows somewhere in the building. I wondered why the fire sprinklers hadn't activated, but an explanation occurred to me. Whoever had "warned" me about the mercs waiting in ambush outside the armory clearly had system access. It was entirely possible they were keeping my smokescreen intact. The fires were already dying down in any case; the WP wasn't left with a ton to work with in the bare, tile hallways.

I watched the clouds thin, and finally heard voices that weren't screams. I heard someone pounding on the door to the armory, which I had quietly shut behind me in my exodus during the commotion. Hushed voices broke through the air, behind the faint crackle of dying flames. I saw shadows in the darkness, lit by the orange glow of the remaining fire. One. Two. A third brought up the rear, hobbling slightly. Two of the three were carrying weapons that looked like submachine guns, maybe something in the HK family.

With meta speed, a split shot on three people would be cake. Preferably Funfetti Cake with white frosting.

As Sienna Nealon, slightly injured and de-powered malcontent, I wasn't so sure. I'd practiced quite a bit with this specific type of gun. With my powers, I could field strip one pretty damned quick. Fast enough for an Army record, at least. Without that additional strength to control the recoil, to keep the weapon centered and on-target? I was definitely hesitant.

Hesitation makes corpses of us all, though, so I leaned slightly out of my doorframe, took aim, and fired at the first guy.

The shots rent the air, thunderously loud without hearing protection on my ears. I aimed for center mass and I saw the target drop after three shots. My barrel climbed with the burst, the blast of the muzzle dying after the third round. The M-16 isn't a fully automatic weapon; it fires in three shot bursts because—surprise, surprise—it turns out that most people can't really control a weapon spraying bullets wildly at the rate of lots per second. I certainly couldn't, not now.

When the barrel climbed for the second and third shots, it was all in a flash and haze. It happened so fast I was stunned. I was not used to firing a gun and having it make that sort of movement. I'd fired fully automatic shotguns and kept them snug to my shoulder the whole time (still hurts, BTW). But I caught a glimpse of an unmistakable pink mist on one of those climbing shots, and I knew the guy was dead.

I recovered from my surprise in time to shift targets but not quickly enough to fire first. I felt my enemy's shots slap the wall behind me. He'd aimed into the darkness, without the benefit of a backlight to guide him, and missed. Not by much, but enough to keep me breathing for a little longer. I didn't panic. I didn't freak out. I just did as I was trained to do and shifted targets, the screaming voice of worry telling me that I could die safely buried in the back of my mind. I squeezed the trigger as soon as I saw the red dot fall on the man's stomach, and I watched the barrel climb again with a three-shot burst.

This time I missed completely with the second and third shots; my gun jumped up and left, placing the follow-ups over his shoulder. I heard him grunt, re-honed my aim to his center, and fired again. I didn't know if he'd had body armor that had stopped my shot, and I didn't want to chance it.

This round hit, dropping him to the floor. He moaned, and I went to change targets again, but the last guy was gone. I put away that thought of major concern and fired another volley into the man I'd just put down; mercy was a sweet concept and all, but I needed injured enemies returning to the fight like I needed more holes in my head. Because I had no doubt that's exactly what they'd do to me given half a chance. Mom was very clear about how we fight—to win, accept no substitutions. If that makes me ruthless, so be it. Fighting for your life doesn't come with rules beyond the one about winning at all costs.

I turned my attention to the problem of the missing man, listening beyond the very slight hiss of a faint fire in the distance for any sign of him. If he was moving, I wanted to know where. If he was about to come out shooting, it'd be helpful to know what direction that would come from so I could anticipate it and fire back. It was a straight hallway, and he'd been down it a minute ago and disappeared. That meant he probably went into one of the side rooms. But there wasn't any way he could flank me from there; the training room I was in lacked windows or another entrance. It was just a big space with canvas mats on the floor for sparring practice, no distractions. There were swords and stuff hanging on the walls, but those were about the last thing on my mind at the moment. I'd have rated them as useful if I had powers, but less than useless in a gun fight without my powers.

I was trying to figure out what my enemy would do next when I heard something hissing in the room with me. It was subtle at first, and it got my attention immediately. Divided attention, admittedly, because I didn't want to take my eyes off the hallway for more than a second in case it was a distraction.

It wasn't.

The wall was burning, the drywall turning blue with a glow that made it look like cerulean energy was dissolving it along a circular line. It took me a minute to realize that it wasn't drywall, it was concrete, and that that was indeed what was happening.

The blue glow traced an ovoid pattern around the wall as I backed up into the room, M-16 held up defensively. When the oval was complete, a kick from the other side sent the cutout concrete block tumbling into the training room, a cloud of white dust billowing forth into the already smoky air.

Miksa Fenes stepped through, hands glowing with what looked like blue energy, and his eyes locked on me immediately. Only one thought pervaded my mind as I stood there, wondering what the hell to do next:

Why, oh why couldn't I have shot him first?

32.

Whatever. This was no time for regrets. I ripped off a three shot burst at the bastard—

—and watched him hand wave with his glowing blue crap and dissolve the bullets.

"Dammit," I said.

Miksa said nothing.

Unnerving.

I shot at him again and watched my bullets dissolve in his fancy-schmancy blue-fire radiation or whatever it was. "Sonofabitch," I said.

"For Liliana," he said finally, his cold eyes watching me with the reflected glow of his hands.

Awww, crap. I guess they were close, after all.

He flung the blue, glowing energy at me and I barely dodged in time. I felt like I was moving in slow motion, throwing myself to the floor and rolling like I'd always practiced. I felt something tear at my shoulder and I screamed as I came back up and reacquired my target, firing again. The recoil sent flames out the barrel and the feel of flames down my open wound, forcing me to take my finger off the trigger at the conclusion of the burst.

Miksa Fenes just stood there, hands still glowing blue. He was calm, absolutely calm. He knew he had me, and he knew I knew it. I glanced back to see that he'd made a dog-sized hole in the wall behind me with that last blast, and I felt a sinking feeling inside.

And then the fire sprinklers activated.

They didn't go for a subtle, light summer rain, either. We went from smoky and hazy to torrential downpour in a half-second, the cold air that had seeped into the room abetted by freezing water dropping on us from on high.

I watched Miksa Fenes's glowing hands peter out in the drowning deluge put out by the sprinkler system. His eyes met mine and I could see the faint panic as he realized just what he was dealing with here.

I felt a wolfish smile play across my lips as I adjusted my grip and fired my underslung grenade launcher at the bastard.

I swore like an angry Belieber at any who dared to doubt my idol when Fenes employed his meta speed to throw himself sideways a the last second. I tracked after him, but at substandard speed. He landed in a sideways roll that was inconceivably fast. It made me feel a little sorry for every human I'd ever dazzled with it.

It also made me wish to have my powers back.

I fired once with the M-16, then again, and Fenes dodged both bursts. He rolled low, closing on me, and I started to panic. The sprinklers were suppressing his powers, meaning I had the advantage at range. But he was blurry with speed, stronger than eighteen muskoxen chained together, and apparently mad as hell that I'd killed an old friend of his.

I fired one more time before he got in under the barrel of my gun and laid a hand around it. I thrust it forward, hoping to jar his hand loose as I discarded the weapon, but it didn't really work. I was trying to go with his momentum, but I just wasn't fast enough to pull it off. He yanked the M-16 out of my hands, and I barely let go in time to keep him from causing some serious damage with it. I was already going for my Glock when he hit me with a short punch to the sternum that sent a surging pain through my chest and put me right on one knee.

He slapped the Glock away as I cleared the holster with it, sending it skittering to the corner. He'd already thrown away the M-16, so fast I hadn't even seen it. I heard it land, though, over the roar of the sprinklers. I got my head up in time to look him in the eye, prey to predator, before he slipped around behind me and put me in a chokehold. I felt his forearm tighten around my neck as he lifted me off the ground, my head squeezed against his chest. Stars and spots clouded my vision, and I felt the blood leaving my head as he pulled me up, up—to my death.

33.

I tried to slow my breathing, tried to slow my thinking, but my mind was whirling at a million miles a second.

I couldn't *breathe.*

My body was in full panic mode, regardless of what my mind was doing. I needed air, needed it now, needed it like nothing I'd ever needed before.

My hands flailed uselessly, slapping at Miksa Fenes's arm, which might as well have been made of pure steel for all the good my little slaps were doing. He said nothing, or at least nothing I could hear, and since I could hear and feel his breaths on the top of my head, I assumed he wasn't doing any talking.

I stopped slapping his arm and searched for another option. I needed something. Anything.

A weapon.

Like the knife on my belt.

I grabbed the Gerber survival knife out of its sheath with fumbling fingers and ran it straight into his hip. He screamed, breaking that quiet tradition. His grip loosened marginally and I brought my head down, then straight back into his nose.

Not gonna lie—it hurt. The crown of my skull met his nose, and I felt the thing pop like full water balloon poked by a knife. Blood splattered into my hair and I spun—slowly for me, but fast enough—to bury the knife in the side of his neck.

I pulled it out and stabbed him in the neck again. He

looked at me, shocked, and reached out to take hold of me with hands that felt like they were about to burst into flames. I backed away, but knew that was a losing strategy, long term. He may have been weak, but he was still stronger than me.

So I reversed my motion and went for a low tackle to the knees.

It did next to nothing to him. He was a super-strong meta, and I was a normal person at the moment. My shoulders hit him and he wobbled a little. Even with blood loss that wouldn't be immediately replaced, he was still worlds stronger than me.

So I bounced off his legs a little, and jammed my knife right into his thigh, giving it a good twist once I knew it was in tight.

He backhanded me with the force of a jackhammer blow and I crumpled, dragging my knife out as I fell. He made a cry, and I felt him fall beside me.

I looked into cold, stunned eyes and felt my grip on the knife slick from what I'd done.

But I wasn't *done* yet.

"You want to know how Liliana died?" I said in a low whisper, all I could manage under the circumstances. He blinked at me, and I rammed the blade into his chest, right under the sternum. Then again. And again. And again, not letting up. He pushed against me, but weakly, barely moving me as he struggled against the inevitable.

The cold eyes found mine, then wavered, blinking, as his sight faded. Miksa Fenes died, the sprinklers raining frigid water down on him from above, showering us both as the red liquid dispersed, washing away the evidence of what I'd done.

I felt cold and weak, trying to stir to my feet, to get the hell out of here before they sent more men after me. It wasn't likely they were going to write the whole thing off as a bad idea, after all. No, Natasya and Vitalik were still here, and still meant me harm, and they had a host of gunmen backing them up.

So I lay there, in the cold water, trying to collect myself and get moving again, and only one thought came to mind that gave me the motivation to do so.

"Two down," I whispered, my breath stirring the puddle of cold water next to my face. The red from Miksa's wounds was spreading through it in a faint cloud, like a wind was blowing it forward from somewhere. "Two to go."

34.

The M-16 was useless, the barrel bent at a subtle angle by Miksa's grab-and-throw maneuver. By itself, this would not have been a problem. I could have just gotten a replacement. But some genius had tossed a whole mess of grenades outside the armory vault and destroyed the biometric scanners that would have allowed me access.

As they say in Latin, *mea culpa*.

Also, as they say in the language of my people, *shit*.

I collected the Glock off the floor of the training room and assessed what I had left. A pistol, some grenades, a couple Claymore mines (just in case), first aid kit, and a survival knife. I also gathered a submachine gun from one of my fallen enemies and made it my primary. I was suddenly thankful that Glen Parks had insisted on familiarizing me with every gun he possibly could. Otherwise I might have been heading into another nasty fight carrying nothing but my pistol.

My new weapon was a Heckler & Koch MP5. I'd used one before, and I liked it. The benefit here was that all my flunky enemies were using them, so as long as I kept killing them, I'd have plenty of ammo. The downside was that it used a 9mm bullet, which had nowhere near the range of the M-16. I definitely wasn't going to be able to pick out a nice spot on a snowy knoll and do some sniping through open windows from a pleasant distance. Not that I would have wanted to anyway, now that I was drenched in water.

The sprinklers shut off just after I started to get up, apparently after my friend on the other end of the looking glass knew for certain Miksa was dead. It happened so quickly that it almost felt like they were apologizing for drenching me. Personally, I felt it was better than suffering death by Fenes's glowjob.

Heh. Glowjob.

I was dripping as I scanned the training building, though, looking for replacement clothes. There was zero chance I was going to find anything here, however, because the sprinklers had been turned on throughout the entire building. While I had thought I'd had hypothermia and frostbite before, going outside in clothes that were soaked through would pretty much guarantee it happening if I tried to run for either the dormitory or the headquarters, a.k.a. the two remaining buildings on campus I hadn't wrecked.

Yet.

We also had a parking garage, but I immediately discarded that possibility with only a little thought. I wasn't going to find clothes there, and trying to assault the main headquarters in a vehicle was about as smart as charging across the field toward the building while flapping my arms like a chicken. *Nice target you got there. Boom!*

I could certainly find some warm clothes across the campus at the dormitory, but the problem was I'd have to get there. If the campus was a clock face, the headquarters was the center of the circle. The building I was in was at roughly the four o'clock position. The science building—mostly destroyed, pretty much empty of anything else of use—was at six o'clock. The dormitory was all the way over at the nine o'clock, hundreds of snowy feet away.

This was not shaping up to be a great night.

Next thought: why couldn't they have come to kill me in summer?

I stripped the wet winter camo off and tried to come up with a plan. I couldn't exactly sit around and wait for it to dry around a fire, after all. But I couldn't go outside naked as the day I was born and expect to survive the crossing, either, especially since my skin was damp from the drenching. It was a long, long run, over open ground. Circling all the way out to the woods would add a considerable amount of exposure to my journey, putting me ever closer to frostbite and hypothermia.

No, I finally decided that the best way to go about this was to take the smartest chances I could. The Russians had to be down to somewhere between 25-50% of their mercenaries, and they were damned sure down half their meta strength. They had hostages, but I couldn't worry about that right now. Sallying forth to try and rescue them in my current condition was a guaranteed suicide. I mean, I'd have to save them eventually, but that was far off. I'd need to access the armory in HQ for a better weapon first, at least. In a way, the Russians' inability to communicate with me was a saving grace. They couldn't issue threats against the hostages to me, and I couldn't get overpowered by emotions and turn myself in because of it.

I should have had a weapons cache built in the dorms, come to think of it. Live and learn. All I had left over there was probably another pistol or—

Or—

My automatic shotgun with a big box of shells? Yes. Yes, I did have it shipped from Vegas to home, and I had been storing it in the top of my closet. It wouldn't be perfect, but it would help. Yay for laziness and failing to store the weapon where it should have been stored.

So, back on focus, they were down on manpower, and at least some of their men needed to stay in place to guard the hostages. If they cared about that. Hopefully they did, since they hadn't sent their full strength out against me yet.

Wait. If they were trying to kill me, why *wouldn't* they send their full strength after me?

I mean, thus far I'd killed one of their metas that they knew of, and killed a half dozen other men. A smart tactical commander would have gone after me with overwhelming numbers the minute I blew up the science building—*if* I'd been her primary objective.

What if I wasn't their primary objective?

I mean, Volkov clearly said that someone wanted me dead, but what if that wasn't all they wanted? I blinked as the thoughts came faster now. What else could they want? High-profile hostages? Well, that certainly fit, because we had senators and congressmen in attendance this evening, along with other political types. That might be an end in and of itself. Because the only other thing they could possibly be interested in that was here was—

Sonofabitch.

This wasn't just an assassination attempt on me; this was a jailbreak.

I slammed a hand into a wet segment of drywall and felt it collapse. It stung. I finished taking off my clothes and wrung them out, as hard as I could, before putting them back on. There was no more time to delay, assuming I was right. I was still damp as a sweaty wrestler, but I had no time for the camo to dry. I had to cross the snowfields around the perimeter of the agency right now and get to fresh clothes and another weapon.

Then I had to figure out how to use the tunnel into headquarters in order to stop them. Because if they got away with this …

Every dangerous meta I'd put away over the last three years could come roaring out of the ground to help them hunt me right to my inevitable—and brutal—end.

35.

Natasya

"You told me you'd be able to access their network," Natasya said, keeping her tone level as she spoke into the cell phone, pacing in front of the second floor lobby windows of the headquarters building. She'd had to leave the place where Vitalik was working on the vault in order to make the call to the voice, and now she was staring out at the night in front of the windows, under the portico that looked out toward the entry to this massive, opulent campus. "You told me to place the little device on their computer and that you would be able to open the doors, show us the surveillance cameras, and open the prison cells."

"I am trying," came the voice, shot through with obvious stress. It ended with a little wheeze. Whoever the woman at the other end of the line was, she was fast approaching her limits. "Someone is blocking me at every turn. Someone is inside their network, putting up roadblocks and—dammit!" The sound of something hitting hard against plastic echoed through the phone. "You have someone on that campus who is thwarting me. Until you stop them, I won't have unimpeded access. I'll have to keep fighting my own little war with them over everything." *And lose*, went the last part, unsaid. Natasya sensed the voice was not used to losing, either.

Natasya stared out into the night, the portico lights a

blinding fluorescent. This entire establishment reeked of waste, of money spent pointlessly. She was hardly a stranger to that, but it bothered her on a strictly ideological level. "I've sent Miksa out to kill Nealon. He should have reported back by now."

There was a rasp at the other end of the phone before the reply came. "You think she killed him?"

"She is quickly convincing me that you misjudged her when you said that without her powers, she was nothing." Natasya straightened, leaning against the bannister rail that separated her from the open air and the granite floor of the lobby below. "She has been trained by someone. This girl is no helpless mouse without her powers."

"I can't help you with that," the voice said. "All I had was a thermal imaging satellite meant to track volcanoes and nuclear launches, and it passed out of range twenty minutes ago. Anything better, anything with real-time imaging would take too long to crack from *here*." The emphasis on *here* imbued it with a certain disdain that told Natasya a few subtle things about where this woman was hiding. It was somewhere she loathed.

"I can't send out Vitalik," Natasya said. "He's busy with the vault. I could go, but if this girl has killed Miksa, she'd be well-positioned to ambush me with a rifle shot—"

"Don't go yourself," the voice said. "Either send minions, and hope they get lucky, or leave her be for a while. Cracking that vault is priority one, and keeping the hostages intact in case the exfiltration goes hairy is priority two." There was a sense of resignation in the voice. "Sienna Nealon will keep. I'll hire someone with a rifle to kill her at a distance in a month, a year, sometime in the future if we miss. Splatter her brains all over the nearest wall." There was a subtle adjustment in the voice's stress level. "But we cannot let Eric sit in that prison another day, do you understand me? You have to get him out."

"I understand," Natasya said. "When the vault opens, I think we'll find more than a few willing allies who'd be happy to help fulfill the last objective."

"Probably," the voice said, seemingly unconcerned. "And I wouldn't mind seeing some of her greatest hits getting a chance to have a go at her, but it's not as important as—"

"I hear you and understand," Natasya said. This woman did like to go on and on.

"What are you going to do about Nealon?" the voice asked. Tentative. She'd surrendered control of the mission to Natasya, but she was still an interested party.

Natasya thought about it for a moment before answering. "I do not like ceding ground to an enemy. I do not like letting this girl wander around unimpeded. Let her work without distraction, given what she's done so far when we are breathing down her neck every moment, and I shudder to think what she will come up with." Natasya shook her head. "No, I will peel off a detail of six more men—all I can spare— and send them after her. They will probably die, but if we're lucky, they'll at least keep her occupied until I can open that prison up and send her a whole host of new friends to hound her to death."

36.

Sienna

I looked out the side door of the training building, my boots squishing in the puddled water, and plotted out my insane, idiotic path. My shoulder hurt where Volkov had driven me through a glass window, my throat hurt where Fenes had choked me, I ached all over from a variety of injuries, and now I was about to have to run—I dunno, five or six football fields over snowy ground in damp clothes?

Like I said before, not my best night ever.

There was no point in delaying, so I started off at a trot, my backpack swaying on my shoulders where I'd tightened it. I had my Glock clenched in my hands as I ran. I'd put the Smith & Wesson with its five remaining shots into my breast pocket, hoping it wouldn't be needed. It probably would, though, knowing my luck.

I jogged across the packed snow, noticing that some fresh flakes were drifting down from above. There were massive lighting poles placed strategically at various points around the campus, enough to break the darkness but not light the place up like the new football stadium in Minneapolis. They didn't help me much right now, providing enough illumination that a sharp eye could pick me out running across the featureless expanses, but I couldn't worry about that.

Because I had a frozen-ass run to make.

By the time I crossed the main driveway I was frigging cold. It was a U-shaped loop, the bottom edge of which ran right up under the headquarters portico, and so I crossed it twice as I threaded my way around the campus. I passed the open-air helicopter pad on my left, giving it and its mighty ground lights a wide berth.

I kept my eye on the headquarters as I made my run. It was probably three hundred feet away from me now, because I'd had to detour to avoid the helipad, and I could see figures in the lobby. They weren't clear, but they were there. I wondered what they were up to, if they were just patrolling.

I kept running, and my breath burned in my lungs. I'd been doing cardio regularly ever since I got back from London the last time. Then, I'd gone face to face with some enemies who had challenged me for the first time in years, made me realize that there were still some tough bad guys out there; now it looked like my training was paying off. Before London, I probably would have collapsed in a heap from a run like this.

As it was, I just *wanted* to collapse in a heap. Or die. Maybe not that last one, not really.

I could see the parking garage ahead, and my skin was tingling from the cold. My uniform was stiff and growing stiffer by the moment, the residual water in it gradually freezing. I could feel ice forming, and it felt like a slow burn, minus the slow part. My bones felt a strange ache, and I wondered if that was from the cold as well.

I huffed onward, planning to pass the parking garage on the far side. It was a massive structure, sprawling, multiple stories, heated inside so as to keep employees' cars—and our government automobiles—out of the elements. Minnesota, she's a harsh mistress, and not so kind to vehicles.

I was practically gasping for breath as I drew near the garage. I chanced a look back and did a double take.

Crap.

I felt the first bullets whiz past to hit the snow a second later. The sound of the shots followed, a sharp series of cracks.

Then came another, then another. I didn't bother to unsling my HK to return fire; the range was improbable, if not impossible. They were using the same guns and were aiming really high. Still not having much luck, fortunately for me.

But my legs felt like concrete and my lungs felt like they'd been poured full of water, so their luck wasn't going to stay bad forever.

There were six guys behind me. They were running full out, and I had to guess that they had longer legs than I did. A pack-a-day smoker could probably run me down if he were six feet tall. Just a matter of time.

So I did the only thing I could. I bolted for the garage.

The garage wasn't locked with biometrics, fortunately. It was still a hundred feet off, easily, and I was dragging ass. I fired the Glock blind over my shoulder, in their general direction, and listened to the deafening roar of the gun going off. I added another bullet to the chorus and listened as they returned fire. Bullets slapped wet snow, flakes falling down around me, as I closed on the garage. The shots got closer as I drew closer, and I fired again, hoping to make them weave or something, anything to buy me a few seconds.

I ripped the door open with what felt like my last breath, and slammed it shut behind me. I had my backpack off and unzipped after a moment's fumble, setting up a tripwire and a claymore in seconds. I faced the helpful "Front Toward Enemy" side toward—yep, you guessed it—the door. Thank you, Glen Parks, for making me practice the setup and defusing of mines until I could do it in my sleep.

I retreated behind the nearest car at a crouch, ducking down and unslinging the HK as I holstered my pistol. I needed to move as far from the door as possible before—

It wasn't the loudest explosion I'd heard tonight, but it was pretty damned loud in a confined space. The sound of the charge followed by pellets beyond number ripping through the open door into legs and feet was a nice sound. I was getting used to agonized screams being the soundtrack of my life, thank you very much.

Every single thing I was doing was thinning their numbers, but they kept throwing more at me. In the long term, that was a losing strategy for them, right? I mean, eventually they were going to run out of numbers. For crying out loud, these idiots had just run straight into an ambush, after all.

That was probably a mark in favor of my prison break theory. It was feeling more and more possible all the time.

There was also the distinct possibility that all my pursuers weren't dead, which was … well, likely. If they'd had any training at all, they should flank me from multiple sides.

Which meant that whoever had just seen the tragic end of their ballet career was probably not the only point of attack.

I cursed into the quiet air and listened as I scrambled back toward the far end of the row and crossed further into the garage. If they'd had six guys and lost—conservatively—two, then that meant they had four left to try and run me down with.

But I had five floors in which to hide. To hide …

… and kill them.

37.

Advantage: Sienna. I know that sounds funny since I was at least four-on-one in this encounter, still hurting, ouchie ouchie, but seriously … compared to what I'd been through so far, evading and killing four guys in a parking garage sounded like a walk in a park. And I don't mean Central Park at night, either, I mean like a walk in a really peaceful park at night. Like maybe the Magic Kingdom or something. I've never been, but it's gotta be peaceful, right? Except for screaming toddlers.

I decided my best plan was to move up to the second floor while these guys were still sneaking their way into the first floor. Then I'd have time to do stuff to distract them, like maybe …

… well, I don't want to spoil the surprise.

I heard someone enter the garage on the far side, the one closest to the headquarters, just as I was heading up the ramp to the second floor. I kept my footsteps as muffled as possible. Surprisingly, my boots helped, making soft whispers only as I crept up the incline and left the first floor behind. The up ramp was a simple rectangle, parking spaces on either side. It was pretty full, too, because we had lots of agency cars on the first floor, along with all the cars of all the reception guests.

And then I got to the second floor and saw the giant, gaping hole in my strategy.

I was used to being in the garage during the daytime, when

all the worker bees of the agency were here, fighting for parking as low to the ground as they could. (There was no elevator.) The ramp was usually full all the way up to the third floor, even in the afternoon.

Now, with the only people here being the guests for the reception, the second floor was nearly abandoned. It was Dodge City at high noon out there. I half expected a tumbleweed to come blowing between the dotted lines. Hell, it could have had five spaces all its own.

I heard whispers behind me and cursed silently as I realized that creeping back down that ramp was certain death. No doubt about it, I was stuck here with sparse cover. Now my best bet was to get to a stairwell and ascend to the topmost floors, where maybe one or two cars were parked, at most. Maybe I could use one of them as cover, or for some of those distractions I'd planned, because the second floor wasn't going to be good for much besides my death. I needed time and some space to maneuver, and getting as far from the enemies as possible was the only way to accomplish that.

I crept on, moving around the three-wire divider that was strung between poles to keep people from falling down the sides of the ramp. I hurried to the corner of the empty parking garage, scrambling under the dull fluorescent lights to keep from making noise as I moved. I made it to the brick stairwell in the corner and paused at the door, putting my ear to it to listen.

I heard nothing.

I eased the door open carefully, taking notice of the fact that my fingers were still feeling particularly numb at the ends. I kept my HK cradled in one hand, ready to sweep into the stairwell firing. After all, at that point my position would be pretty well given away, might as well go out in a blaze of glory. And bullets. Mostly bullets; killing these faceless idiots wasn't going to do much for glory. I'd killed the strongest man on the planet, after all. Nameless mercs weren't much of a feather in my cap, so to speak.

I opened the door, and it squealed just slightly. I froze, listening. I doubted the sound was easily audible on the floor below, but if someone—by chance, which was one in four, since there were four stairwells—happened to be in this very one, they had almost certainly just heard me.

I waited. Listened.

Heard nothing.

I slowly shut the door, easing it through another squeal as it closed, hoping that wasn't the noise that gave me away. I kept my eye fixed on the downward path, making sure someone didn't sneak up on me.

Once the door was closed, I started up the stairs with a confidence. This might actually work. I might actually be able to get to the top floor and—

The sound of gunfire from below was a rude interruption to my train of thought, and I felt bullets spray against the wall, showering me with concrete shards. I felt a sudden stinging in my right eye and dropped instinctively.

It saved my life.

The next stream of bullets spattered the wall behind where my head had been a moment earlier. The firing came from below.

Yep. Wrong staircase. What were the odds?

Oh, right. One in four. Crap. Looked like their luck had changed. Mine, too, but not for the better.

I started toward the squeaky door, figuring maybe I could get back into the main garage area. My backpack clung to my back, my frozen camo starting to melt in the warmth of the heated garage. Clearly the camo wasn't doing much to hide me, dammit.

I reached up for the door, pulling the handle. I couldn't see the gunman who was spraying the area around me with liberal amounts of lead, but it wasn't a stretch to assume he wasn't far down the stairs. I opened the handle, listened to the squeak as I pulled it open—

And felt the door rattle under a hail of bullets from inside the garage. I shoved it closed, hard, with my shoulder, sick in my gut from knowing what this meant.

My retreat was cut off.

38.

Feeling cornered was not exactly a new experience for me, even before this marvelous night in which I wore formal wear and metaphorically tangoed with more men than I cared to. As in, "Tango down!" It was looking like this time I was the tango, though, because another spate of bullets pelted the door above my head, as the merc in the stairwell with me made his own play to kill me with another burst.

Being powerless really cuts down on the available options. I hate that. Also, I never wanted to leave my couch again.

Footsteps closed in on the door, and I knew I had only a few seconds. Rummaging through my backpack, I grabbed a smoke grenade and tossed it down. It clinked on its way to the bottom of the stairwell. I thunked my boots against the ground on the side of the walkway, trying to produce a false impression that I was bolting upstairs, then waited for the response.

It didn't come.

I heard the smoke grenade pop down the stairwell. I'd thought about going with a flashbang, but those were a little more chancy. Grey smoke flooded the stairwell, surging up to my level before the footsteps outside the stairwell had even reached the door.

As quietly as I could, I slid headfirst down the stairs, careful not to knock the butt of my gun against anything at all. I was as noiseless as a young woman could be while swimming down stairs. Fortunately the hiss of the smoke grenade covered some of it.

I made it to the landing below and waited until I heard the sound of gunfire from the guy who'd kept me from going up. A flare of muzzle fire lit up the smoke, and I realized he was about ten feet in front of me, heading up. He was working on instinct, his actions guided by what he thought I'd do. In the face of overwhelming odds and a bunch of guys about to reinforce him from the second floor, my smartest move *would* have been to head up.

But he'd already inadvertently given away the fact that he was the only one between me and the first floor exit because he hadn't shouted, "Grenade!" when I tossed that smoker down there. He'd just quietly gone about the business of covering himself. Which meant he was either alone or the worst team player on the face of the planet.

I was banking on the former; mercenaries generally have some military training, and that's the sort of thing you don't just forget to do.

Besides, if I was wrong, I was going to end up no more dead than if I tried to escape up. That was certain doom.

I made myself a part of the wall, leaning hard against it, clearing myself out of the stairwell path as the guy charged up, firing willy-nilly and blind in an effort to keep me from getting up to the third floor and beyond. If I'd still been trying to go up, I would have seriously reconsidered my actions right about then.

Instead, I popped up from behind him as he passed me in the smoke without a thought that I could have been lingering on the landing. I drove my Gerber knife into the place where the skull meets the base of the spine and twisted. It was harder without my meta strength, but I got it in there. He didn't make much more than a noise of protest before it was done, and he dropped. I had to step quickly to keep from having his falling body knock me over. I dodged neatly over him, and I pushed him to the side then listened to him thump down the stairs, keeping my steps only semi-quiet as I charged to the first floor.

There had been a decent interval of time since I'd heard shots at the second-floor entry to the stairwell. I'd figured this was where things would get troublesome, with those reinforcements pouring into the stairwell and hampering my progress. But they were taking their sweet time, messing around with the door handle and opening it oh-so-slowly. It took me a moment to realize why: the claymore I'd left at the first door had made them cautious. Fool me once and all that. Well, I could certainly use the delay.

I slammed against the exit bar on the first floor and burst out of the smoky stairwell into fresh, cool air. The fluorescent overhead lighting was a welcome change from the obstructed view of the stairs offered after I'd tossed the grenade, and I immediately ran, doubled over, for the cover of the nearest car. No shots greeted me, so I assumed I was alone for a brief moment in time.

Which was good, because I had plans that required at least a brief moment of time.

I could hear shouting in other parts of the garage, and muffled yells from the stairwell behind me that told me someone had probably discovered my handiwork in there. Not to brag, but that was an ace sort of kill, pulling that off. Totally ninja.

I crept along, sneaking in front of the bumpers of cars, keeping low and watching through windshields and out the back of vehicles as best I could. I didn't see any movement, which was the biggest giveaway. I made my way as quickly as I could to the part of the garage where we kept the agency vehicles.

There was a keybox like the kind valets use, with a numbering system to denote which keys go to which parking space. In space one was the car used for the director, a lovely SUV made to government specs, complete with armor. It wasn't exactly Nick Fury's car from *The Winter Soldier*, but I liked it. I seldom used it myself because I don't really love driving, but in a pinch it was a hell of a vehicle.

Now it belonged to Andrew Phillips, I supposed, so I didn't really think anything of it when I grabbed the keys and planned my next bit of mayhem. This one would involve vehicular homicide and more destruction of government property, so I felt like I'd picked the right car for the task at hand.

The garage attendant, bless his soul, had always parked the car for me. It was a big damned SUV, and the genius who'd designed the parking structure had made the parking spaces with Honda Civics in mind, forgetting that this was America and we drove cars big enough to challenge garbage trucks for road dominance over here, dammit. As a result, the attendant always parked the cars he drove backward, front end facing out so that if I desperately needed my car, I could just get in and go. He said he did it for insurance purposes, whatever that meant. He had a whole monologue about it, but I just nodded politely and tuned him out.

I crept up on the car, unlocked the door quietly with the fob (one click) and opened it wide enough to thrust my backpack in first. Then I slid up into the driver's seat and kept myself low in the seat, so that I could look out through the steering wheel and see what was going on in front of me. For now, there was nothing going on.

But I suspected that was about to change.

I waited, undertaking a little modification and preparation while I did so. I'd once heard in a movie (*Under Siege 2*, a classic of American cinema) that chance favors the prepared mind. I wasn't leaving much to chance here. These guys wanted to find me, they probably figured I was here on the first floor, and I wasn't going to disappoint them in their search. They were definitely going to find me, all two or three of them that remained.

Of course, they were going to be sorry they found me, but hey, no plan survives contact with the enemy, guys. (That one's Sun-Tzu.)

I'm detecting a pattern in my quotes. It probably says something about me.

I waited and waited, for what seemed like hours but was probably only minutes. The fluorescent bulb just ahead of me had developed a flicker, but the insulation in my car was so good I couldn't hear the hum. Points for that, because it's an irritating noise.

Pretty soon I saw the first mercenary emerge. He crept along, breaking cover in the row of cars to my right and crossing the row to wait behind the hood of a sedan. He'd just checked the exit door over there, I figured, and determined that there were in fact no footprints heading out.

Just like I figured they would. Predictable.

Two other guys came creeping along the row, one just in front of me, and I slid down even further, counting out thirty seconds before I bobbed back up enough to peer out again. He'd hardly made an exhaustive search; it looked like he was coming together with his buddies for a confab. I counted one, two, three of them, and breathed a sigh of relief as they congregated near the trunk of the sedan.

They were on either side of it, trying to keep themselves from being exposed in case I was waiting somewhere in the garage with a gun, but also leaning toward each other enough to minimize their volume. I realized in that moment that these geniuses—these super geniuses who'd been trying to kill me—didn't have radios. Why? Maybe they figured the government could overhear them?

It all worked in my favor, though, because I quietly buckled myself in and started my car, making sure to set the lights to the "off" position first, rather than let them snap on automatically. I figured that might buy me an extra second of surprise as I threw the car into drive and floored it.

Someone with a gentler temperament than me—like, oh, I dunno, Conrad Hilton—might have used this opportunity to escape. Not me, apparently. I'd felt the fear for my life and it had passed somewhere around the time Miksa Fenes tried to burn me into ash, around the time I figured out what these Russians were planning to do to my prison. Leaving aside the obvious worries of what could be happening to the hostages, I was left with one overwhelming emotion: rage.

Yep. Now I was just pissed off.

I mashed the accelerator all the way to the floor and listened to the horses run. The mercs wasted precious seconds trying to figure out where the noise came from in the echoing garage and then at least another precious second deciding internally what to do about the black SUV barreling at them doing about fifty. The guy closest to me leapt sideways as I slammed into the back of the sedan they'd been meeting around. I didn't hit the other two guys directly, but I whipsawed the sedan sideways as I T-boned it, and it smashed flush into the car next to it, leaving no room for space between them.

Take a government car, weighing several thousand pounds, add a dab of velocity for several seconds, then a parked car, garnish with two assholes who were out to kill me. Voila! That's my recipe for mercenary puree. Put it in your cookbooks, kids, because it's one that the whole family will love.

I was dazed after the impact, but I could see through the dust that the deflated airbag had left behind that I'd gotten two of them. One was screaming at the top of his lungs, his groin and everything below crushed between two cars. The other hadn't been quite so lucky; he'd dived for the open aisle to our right and didn't quite make it. Now his body was hanging out in the open, pinned from the middle of his chest down. If he wasn't dead, he was close; there wasn't a doctor in this world that could fix him.

I didn't exactly admire my handiwork, but I felt a sense of satisfaction for a brief second until the bullets peppered my window. They did what bullets do when they hit bulletproof glass—spidered the hell out of it. This stirred me back to life and I made a quick, last-minute adjustment before I scrambled into the passenger seat and prepared to bail out.

I almost got out before the last idiot got the driver's side door open. I'd hoped I'd have a second or so due to the mangling of the car in the crash, but luck was only kindasorta on my side this time. This guy was enraged, livid at what I'd done to his buddies, and it was obvious on his face. He jerked the door open just as I was tumbling out the passenger side, and I got an unfortunate and undesired boost as the claymore I'd just finished wiring to the door blew up behind me.

I knew it was going to be loud, but this was like a 747 taking off in my frigging ear. The force of the explosion sent me end over end as my legs—which were still on the passenger seat— flipped over my upper body, which was almost slithered out of the car. I landed on the concrete floor with a WHUMP! and all my air left me.

I lay there, staring up at the still-flickering light above me, for several minutes. I wanted to get up, but I couldn't. My ears were ringing like I'd listened to a death metal concert from inside a speakerbox, and my entire head was shaking.

My only consolation was that I'd probably killed the last of these douches, so there was that.

I peeled myself up off the floor after another minute, still hearing that ringing in my ears. I shuffled off toward the nearest door and bailed through it, losing my balance and pitching forward into a snowbank just off the sidewalk outside. Someone was playing cymbal in my head, with a whole chorus of triangles to add to the pitch and wail. I tried to push myself up but my shoulder screamed at me in a voice that resonated throughout my whole body. I told it to shut up, but I had a feeling that those bandages I'd attached had pulled free in the crash. *Shoulda known better*, a faint voice of reason in my brain told me.

You should shut the hell up, I told it in reply. I was in no mood.

I crawled on my knees, the dormitory building rising up in front of me. It was an angular building, with balconies and a long L shape that left one wing of it stretching out to meet me.

There was an entrance over there, and I was by God going to find it, even though the lights were off and all I could see was blurry shadows along the length of it.

Wait, why were the lights off?

I felt the cold press against my gloveless hands as I crawled, my clothing once again freezing against my skin. I felt the sling with my MP5 fall into the snow, and I dragged it back up with useless hands. I was shaking, from cold or injury or shock, maybe even some combination of all three.

"You bastards sure know how to show a girl a good time," I said as I collapsed into the snow again, but I couldn't even hear my words over the ringing. I saw snowflakes dancing past my eyes. One fell on my nose. It tickled.

I wanted to collapse here and sleep for the night. It had to be late, past my bedtime. My brain wanted to trick me, wanted me to take this opportunity to just rest and attack the problem by dawn's light. I'd be rested. I'd be refreshed. My shoulder wouldn't be crying and moaning in pain. It felt cool and wet, like it was bleeding again. Or was that just sweat?

I hauled myself up to all fours again and made another start across the field. The dormitory building was impossibly far away. Miles, maybe. It didn't feel like it was getting any closer. I thought maybe walking would get me there quicker, but my body vetoed the idea of standing. My shoulder pleaded for mercy with each movement I made to crawl forward, but my legs told it to take a flying leap. You're on your own, they said, we're out for the night. Assholes.

I made it another mile or five, but the dormitory grew no closer. I flailed my arms to try and crawl, and then realized my belly was firmly in the snow. I couldn't make myself move. Hell, I didn't want to move. I wanted to sleep.

Hypothermia, a distant voice whispered. Did it have a Russian accent?

Shock, another one added.

Death, came the most compelling of all, deep and gravelly.

I felt myself stop shivering, but only dimly. I felt strangely

… and suddenly … warm? And sleepy. Oh, so sleepy.

I curled my legs up to my chest and wrapped my good arm around them, lying there on my side. I saw my breath frost in the air, go misty and float off into the dark of night, lit by only a faint and distant light from headquarters.

Headquarters? Wasn't I supposed to go there for some reason?

It didn't matter now. Now was a time for sleep. It was night, after all, and night was a time for sleep.

I heard the sound of crunching snow over the distant ringing in my ears, and then I felt strong arms roll me over. I blinked at the shadow of the figure stooping over me. My gloveless fingers caught his arm and I felt smooth leather, slightly wet from the falling flakes melting on the surface.

I felt him gather me up, like a child being picked up by a parent, cradled safe and warm. The darkness was near-complete, and he started to walk, to carry me. Something in my mind said, *meta*. I told it to shut up, because I needed to sleep.

"Hi," I said, my voice dragging, muted, barely audible above that persistent ringing.

"Hey, Sienna," the man said, and even though I couldn't hear him all that well, I knew that voice. It was smooth, it was calm, it was … sweet?

The steps were slow, steady progress over the snow field, and I could see the dormitory building looming over us in the shadows. Why were the lights off? That was weird, wasn't it?

I wanted to close my eyes, but felt strangely riveted to this man, his shadowy face that I couldn't even see, his smooth and familiar voice. He carried me on, and I felt him adjust my weight as he did something. Then I closed my eyes in shock as light flooded my senses. I cracked them back open again, blazing brightness overwhelming me as I stared up. I locked onto his face at last, even as I felt the tiredness—the darkness—welling up to get me for the last time.

It was Scott Byerly.

I stared at him for a moment, his dusty blond hair all but hidden under a ski cap. Then my muscles gave out, and I felt myself go limp, safe in his arms, as I pitched into a deep, deep sleep.

39.

Natasya

"I think we can conclude that the men I sent after her are either dead or incapacitated," Natasya said into the phone, waiting for the judgment on the other side.

None came. "If they kept her busy, then they've fulfilled their function," the voice said.

Natasya stared out into the night. She was at the corner of the building on the fourth floor, looking out into the darkness at the parking garage in the distance. She'd heard gunfire as the mercenaries she'd dispatched after the girl caught her trail, but they'd disappeared inside some time ago and no significant noise had emerged since save for a subtle pop that could have been a muffled explosion.

The garage was little more than a cluster of lights in the distance, a looming shadow only slightly less dark than the dormitory building in the distance. With one last look, Natasya turned from it and strode back into the headquarters, leaving the perimeter office behind.

"How much longer?" the voice asked.

"How long until you're in the network?" Natasya replied evenly.

"I am working on it, but I'm being perpetually thwarted," the voice said with a coolness all her own. "You should nearly be done executing the first contingency now."

"And we are," Natasya said. "If you want a status report, you should contact Vitalik."

There was a moment of pondering. "I will. Call me if the situation changes."

"Very well," Natasya said, threading her way into the interior bullpen. This was a working space that had been cleared through the supervised labor of the party guests. It had been good for them, these fat, slovenly pigs, forced to put their backs into clearing a space where they could sit and have men point guns at their overfed faces. They'd sweated, some cried, a few stubborn refusals had bruises to show for their defiance. None had gone so far as to warrant a bullet; their resistance was pathetic. And predictable, in her view. They were soft.

She had eight men left up here. That was all—all that remained of her force of mercenaries in this place, save for the two watching Vitalik's back downstairs. Ten men, two metahumans. All she had after throwing some two metas and eighteen mercenaries after Sienna Nealon. It was a depressing loss of personnel.

But it was acceptable.

For now.

Every single one of her guards was watching the crowd, save for two patrols working their way around the ring of the building. They strolled through the lushly carpeted hallways, striding between the walls hung with canvases, tall potted plants giving the place an air of green, and she tried not to be sick at the wasteful display.

She wandered into the middle of them, looking at the cowed and cowering hostages. Not a fighter among them. Not a soul of resistance in their midst. The security force had all been drugged, disarmed and locked away. If it had been up to Natasya, she would have made the poison lethal, but the voice had insisted on a compound that would merely knock them out. That left a question mark in Natasya's mind, having those men still breathing, but she did as the voice commanded.

After all, she'd laid siege to two different bastions of

America's government in the last two days, and whatever success they'd had was due to the voice's planning and knowledge. While she'd lost two of her own men, that could happen on any operation. Especially one this deep in enemy territory, and against such an unpredictable foe.

Still, she'd learned long ago that objectives mattered more than losses. While she felt for her lost comrades, Volkov had died stupidly, and through no one's fault but his own. Whatever had happened to Miksa was more ambiguous, but still well within the realm of acceptable losses.

And she intended to lose absolutely no one else.

"Who is in charge of this place?" Natasya asked, wondering aloud. She hadn't even thought to ask before, because it was utterly irrelevant. The voice had been so certain that as soon as they were under siege, the prison would be locked down against any access, even that of high-level administrators. There would be no option but to unlock it electronically or physically.

A large man, sandy blond, cool and composed, stood up. His legs wavered as he did so, though Natasya couldn't be certain whether that was from nerves or simple prolonged inactivity coupled with age. "I am," he said. "My name is Andrew Phillips. I'm the director of this agency." The tone was neutral, absent any defiance or fear, just a simple statement of fact.

"Oh, yes," Natasya said, staring at him. "I met you before, when we came here." She felt herself smile, lightly amused. "How tragic it is for you, to be so forgettable."

He remained expressionless. "It hasn't worked out too bad so far."

Natasya felt a laugh bubble up from within. "An excellent point. Sit down, Director. I have no need of you for anything, and if you keep your people calm, you may live to see the morning."

Phillips hesitated, and she could see the wheels turning. "What is your intention here?"

Natasya blinked, then shrugged. "I intend to open the

doors to your prison and free our captured brethren within. Then, under cover of you … lovely, high-profile hostages, we will go to the helipad on your roof and take a chopper to the nearby airport, at which time we will board a waiting plane bound for the tropical paradise of Cuba. There we'll let our comrades decide what to do with your senators and congressmen, while we soak up the sun."

Phillips did not even blink. "That's a very ambitious plan."

Natasya inclined her head in acknowledgment. "Now sit, please."

"One question," Phillips said. "Do you really think the authorities will let you get all the way to Cuba without opposing you?"

Natasya met his fearless gaze with her own. "If they wish for your people to continue breathing, they will. Though I doubt very much that your police and FBI will even be awake before I am sitting in the airport in Havana."

Phillips stared back at her for a moment, like he was pondering pushing his luck and asking another question. Instead he seemed to decide the better of it and sat back down, folding his long legs underneath him and using a cubicle to rest his back. He stared straight ahead, at the floor, as though there were something of great interest there.

Natasya's phone rang, and she answered it without saying a word. "I have something for you," Vitalik said on the other side. She could hear the triumph in his voice.

"Are you done?" she asked, already almost certain of the answer.

"I am done," he said, and she could hear him smiling from here. "Only one task remains, and for that I will need your help."

"I am on my way," Natasya said and put the phone back in the case on her belt. She'd changed out of her party dress hours ago, and felt the better for it. Fatigues: this was the attire appropriate for the party she wanted to attend.

And now all she needed do was descend to the basement prison, and the party she had planned could begin in earnest.

40.

Sienna

I awoke with the natural start of someone who'd been carried off by her ex-boyfriend while in the midst of a deadly game of pursuit by people who wanted to kill me. I went through the rapid cycle of wondering if I'd been dreaming the whole thing, followed by the confusion inherent in finding myself in my own bed, with the room dark around me.

Then I heard Scott's voice in the living room and knew I hadn't dreamed it.

I was clad in nothing under the sheet. I might have been more offended that someone had undressed me, but I'd been wearing camouflage soaked with snow and ice before, so I let it go. I clutched my blankets close to me and heard Scott cease speaking in the other room, followed by a gentle, "You want to get some clothes on and come join us?"

"Maybe," I said, my throat thick with dryness. How long had it been since I'd had a drink of water? "Who is 'us'?"

The door opened and I pulled the sheet close to my body as a purely reflexive measure. I saw long, dark hair and a woman wearing a cocktail dress, and I felt the urge to in sigh relief and exasperation all at once. "Dr. Perugini," I said.

"I sewed up your wound," she said, pulling the door shut behind her. "Nasty little cut, but unsurprising given the window stunt." She shook her head at me. "Stupid. Very stupid."

"I didn't choose to go out the window," I said, irritable. "It was sort of forced upon me. Also, it didn't turn out so bad, since I'm still alive."

"Through no fault of your own," she said, glaring at me.

"Sienna," came my brother's voice from the living room. "Would you mind saving the bickering for later? We've got things to talk about here."

"Yeah," I said and threw the sheets back, flashing Dr. Perugini, who rolled her eyes to avert them. I opened the closet door and ignored the square, empty space that greeted me under my clothes. I grabbed jeans and a shirt, then made my way over to my dresser and pulled fresh socks and underwear, and threw them all on while Dr. Perugini faced the door. As an afterthought, I went back to the closet and stood on my tiptoes, grabbing my auto shotgun off the top shelf and snatching up the big box of ammo with it.

Perugini's eyes got wide, and she shook her head at me. She didn't say anything, but I got the sense she didn't like me playing with guns. I gave zero craps, and walked past her into the living room to find Scott and Reed huddled around a cell phone that was plugged into the wall, charging. They were just standing there, like it was an object of worship for their primitive Neanderthal society. "It's a cell phone," I said, causing both of them to look at me in confusion. "Are you two mesmerized? I feel like I'm staring at cavemen who just discovered fire—"

"Hey, Sienna." A weak, whispered voice came from the cell phone speaker.

I frowned. "Is that … J.J.?"

"In the not-so-flesh."

"He's in headquarters," Reed said, giving me an appraising look. It took me a second to realize he was scoping the damage rather than checking me out. Because that would be *ewwwww*. "He's tapped into the network, trying to block the terrorists out of the system."

"And so far succeeding, despite some pretty impressive efforts on their part," J.J.'s voice came from the speaker. "Whoever they've got on their side is very, very good. I'm holding on by the skin of my cuticles here."

"Were you the one who's been helping me?" I asked, easing closer to the phone. Perugini was at my side, but at an appropriate distance since she and I didn't like each other.

"The very same," J.J. said. "Sorry about the sprinklers."

"You had to do it," I said, staring at the little box producing his tinny voice. "Are you safe?"

"Mmm, probably not," he said. "But I've got access to every camera on campus, and I know where all their guys are, so even though I'm in the belly of the beast, I'm okay for now. I'm hiding in a closet on the second floor."

I felt a thrill of excitement. Full recon will do that to a girl. Well, at least to a girl like me. Maybe geeks really were a girl's best friend after all. "How many are there and where are they?"

"How did I know you'd be straight to business?" He didn't sound like he was surprised. "Two on roving patrol on the fourth floor, six guarding the hostages, two mercs plus the remaining Russkie metas heading down into the prison as we speak."

"Shiiiiiiiit," I said, and Reed nodded along. I glanced at Scott, who was watching me with only minor interest, comparatively speaking. "Are they through the final door, yet?"

"They're in," J.J. said. "But the cell doors are still locked down, so they've got a little ways to go. I'm keeping the place in lockdown—"

"Wait, how did they get into the prison?" I asked.

"Vitalik is a frost giant or something," Reed said, not looking all that thrilled. "He froze the door all the way through and they busted it to pieces. Then he and the mercs set off a chem bomb of some kind in the corridor of death and smoked out the guards, rinsed and repeated the freeze trick on the door to the prison."

"Crapola, crapola, and crapola," I said. "What are they doing now?"

"This Vitalik guy made a quick beeline to one cell in particular," J.J. said. "Eric Simmons."

"I just put him in there," I said plaintively.

"Well, he's almost out now," J.J. said. "I give it five minutes and he's going to be a free man."

"What's their next play?" I asked, then shook my head. "Never mind, you couldn't possibly know that—"

"The Russian lady told Phillips they're going to evacuate under the cover of hostages before the authorities can arrive," J.J. said. "Gonna take the high-level ones on a helicopter ride to a plane, then jet out of the country to Cuba."

"How could you possibly know that?" I asked, mystified. "We don't have microphones on our security cameras."

"True," J.J. said. "But we do have them on pretty much every computer in the building, built-in and ready to transmit to anyone who can access the network. Webcams, too." He sounded a little sheepish. "Plus, I might maybe have hacked into our VME Dominator. Not quite as skilled with it as Roche, but I can do a few things—"

"Are the Russians working for someone?" I asked, suddenly urgent. My time was expiring, and fast.

"Yes," J.J. said. "But I can't hear the voice, even though I've intercepted a couple calls. It sounds a lot like what Rocha reported in New York. I'm picking up one side of the conversation only, direct through the microphone."

"That explains why Simmons is the priority rescue," Reed said grimly. "The brain decided to spring him."

"Seems like this is our mystery brain's go-to move," J.J. said, "the cell phone thing? Most people would just carry a radio."

"When I catch up with this mystery brain, I'm going to turn them into mystery meat," I said. "We've got to stop them. If Simmons gets out—"

"Yeah, yeah," Scott said, nodding along. "Sounds like this

guy can make the San Andreas fault look like a gentle shaker."

"If he was of a mind to," I said. "I don't really want to deal with that, personally."

"How you feeling?" Reed asked, nodding at me.

"Weak," I said. "Powerless." I lifted a hand and placed it on Scott's cheek. He recoiled, a little surprised, frowning all the while. I held it there for ten seconds, then twenty. "Yeah, still powerless."

"Why would you use me to test that?" he asked, more than a little cross.

"Because you've still got your power," Reed said, and now I knew why he was glum.

"Et tu?" I asked, staring at him.

"I was getting you a drink when I realized the barman was a plant," Reed said and nodded to Perugini. "Didn't know how to make anything. When the suppressant bomb went off, I was trying to get Isabella to the exit. When I went to clear the air after the blue smoke …" He held a hand up and cringed, not so much as a wisp of air moving at his command. "Performance issues."

"Getting old, eh?" Scott cracked and snapped his fingers, causing water to splash lightly from his hand in a line as thin as a kid's squirt gun.

"At least I don't go spraying all over the place," Reed volleyed back, amusement creasing his forehead.

Dr. Perugini made a harrumphing noise a moment before I could make one of my own to bring us back on target. "Prison break, yes?" She shuddered. "Do not forget, Anselmo and his hench-loons are in there."

"We need a plan," I said, staring at the blackout curtains strung in front of my windows. Now I knew why the lights were off; J.J. was trying to make it look like no one was home.

"Ooh, I got one," J.J. said. "Come over here and kill all the bad guys. You seem like you're good at that."

"Priority has to be the prisoners," Scott said, jaw tight. "They get out, you've got pretty much just me, a water-thrower, against … whatever you've been capturing lately." He said it without an ounce of disdain, which was … predictable, in its way.

"Angels, only, I assure you," Reed said with a smirk. "Of the fallen variety, maybe. Hell beasts, and Anselmo is pretty much the worst. But I think we should make the hostages priority." He shrugged when all eyes turned to him. "They're innocent people."

"Politicians and bureaucrats," I said without sympathy.

"Ariadne," Reed said, looking at me seriously. My smug glibness dissolved in an instant. "Jackie. I know the tribal instinct is strong in you, so remember that some of them are our people."

I grudgingly had to admit he was right. "Still, those prisoners get loose and it's going to be a free-for-all. We need help."

"Oh," J.J. said, "I called the FBI right before I called Scott. There's a perimeter around the campus, out of sight. The police have the place cordoned off, but they're playing it super cool at the moment. FBI Hostage Rescue Team is already en route from Chicago via helicopter and should be here in about an hour."

"We need a SWAT team of our own," I groused, not for the first time.

"Hey, if the Department of Education can have one, it seems fair that we should," Reed quipped.

"Whatever you're going to do, guys," J.J. said, "you might want to do it fast, because their bench strength is minutes away from getting on the field." He paused. "Or whatever. Did I say that right? I'm not a sports kind of guy."

"Hard to believe, that," I said, and shook my head. When I raised it again, my eyes fell on my backpack, leaning against the side of the couch in my living room. My MP5 was right next to it. Our numbers were improved, but Reed and I were still powerless and about to switch from ambushes and traps to assaulting an enemy in a dug-in position.

"The Russian lady is in the prison," J.J. said. "I'm thinking this is not good. "

Not good? This was all my nightmares in one.

Stalling for time was only going to make the problem worse from here on out. If we waited, we were screwed. Every minute we let them work was another chance for them to add a player to their team. At this point, time was on their side, the numerical advantage was on their side, and the power gap was all in their favor.

All I had was guts, some guns, and a guy who could spray water hard enough to hurt, maybe kill. Against an ice-type and a … whatever Natasya Sokolov was. Unknowns made me nervous. This was so much worse than what I'd done before. That was running, playing defense as I went.

This was going on the attack against a machine gun nest with inferior numbers.

I thought about it, for one brief second, the idea of running, or doing something similarly cowardly. It didn't even get fully unpacked before I shoved it out the door like an unwelcome guest. Power or no power, that wasn't who I was.

"Saddle up," I said, shaking my head. "We've got no choice." Scott looked at me with a grudging nod, and Reed just looked a little reticent before he gave me a nod of his own. "We're going in."

41.

Simmons

Eric Simmons could hear the freedom train, man, and it sounded good. However long he'd been in this timeless pit in the ground (and he wasn't real sure, since they didn't dim the lights, ever) it had been way, way too long. He couldn't live without the feel of sunlight over his head. He'd bounced around these gel-pack walls itching to let loose with a righteous burst of quake that would send this whole joint shaking.

He hadn't, though, because that lady with the sweetness-proof soul hadn't been lying, he didn't think. Sienna Nealon. That bitch.

So he'd waited, bided his time, sat back and trusted in Cassidy to do her thing. She was good at that.

No, she was the best at that.

And now he watching a guy with ice hands frosting over his cell door, and Eric Simmons couldn't have been happier. He thought he recognized the guy—one of those Russians, right? The ones that had been doing some time themselves not that long ago? Man, the wheel turned fast for them. Now they were a cause célèbre—or however you said it. After the press got a load of how he lived in this dive, maybe he'd be a cause célèbre, too, because this place was crazy inhuman. No exercise? No TV? No one to talk to? All he did was watch the guards make circles around the Cube all day long until they changed shifts. Lie down, sleep, wait for a meal to come out of a slot in the ceiling. All prepackaged, and nothing left at the end that couldn't be flushed away down the toilet hole.

It was like hell, if hell had been quiet.

No, Simmons was damned glad to be seeing the end of his days in this place. The door was all frosted over, the gel covered with ice. Now he was just waiting, waiting and trusting the Russians to do what Cassidy had probably convinced them to do. Waiting and—

There it was.

He heard the crack. It was subtle at first, like the noise a tuning fork makes, or like something bumping against something heavy. A thump, but with resonance. He listened, and he heard it again, louder this time.

Eric Simmons couldn't help but smile. This was why he did what he did with Cassidy. It wasn't because she was the greatest lay, because there were way, way better out there.

It was because when trouble came his way, she was the best damned insurance policy he could imagine.

The door shattered and collapsed inward, and when it finished, Simmons just stood there staring out at the Russian guy with a big ol' smile on his face. "Nice job," he said, feeling like he should say something to the dude. It was like looking in a dark mirror—tall guy, dark hair, handsome. His kind of friend, really. "I'm Eric Simmons," he added, like he had to.

"Vitalik Kuznetsov," the guy answered, gesturing him forward. Eric stepped out and gave the prison a look around. Still a cube. He could see a little more of it now than he could through the door, and now it didn't look so distorted. That was another bad thing about the gel. It made everything look a little funhouse mirror-y.

"Simmons," came the voice of a woman who had been lurking just outside his cell. His initial impression of her screamed *dangerous* in bold letters. "You're wanted on the phone." She extended a cell phone to him, which he took.

"Hey, babe," Eric said without even waiting to hear who

was on the other line.

"It's so good to hear your voice again," Cassidy said on the other end, relief rushing through with a little wheeze. That was her asthma. It was weird that she had it, because he didn't know any other metas that had any problem like that. Not that he knew a lot of them. "How did they treat you?"

"It sucked," Eric said, shaking his head. He was looking the Russian woman up and down. She was fit. Dangerous, too, obviously, but … how long had he been in there? "What's the play? We just gonna waltz out of here?"

"The Russians dusted the place with a suppressant that took away all metahuman powers," Cassidy said with a little undisguised glee. "They got Sienna Nealon and her brother with it, but they both slipped away. She's been making a lot of noise since, raising some hell all over their campus."

"You want me to bring the place down around their ears?" Eric asked. He looked around the prison, the Cube. He wouldn't mind sending this place down on itself, rubble crashing down for five stories and burying this hellhole forever. Maybe it'd bury his memories of this boring dump with it.

"I want you to come back to me, baby," Cassidy said softly. She was echoing a little, which meant she was in her chamber. He wondered if she'd been in there the whole time he'd been in here. It would have been like doing a prison stint for both of them if she had, though she didn't mind as much. "I want you to come to me, and we'll deal with Sienna Nealon later, on our terms."

"Seems a shame not to get a hit in while I'm here," Eric said, "and while you've gone and declawed her and all. Without her powers, she's gotta be a nothing, like—"

"She's killed twenty of my men," the Russian broke in, her frosty eyes flaring cold. "Including two metas."

Eric felt his mouth dry out. "Live to get revenge another day. Got it. Sounds like a good idea."

"There is one thing we could do to cause her a few

headaches," Cassidy said on the other end of the line. He could almost picture her, in his head. Bad lay or not, she'd be a damned welcome sight after his last few days. And a welcome—well. She'd be welcome.

"I'd like that," Eric said. "I'd give her a brain hemorrhage if I could. What do you want us to do?"

"I need you to have Vitalik open one of the cells," Cassidy said. "More than one if possible—"

"It's possible," Eric said, glancing over at Vitalik. "Dude can frost these suckers over in no time. Cracks 'em open like a crab leg. Which, I am totally in the mood for lobster right now. Or seafood of some kind. They didn't feed me anything but pre-fab shit in here, baby, like you wouldn't believe—"

"Eric," she said softly on the phone, and Simmons came right back to himself. He looked over the Cube, looked at the Russian lady, and at Vitalik. They were both waiting on him for instruction. "We need to help cover your escape. You need some help."

"Help, yes," Eric said. "Got it. Who in here is gonna help us, though?" His eyes swept the whole square of prisoners, and he'd counted something like twenty of them. "Kind of a lot of choices."

"I did the research," Cassidy said, cool, smiling through the phone. God, he wanted to get his hands on her right now, she sounded so good, even with that slight wheeze. "I want you … to open the cell with Anselmo Serafini in it.

42.

Sienna

"Simmons is out," J.J. said in my earpiece. We'd set up a quick conference, and now—for better or worse—the geek was a temporary replacement for the normal voices in my head. Whom, I have to say, I strangely missed at the moment. Maybe it was the contrast of having J.J., Reed and Scott echoing in my ear in their stead, but having the viciousness of Wolfe on call was occasionally useful, even if I didn't talk to him or the others as much as I used to.

I should probably do more of that, I conceded.

"What's the plan here?" Reed asked as we stormed through the tunnel toward the headquarters building for the second time tonight. This time, though, I was dressed for the occasion. My AA-12 fully automatic shotgun was slung over my shoulder and ready for the dance. It was a much better choice than a dress, I had to concede. More comfortable for me, too, even though it felt a lot heavier without my meta strength.

I missed my meta strength like a dieter missed carbs.

"Follow me and don't die, Sean Bean," I shot at Reed. I knew it would elicit a frown without even turning around, but I did it anyway just to see the look on his face.

It was sour. "Thanks for that," he said, the MP5 slung around his shoulder, ready to go. I knew he knew how to use it, but I was a little unsure if he *would* use it when the moment came. I had to assume so, though.

"They're moving to Anselmo's cell," J.J. said with a rising note of panic.

I said something distinctly unladylike and caught a sidelong glance from Scott. He shouldn't have been surprised, because he and I had done it numerous times. Then I remembered that he couldn't recall it even if he wanted to, and I felt a surge of guilt that I ignored, ignored, ignored.

"You're clear through the lobby," J.J. said. "One guard at the entrance to the prison tunnel."

"What are we gonna do about the hostages?" Reed asked, and I could hear the nerves.

"Punt," I said, not really sure. "We can lock down the prison on our end, maybe, trap them down there. J.J., the prison guards—"

"They're … not gonna be of any help," he said, in a tone that left me in no doubt that they were dead. Damn.

"The mercs are gonna kill the hostages if we don't deal with them, Sienna," Reed said, catching my attention again. "They have to be first priority."

"Anselmo getting out is my first priority at the moment," I said, with a snap. "That and the guy who could send our whole world crashing down with the touch of a finger against the ground."

We emerged into the stairwell, and I could mentally feel Reed digging his heels in. "You've always been the boss," he said, taking hold of my arm, dragging me around, "and I've gone along with everything you've said because you're almost always right. But this time? You're wrong." He said it with enough certainty that it rattled me down to the teeth. "You want to protect the world against Anselmo and Simmons walking out of here, and I understand that. But there are like a hundred hostages up there who are going to die right now, today, versus the threat that those guys might maybe kill someone tomorrow, if they get away." His dark eyes were serious, pleading. "Those guys with guns will mow through the hostages, and it'll be guaranteed blood and guts right *now*, today. You want to be a protector? Save those people."

"I told you I didn't want to—" I made a hissing sound. I felt my fist ball up as I stood there on the first step of the staircase, looking up at him. "You realize Anselmo and Simmons have a serious grudge against us? And now the Russians do, too, if we let them get away. They'll sucker punch us when we least expect it." I leaned closer to him. "You have people other than yourself to worry about, now, you know. Because cowards like them will not come at you head on. Especially a worm like Anselmo. He'll go right for—"

"I know what he'll go for," Reed said, but his face was pale. "But saving these people now is the right thing."

"Time's a wastin'," J.J. said.

I glanced at Scott. "I'm in for whatever," he said. He always was easygoing. Except for that one thing.

I felt the waver of uncertainty. I knew what kind of trash Anselmo, Simmons and the Russians were. What kind of trouble they'd be later. I should have killed Anselmo Serafini three years ago, should have broken his neck when I landed on him.

But I'm not a murderer. I'm not a stone cold killer. I do what I have to do, but I don't enjoy it ... I mean ... grim satisfaction at a job getting done aside, this isn't how I would have chosen to spend my evening.

Is it?

Who was I, really? An unrepentantly vicious killer like Eric Simmons had accused me of being? Someone who used my powers to stomp all over anyone who got in my way?

Well, sometimes. When necessary.

When *I* thought it was necessary.

And now *I* somehow thought it was okay to leave a hundred people at the mercy of a group of mercenaries to stop men who I knew wanted to kill me from escaping. What were my real priorities here? Saving lives, protecting people, or covering my own ass?

Dammit.

Even with no clear answer, I didn't like the trade-offs here either way. Risk Anselmo, Simmons and company escaping or risk the mercenaries going on a killing spree when we hit their bosses. Because they'd be backed into a corner, too, and if they reacted anything like I did … the agency carpet would be soaked with blood.

"All right," I said, and started up the stairs. "J.J., we need intel on the top floor. Disposition of mercs and hostages."

"You sure about this?" J.J. asked. "They're gonna have Anselmo out in like … minutes. And after him—"

"J.J.," Reed said quietly.

"Two mercs in orbiting guard positions on the top floor, roving lookouts. They're keeping their eyes open out the windows on the blind side of the building. The other six have eyes on the hostages and out the window of the bullpen to guard that approach." He dropped into the realm of the sarcastic. "Clearly not expecting an assault from below."

"We've got minutes until Anselmo potentially enters the fray," I said.

"You sure he's going to?" Scott asked.

Reed and I exchanged a look. "Pretty sure," I said tightly. "He's an Achilles, so he's impervious to physical harm."

Scott blinked at me. "How'd you beat him?"

I shrugged. "Threw him to the ground, partially drained him, threatened to break his neck—which I'm told is possible. He's not invincible, just kinda like iron to hit."

"I had an idea for how to deal with him," Reed said sadly, "but I'd need my powers." He held out a hand experimentally, and shook his head after a minute. "Maybe after this is over, we can spend some time asking ourselves why the government has a chemical weapon that suppresses metahuman powers and we've never heard about it?"

"Because they're scared," I said, cutting off that potential avenue for dickering. "J.J., I know you're not a tactics guy, but maybe you could—"

"Wait until one of these guys passes near your door, and I'll give you the heads up," he said, forcing me to reconsider my assessment of him. "Then you can sneak up on the other roving guy without too much trouble, take him out quietly. Then maybe a distraction or two to get the other six looking different directions, and you guys can sweep in and clean house."

I blinked and caught Reed's eye. He covered his microphone and whispered, "He plays a lot of videogames."

"Oh," I said.

We stalked up the stairs and waited in the white concrete hallway under the lights, silent as thieves about to pull a heist. I stared at Scott, and he looked back at me blankly before smiling politely. As well he should.

I thought about my touch, about how long I'd been unable to lay a hand on people—like Scott, for instance—without draining their soul. I averted my eyes from him but kept watching him in my peripheral vision. We'd been together for a while before we broke up, and physicality hadn't been a problem for us. I'd taken some advice given to me long, long ago by my aunt and had figured out how to carry on a physical relationship that worked out adequately, if not great. It was a little cold, a little distant—like me, in general—but we could do … things. Fun things. Lots of fun things.

But now, he could reach out and take my hand and hold it for hours if he wanted. Hours and hours. Forever.

I sucked in a deep breath and turned my attention to the stairwell door behind us. This was probably not the thing to be thinking about just now.

"Guard's coming," J.J. said into my ear. "Passing the door now."

I had my trusty knife back on my belt. After this, I was seriously thinking about carrying it all the time. Reed opened the door enough for me to slip through. We'd never discussed it, but the breakdown of labor in our relationship always seemed to mean I was stuck doing the killing. Funny how that worked.

I ended the mercenary with the same back-of-the-skull stab-and-twist that I'd employed in the parking garage, and Reed slipped in place to grab him and drag him sideways into an office. Big guy, my brother. I didn't mind defaulting to his strength, because he was fairly buff. And trying to manage that lummox as he fell would have been more than I could easily handle.

We were standing in an office corridor on the back of the building. The majority of the fourth floor was a large, open bullpen where all our cubicle workers did their thing. But on the back side of the building was a hallway that led past conference rooms and empty offices used for consultations or private meetings. Flex space, basically. Dull, white-painted generic rooms that were devoid of personality. I'd suggested beanbag chairs and some sprucing up of the décor, but Ariadne overruled me for budgetary reasons. Her words, not mine. I suspected it was an excuse for her to keep things nice and uptight.

"Around the corner to your right," J.J. said, whispering like he was there with us. "He's facing away and has no clear line of sight to the other guards."

I stalked along the corridor and peeked around. There was a good twenty feet of distance between me and the back of the mercenary. That was twenty feet of ground that I had to cross, silently, without him turning around.

I stared down the hall with slightly widened eyes. J.J. could not possibly be serious. This was pretty much guaranteed to turn noisy, and fast.

"He hasn't turned around in five minutes," J.J. said, as if he sensed my unease. "And you can sneak into the conference room that's the first door on your left and crouch until you come out of the second door right behind him. Trust me."

Who was I to doubt a guy who probably trained himself watching computers and trying to determine how the programmers had coded his enemies' patterns? Hell, hell, hell.

"I'll keep an eye out. If he spots you, I'll pop out and shoot him," Reed whispered from behind me.

I found little reassurance there, but what was I going to do? If we fouled this, it would only cause the other six guards to start shooting hostages, including a few people I actually knew and liked. No pressure or anything.

I came around the corner stooped over, scrambling along at a walk and trying not to make a whit of sound. None. Do you know how hard that is? The natural noise of even scuffing your shoe wouldn't do in this case, because tipping this guy off in the slightest would be very, very bad for our plan.

I was pretty sick of the zero alternatives posed by me not having my powers. If I ever found Eric Simmons's brain, I was going to kick its ass just for all the crap they'd put me through tonight.

I made it to the conference room door and kept low. The place had a faint smell of new paint, or maybe old paint that had been enclosed in the room for a while. I made a mental note to leave the doors open if I made it out of this alive.

I came out the other door and launched up at the back of this guy's head. I caught him flush, did the twist, and he fell.

And then I realized there was no one there but me to catch him.

I tried, really I did. If I'd had my powers, it would have been oh so simple. As it was, I caught his weight, but it was like a single crane trying to keep a bridge the size of the Golden Gate from falling down. Too little, too late.

We dropped, me trapped under his weight. I hoped for Scott to keep it from happening, but he wasn't quite fast enough to stop it. I strained, tried, but I was already weak from exposure, from a shoulder injury that flared back to angry life as I tried to muscle the guy into staying upright, and ultimately I just buckled.

My ass hit the carpet like a teenage girl the first time on a roller rink. Wait. Do teenage girls still skate? I hadn't, when I was a teen, but I spent most of those years locked away or fighting for my life.

Either way, I hit, hard. A carcass landed on top of me a moment later, and I felt the warm splat of liquid on my front. I stifled my urge to grunt in pain, but the thump was still terribly loud. The floor was near-silent save for the sobs of the hostages in the distance, and I felt the whole world go so quiet I would have sworn the beating of my heart was the loudest thing in it.

I didn't dare take a breath, didn't want to speak. Scott appeared with Reed a moment later, whisper quiet, but the damage had already been done. That thump had surely been heard around the world, or around the floor at least. We had to have been blown, and men with guns were surely on their way even as we sat there, paralyzed—

Except no noise came to herald the running boots of men with guns, no shouts and cries of anger at the loss of their comrades came from the mercenaries. We were safe.

Well, as safe as three people who were outnumbered two to one by armed men could be.

I didn't even have to ask; Scott hauled the guy's corpse off of me and dragged him quietly into the conference room, depositing him behind the table. My shirt was bloody, and Reed nodded at it, like I couldn't feel it on my skin. Yes, bro, I've got blood on me. A totally new experience for your sister.

Scott emerged from the conference room, his feet whispering on the soft carpet, and I nodded toward the corner ahead. Then I sighed, quietly. We still had six guys to deal with, after all. At least if they'd come charging it would have been over, one way or another.

"Now what?" Reed asked, whispering into his microphone. I could hear him digitally and in person, which created an irritating stereo effect.

"Now we storm a room with six armed men who have a hundred targets to turn their weapons loose on," I said. I was keeping my voice pretty even to hide the fact that this scared the crap out of me. Going at Natasya and Simmons was easy compared to this. If I failed against them, it would be me who died.

In this scenario, the consequences for failure were … steeper.

"Uh oh," J.J. said, voice in our ears. "Uh … guys … you're not going to like this."

I didn't even need to hear him finish to know what had happened. It was like a nightmare that followed you after you woke up, that dread feeling in your stomach that haunts you after the awakening settling over me as I stood in that hallway, pondering my scary, immediate future and the worse moments to follow if I succeeded in rescuing the hostages.

Anselmo Serafini was loose.

43.

"Set a timer for sixty seconds," I whispered, "because that's about all the time we'll have once we start shooting before he's up here and has to be dealt with."

"He's pretty much invincible against bullets," Reed said in a whisper, "but you think we can deal with him?"

"We'll have to," I said, inching up to the corner and peering down the straight hallway into the bullpen ahead. I was fortunate in that Ariadne had made a concession to livability and we had some potted plants out for decoration in the hallways. It gave me cover to look around the corner and peer through the branches.

They were a long ways off and partially occluded by the cover of the plants, but I could see three guys on my side. I ducked back around the corner and whispered, "Reed, Scott, go check the other side. I didn't see any of the guards when we came up, so I doubt they're in quite the straight line these are."

"They're not," J.J. said, "they're farther around the corner on that side because all the cubicles and desks are broken down and piled up on that side of the room. But all three of them are over there, similar pattern, and they're all looking out the office windows in alternating turns to see if they can spot you coming."

"Okay," I said, peeping out again. These guys were actually in a perfect position to guard. I watched them looking around, and they were pretty alert. They were expecting outside threats, though, not one coming noiselessly from inside, so they didn't tend to look down the hallway I was observing them from. That was the job of the two sentries I'd killed. I gave it another minute at most before they got suspicious of those guys' absence and the wheels started to come off the wagon.

The three guys on my side were spinning, but they were doing it in a slow, controlled manner. If you were watching them, you'd just think they were sort of standing there, inching around to look slowly in a 360-degree turn. One of them had eyes on the hostages at all times, and most of the time at least two of them did. The last guy would be looking through the offices and out the windows to the snowfield below.

I ducked back again and confirmed that Reed and Scott had moved around to the other side of the hallway. I caught sight of Reed retreating around the corner back toward the stairs just before he disappeared. They'd have a clear approach all the way up to the bullpen.

"Sienna, you should move up," J.J. said.

"Can't," I said. "They're watching."

"They're facing down the hall like once every two minutes or so. You'll be fine."

I felt my face crease into a sneer. "This isn't a videogame, J.J. They don't have clearly defined cones of vision, okay? If they see movement, they'll assume trouble, and everything will hit the fan. I can't chance sneaking up the hallway, because if I get seen, this game's over, and they're not turning in any sort of regular pattern." I watched one of the guys turn around at random, straight back to the hostages. "See?"

"Hmm," he said, and I could tell that the unpredictability of humans was something he hadn't taken into account.

I stared straight ahead, through the leaves, making as little motion as possible. Something occurred to me about the way those guys were standing …

I drew back around the corner, analyzing it in my head. It might work. Maybe.

Maybe.

I glanced down at my shotgun and let it rest in its sling. This was not the weapon I needed for this occasion. I unholstered my Glock, reflecting that it wasn't really the right choice, either. My M-16 would have been preferable, but I didn't have it, thanks to Miksa Fenes. Dick. I would have asked Reed for the MP5 I'd given him, but it wasn't that much of an improvement over the Glock for what I was planning. Which was craziness. Absolute craziness.

"Do you have a shot?" I asked, breathing into the silence of the hallway. I felt a rising sense of urgency and stripped my backpack off my back for a quick inventory. I'd already done one, but like an addict I needed to do it again, just to confirm that I wasn't wrong.

A bandolier of M209 grenades. Not gonna be much help in a place where civilians could get killed by shrapnel. I thought about discarding them, but wrapped them around my chest for later. Waste not, want not.

I had one white phosphorus grenade left. I stuck it on my belt for safekeeping.

I had several magazines of 5.56 ammo for the rifle I no longer had. Discard.

I had a first aid kit that had mostly been stripped bare. And I wasn't going to have much time to patch up from here on out, I figured.

I slid the last couple of mags for the Glock into my belt along with a couple spares for the shotgun. Then I left the backpack on the ground. No need for excess weight or drag at this point, because shit was about to get real. We were going to need to move fast in order to pull this next part off.

J.J. was the one who finally answered for Reed and Scott. I should have figured with them lurking just around the corner from the enemy, they wouldn't be able to speak. "They're nodding yes, I can see them on the camera. Looks like they're ready to go if you are."

I looked around the corner at my targets again. Reed and

Scott were two guys against three targets. Manageable. That's like one and a half each. I was one against three, and I didn't have my meta reflexes or strength, which was going to slow my target acquisition and make a mess of my ability to control the recoil from my handgun.

And this was a long, long shot.

"I've got HRT on the line, and they're on a chopper, inbound," J.J. said. "ETA five minutes. Can you wait?"

"Nope," I said.

"Is there a chance any of the hostages are armed and could help?" J.J. asked hopefully.

I stared at my three targets, just down the hall, dark silhouettes in tactical clothing. Probably a good choice on their parts that they'd shed the bright white catering uniforms they'd infiltrated in. Made my job marginally harder. "Unlikely. We don't have that many people here, no one from ops, and most of the guests are soft political types." We were on our own. "Go on my signal," I said, taking a slow breath.

I waited until they were all facing the other way and crept down the hall to the next potted plant, hiding behind it as best I could to obscure their line of sight to me. It wasn't perfect, but it got me about thirty feet closer. I repeated it again, making it to the next plant in the line, and figure that was about as good as it was going to get without blowing my luck.

I looked at my targets, all in a row, and hoped, hoped, hoped that this would go the way I saw it in my head. I took another slow breath, ran my tongue around in my dry mouth, and felt like I was tasting seven hours of accumulated hunger writhing around in my belly. But there was another hunger driving me on, one that was primal, one that filled me with a numb, cold anger that seethed through like the hypothermia, one that was told me the job wasn't done. Not yet.

I stared straight ahead, blinked one last time, and whispered, "Go."

44.

Simmons

When that Anselmo guy popped out of his cell, it was like looking into his own future, Eric thought. The dude was probably pretty cultured before he went in. He had that look, that old-school European elegance, but it was completely shot to shit by however many years of beard and hair growth. The guy was shaggy, like he'd been living under a bridge for a decade, but he was still in okay shape for all that. Maybe from perpetual showers or something, because they'd had a functional setup for one in their cells.

"I cannot tell you how good it is to breathe the free air once more," Anselmo said, his all-white paper prisoner uniform a little crinkled. Simmons didn't get the "free air" thing, really, because it smelled like this place was seriously recycled and unhealthy, but he let it pass. Anselmo adjusted the uniform, like he was gonna straighten all the creases with his hands. Simmons thought he had a gleam in his eye, like he was living la vida loca or whatever, ready to tear up the town. He had a good energy. "I cannot thank you enough," he finished with a bow toward Natasya.

"No need for thanks," Natasya said, stiff as a brick. Simmons had been watching her since he got out, and his considered opinion was that she was the stick in the mud sort. Or the stick up the ass sort. He'd been on jobs with those kinds

218

of guys before, the ones who always brought a really negative vibe, always thinking of how things could go wrong. He hadn't exactly known her for very long, of course, but ten minutes was enough to form a basic opinion. "When the moment comes, perhaps you might help us with Sienna Nealon?"

"I would be more than glad to assist you," Anselmo said, and the gleam in his eyes grew. "I have very bitter feelings about how our last encounter proceeded, and a desire to … express them to her personally."

"Well, this is the time," Simmons said, feeling like he was stepping into the grown-ups' conversation, "because she is currently sans powers, man. She's weak like a kitten."

Natasya gave him a pretty pointed look. "She's still dangerous."

"Perhaps to others," Anselmo said with a shrug that reaffirmed Simmons's opinion of him. The dude had game. "I doubt I will have any great difficulty with her. She can shoot me all she pleases, and it will do her little good. I will simply smile," which he did, a great big infectious grin that made Simmons smile a little too, "and then I will remove her skin a few inches at a time."

Natasya didn't show much reaction to that, but Simmons couldn't help himself. "Dude, you are like … my new hero. I would love to see you do that." Anselmo beamed at him, and Simmons couldn't help himself; he nodded and smiled back. "I would pay to see you do that. In slow-mo. With popcorn. Maybe a green tea or something—"

Natasya let out a sudden, harsh outflow of air. "Who else should we let out of here? We could use assistance—"

"I have two friends," Anselmo said, nodding toward a cell around the bend, and then one a couple doors down. "Their assistance would be appreciated—"

A sharp trilling noise interrupted them, the sound of Natasya's cell phone, which she'd taken back from Eric as soon as she could. A little possessive, he figured, but it was okay because he didn't have anything else to urgent say to

Cassidy anyway. He just wanted to get out of here, maybe throw a little hurt first, drop this place down a few hundred feet into the earth on the way out if he could manage it.

"Yes?" Natasya asked. Simmons could tell it was Cassidy just from the look Natasya got when she answered. Her face was still, and she barely reacted to whatever news was given, just enough to take her mouth away from the speaker to talk directly to Anselmo. "Our guards with the hostages are being attacked right now. Fourth floor."

Anselmo stared at her, placid. "Do you know that it is the girl in question?"

Natasya waited just a moment before delivering her answer, like she was waiting to hear for herself. "It is."

Anselmo made an abrupt right turn, his paper uniform trailing in the breeze created by his sudden, swift motion as he took off for the door. "Upstairs?" he called back.

"Straight up," Natasya said, watching him retreat into the tunnel that led to the surface.

Simmons couldn't help himself. He knew he was wearing a goofy, awed grin, just watching that walking badass heading up to rip the limbs off that silly little chick. He was tempted to follow, really did want to watch her get her comeuppance. "This is gonna be so awesome. He's gonna rip her to pieces."

"He's overconfident," Natasya said, causing him to spin around in surprise to look at her. "That's a weakness in this situation."

"The dude has invincible skin," Simmons said, looking at her in sheer shock, pure disbelief. Was she not listening to anything that had been said? "She can't shoot him, she can't cut him, she can't overpower him." He held up his hands, like, *Explain it to me, you dumbass.* "What do you think she's gonna do? Tickle him to death?"

Natasya shrugged, like it didn't matter, and put the phone back up to her ear. "Get the helicopter here now. We're leaving right this minute."

"You said you were gonna let his friends go," Simmons

said, waving at the two cells that Natasya had indicated. Vitalik was already working on one, with a swarthy young guy watching from the other side, slowly disappearing behind a wall of ice. "What's up with th—"

Natasya grabbed him by the arm and started walking. Simmons made a split decision to follow her along the metal catwalk rather than let her tear it out of its socket. "What the hell?" he asked when he got his feet back under him, following along behind her.

"He's going to die horribly," Natasya said flatly. "I don't intend to join him." Simmons looked back to see Vitalik and an armed mercenary trailing them.

"She's one frigging girl!" Simmons shouted as they entered the tunnel, his protest echoing off the walls as he was dragged bodily out of the prison—surprisingly against his will.

"Everyone keeps thinking that," Natasya said as she hauled him closer and closer to the apex, the glow of outside light of some sort filtering in from a room at the top of the ramp, "and she keeps killing every person we send after her. At some point," she said, giving him a look back that returned his earlier one, unmistakably—*dumbass!*—"an intelligent individual might stop thinking of her that way and see her for what she is."

Simmons could barely believe his ears, but he was still having trouble keeping up with his legs. "For what she is? Man, she's a nothing!"

"No, she's not," Natasya said, shaking her head as she hauled him through the security room at the top of the steps and into an eerily empty lobby. Gunshots were audible now, somewhere far above them, and the Russian paused, looking up like she could somehow see their origin.

"Fine, whatever," Simmons said, and even to his ears he sounded annoyed, petulant. "What is she, then?"

Was it the chill of someone having opened an outside door recently, Simmons wondered, or was it the cold, penetrating eyes of this badass Russian who'd somehow pulled off the impossible in taking over this place that made him shiver? It was worse than being herded out of that plane when he'd first gotten here, without a coat, without anything. He felt the chill, felt it ripple over him, and he shivered, then broke eye contact. He knew what he'd seen there, though, and it wasn't a good sign, not from a bad, bad mama like this lady. She was tough. She'd seen shit. She'd done a prison sentence of three decades and looked like she could handle thirty more without blinking.

But he knew what he saw in her eyes. It was obvious as hell.

Fear.

"She's the most dangerous person on the planet," Natasya Sokolov said, and her voice told Simmons she was serious as she could be. She grabbed his arm again and hauled him off, and this time he didn't try to fight it.

45.

Sienna

Like the saying goes, I'd rather be lucky than good, but when we started to take out the mercs guarding the hostages, I got a bit of both.

I leaned out from my position and steadied my aim. The nearest guy was about forty feet away. Not a tough shot for me on a normal day. The next was about twenty feet past him. Getting trickier. The last was at least twenty feet beyond that—an eighty-foot shot with a 9mm pistol when my aim had become much less certain than it usually was.

Still, ducks in a row.

I fired the first and that was where my ceaseless practice came in handy. I double-tapped, and while I was pretty sure one shot missed (the second, if you must know), the first caught bad guy number one right in the temple.

And then kept going and hit the second in the chest.

Luck.

I stepped slightly out of cover and fired again at the second guy, not believing for a second that he was dead or any more than briefly stunned. These guys were wearing some sort of body armor, and while a shot could put him down, I didn't think it would put him out permanently.

The third guy, he was the wild card. All it would take was one of these yahoos to start shooting up the hostages, and we'd be cooked like a Thanksgiving turkey. Which, in my house, was always overdone. The Nealon women are not great domestics, okay? Also, our patience is not infinite (which is how long it takes to cook a turkey, or so it feels).

His instinct saved me from worst-case scenario, because he went for self-preservation rather than chaos. He leveled his HK submachine gun down the hall and let off a burst in my direction.

Yay for him not shooting at hostages!

Not so yay for him shooting at me.

I felt the bullets go skipping past as I took cover in an office doorway. This one belonged to one of the guys who handled admin for transport, and the glass window just past me shattered as it took a few rounds.

"Tango down!" I heard Reed shout in my earpiece. I'd expected it a lot sooner, frankly. Another round of shots skipped past me and painted the far hallway door. I wanted to blind-fire to cover myself, but I was afraid an un-aimed shot might hit a hostage, so I waited a second.

"Another down!" Scott called. They were rolling theirs right up, and I had one to go.

I had a bad feeling that my last guy had the hallway pretty well covered, but Reed and Scott's actions were raising enough of a ruckus that I could hear them now. If my last target got distracted, his natural instinct would be to sweep his weapon over the crowd to fire at them. I could imagine Reed and Scott, out of cover, ganging up on the last of their targets, not realizing I hadn't held up my end of the bargain. Then my guy would shoot, and either they'd get sprayed or shots could go into the crowd or—

I didn't want to think about what might happen after that. Madness lay that way, and I was crazy enough most of the time.

I leaned out in time to feel another burst miss me by nearly nothing. A quarter second sooner and I would have died right there in the hall. My target was firing in bursts, controlling his shots, not letting his barrel climb too much before re-centering his aim on me.

Why did I get a competent guy? Why couldn't I have pulled a moronic henchman that couldn't hit the broad side of an airplane hangar?

I ducked back into cover and waited, tense, hesitant. That pulse-pounding feeling of adrenaline was giving way to a gripping fear. Not that I was gonna die, but that I was about to fail, big time.

"Your last guy is loose, Sienna! We've got no shot!" Scott's voice called breathlessly into the microphone.

Another burst of bullets hit the frame I was leaning against, sending fragments of wood into my face. I felt a dozen stings on my cheek and blinked, realizing that my eye, thankfully, hadn't been hit. "I have no shot," I said, and I felt like I was ready to cry. I don't like to lose, and I was set up for a big one here.

"He's got us covered in the hall again, Sienna," Reed said, and I could hear the edge of desperation in his voice. "We couldn't get him for you."

"I'm sorry, guys," I whispered, and another staccato discharge of fire went thudding into the frame behind me. I stiffened, wondering how long it would be before he managed to send a lucky shot penetrating through to me. I guessed it wouldn't be long.

A loud *pop!* was followed by a thud, and I heard a deep rush of relief from J.J. "Tango down!"

"Good shot, guys!" I breathed, feeling my body slump against the frame. Splinters poked at me back from where it had taken a few shots, and the Glock in my hand suddenly felt like it weighed ten million pounds.

"Wasn't us," Reed said, sounding a little baffled. "That dude had us pinned. Scott was gonna work around to you and try and hit him from both sides of your hallway, put him off balance."

I felt my spine stiffen, and I eased around the corner,

Glock up again as I quickly covered the distance down the hall. "J.J., what am I looking at here?"

"A hell of a surprise, I'd say," J.J. replied, and he sounded like he was grinning on the other end of the transmission.

I slipped into the bullpen and saw Reed do the same from the other direction. Our hostages were there, tuxedos ripped, fancy shoes discarded, dresses glistening not nearly so much as they were a few hours ago when the party had started. A few of the men were standing now, or crouched, looking like they were finally ready to get in on this fight, now that it was over. I saw a certain senator looking like he needed to breathe into a paper bag, I saw Andrew Phillips sitting calmly, legs crisscrossed, in the middle of the floor, Jackie next to him with a look of relief on her face.

And I saw Ariadne with a smoking pistol in her hand, still pointing the weapon at the mercenary she'd killed, a look of bare shock on her pale features, her red hair mussed and her mouth agape.

I swept over the downed mercs quickly, kicking aside their weapons just in case. The first of mine was definitely dead, the second was less certain until I fired a round into his skull— drew a few gasps from the crowd, but I had zero time to deal at the moment—and Ariadne had hit the last with a shot to the cheek. It had gone through and out the back, and the guy's eyes were glassed over.

I looked at her for all of a second and knew it was her first kill.

"Nice shot," I said quietly, and she seemed to shake out of her comatose state long enough to lock eyes with me.

"Sienna?" she asked, like it wasn't obvious that it was me.

"None other," I said, that sense of post-battle fatigue falling over me. "You all right?"

"We're fine," Andrew Phillips said, slowly pulling himself to his feet. He was a really big guy, probably could throw a decent punch if he put his mind to it. "None of the hostages were harmed." He looked me up and down. "Thought you were dead for a while, though."

"I bet that really pricked at your conscience," I said, feeling my smartass oats.

"Yeah, it really got me down for about five seconds," he said, and I couldn't tell if he was serious or not. "We need to get these people out of here."

"Agreed," I said. "J.J.?"

"Umm, well, the staircase behind you is clear," he said, suddenly afflicted by nerves, "but I'd hurry if I were y—"

"EVERYBODY OUT!" I shouted, pointing in the direction I'd come from. "Ariadne, get them to the ground floor, now!"

To her credit, she didn't hesitate. "This way, people!" she shouted, waving her gun in the air. I cringed at her cavalier disregard for the rules of gun safety, but at least she was keeping it pointed in a safe direction. She ran, her evening gown flapping in the breeze as she charged down the hallway. I knew her well enough to know she was just masking her feelings; she'd been around me, around here, long enough to have seen some serious stuff. She knew when to run.

The herd was moving slow, and I cut right through them without hesitation, shoving where I had to. I gave a two-term congressman from Oregon a hip-check that would have made a Minnesota Wild player proud when he tried to run me over in his flight to the stairs. It wasn't as easy without my power, but I didn't take any crap from fleeing chickenshits while I had a fight coming my way.

"Where is he, J.J.?" I asked. Reed and Scott were there waiting, my brother with his gun pointed at the hallway and Scott with his hands out.

"Coming out of the staircase now," he said, with a touch of nerves. I was feeling more than a touch myself.

"Where is she?" he announced in grand style, voice booming down the empty hallway. I could hear the crowd moving behind me, scrambling, cattle fleeing from a wolf.

And he was the wolf.

Reed slid out in front of me. It was subtle, like he was taking possession of this bad guy. If I thought he had a chance in hell of dealing with him, I would have let Reed take Anselmo.

But a snowball's chance in hell would have been generous in this case. Reed didn't have the heart to do what it would take to put down Anselmo, even when he did have his powers. He just didn't have it in him to get mean and vicious, to fight a dirtbag like Anselmo on his own level and win.

Me?

I was born for this.

"I'm right here, shitheel," I said, fearless. I pushed all the fatigue back, knowing I was about to go mano-a-womano to with the meanest rattlesnake I'd seen in quite some time.

He came around the corner with a smile on his face. "And so you are," he said with that Italian accent. He was wearing his paper outfit, which was more than I could say for the last time I'd seen anything other than his eyes. He bowed like he was Don Juan, and when he came up his smile nearly made me sick. "I cannot tell you how pleased I am to see you."

46.

"Not running, little lamb?" Anselmo asked as he eased into the bullpen. To his left was the massive pile of discarded rubble that used to be our office furniture. I felt a small sense of relief that I was no longer involved in the budgetary process of replacing that crap. Enjoy it, Phillips. You tool.

Anselmo monologued on. "Do you not find yourself with a desire to run now that you're … weak? Do your knees not tremble at the thought of what I will do to you?" He smiled. "Do you find yourself anticipating—"

"That's about enough of that crap," Reed said. He had his weapon pointed at Anselmo's face.

"Where is your beautiful companion?" Anselmo asked, taking a deep sniff of the air. I imagine he thought he was erotic or something, but I thought he looked a little like a dog sniffing a crotch. Actually, scratch that—my dog didn't look like that when he sniffed at anything. "Your … lady doctor?"

"She's otherwise occupied," Reed said tersely. Perugini was probably on the ground floor by now, helping the hostages with their exit. No need to tell Anselmo that, though. Reed was buying time, kinda like me. When this fight started, it was gonna get nasty quick. I doubted Scott would attack with any more killer instinct than Reed did, especially since he likely hadn't been in a fight in three years or more.

Which meant it was going to be up to me to get so vicious with this psychopath that he would either run from the fight or lie there until he died.

As usual, I had one good idea about that, but it was going to require proper positioning.

"I have dreamed every night of wrapping my hands around your throats," Anselmo said, looking from Reed to me. As far as dramatic revelations went, I wasn't shocked. "I have considered so very many ways to end your lives. Knives were a favorite, for a while, for their intimacy, and the ability to carve pieces … to inflict pain … the maximum amount of pain." He took a breath, luxuriating in the thought. "Then I had a brief flirtation with the more, shall we say, straightforward? I imagined shooting you both in the head from behind." He rubbed his hands together as though he were cleansing them. "Quick, disdainful, a problem solved and nothing more."

His lip turned up at the corner. "But then I thought … you have stolen precious, precious time from me. You have debased me. Stolen my home. What is the appropriate response for this insult?"

"You're going to bore us to death with your monologue?" I asked.

"You're going to—dammit!" Reed said, too slow, casting an irritated glare at me. You gotta be quicker than that if you want to out-smartass me, brother dear.

Anselmo's face was consumed with dark clouds. He was not amused. "You are swine, and here I waste my time casting words before you like pearls."

"Pearls?" I snorted. "Your words are butt plugs; go shove them up your ass."

He came at us, and he was damned fast. Too fast, really, for us to handle. What the hell could a normal human even do against someone who moved like that? He crossed ten feet in the space of a half-second and elbowed Reed aside. I saw my brother stumble into the wall, smashing into it and leaving a solid imprint where he'd cracked the drywall with his head.

Anselmo put a hand around my neck and lifted me up. He

glared at me, held me in the air. I hadn't even bothered to draw my gun. Why did they always do that, the lift and dangle thing?

Oh, right.

Power.

"I will kill you, you dirty, rotten whore—"

Reed rallied and charged into Anselmo with a shoulder. If I'd been able to speak, I would have told him not to bother. I'd already signaled Scott to back off and he was keeping his distance, cautious. I had a feeling he wanted to charge, but he saw what I was doing and knew I needed a few seconds. Reed bounced off like he'd hit a steel wall, falling at Anselmo's feet.

Aw, hell. He needed to not be there, and damned soon.

Anselmo deigned to notice him, putting a foot on his chest like a conquering asshole, and suddenly my plan was not going to come off nearly so well as I hoped for. I estimated I had about five seconds left.

What do you do when you want to get some misogynist, testosterone-laden alpha dick's attention?

I kicked him square in the balls.

His eyes went wide with rage, not pain. Like he couldn't believe I had deigned to kick him in his holy of holies. He forgot all about Reed for a second and took a step forward, leaving my brother on the ground in a heap.

Yay!

Also, yikes.

He moved me toward the pile of debris that had once been office furniture, and I had a feeling a choke-slam was in the offing. His rage was kinda predictable. I hoped my plan was not nearly so.

"I will enjoy this," he promised, lifting me higher. "I will enjoy your pain, enjoy your cries, your protestations—" His mouth was wide as he said protestations, and I shoved the grenade I'd been cooking in my hand for the last five seconds right in his gaping trap. Then I kicked him in the throat while he gawked at me in surprise, mouth wrapped around the green canister, and wriggled out of his fingers. I was already rolling away when I hit the ground, and I didn't stop until I had a good fifteen feet of distance from him.

Anselmo pulled the grenade from his mouth, held it in his hand, and started to laugh. "You think this wil—"

He didn't get anything else out before the Willie Pete lit off in a flare of heat, and Anselmo Serafini disappeared in a white-hot burst of flame.

47.

I'd seen people burned to death before, but I'd never seen someone with nearly impervious skin get exposed to that level of heat before. It was sickening and amazing all at once. Anselmo let out a piercing scream, high and agonized, like the girls he hated so much. It smelled like chemical scorch, pervasive and heavy, roasted meat that flooded my nose and choked my mouth, like I could taste it. The heat fell off the white phosphorus like I'd pulled an Icarus, gotten too close to the sun, and when I got to my feet, I did so in awe of the miniature star that had been born before me.

The idiot had held it up in his hand and was staring at it when it went off, and the flames covered him now. He was a top of the scale meta in terms of power, and that meant his ability to heal from injury was presumably right up there with my boy Wolfe. Using Wolfe's power, I could regrow a limb in ten seconds, heal a cut in less than one second, and even harden my skin against future injury of the same type. Wolfe hadn't had the innate invulnerability to physical damage that Anselmo had; he'd picked his up through several thousand years of flesh damage of all kinds, from burns to bludgeons.

In the days of yore, against hordes of fighting men, a meta of Anselmo's type had taken on entire armies and beaten them. They were nigh invulnerable against spears, swords, horseman and all the other weapons available to the men of the day.

But apparently, no one had ever tried burning an Achilles'

skin off with white phosphorus.

It was definitely sloughing off, and his body was fighting back to heal him—and succeeding, to some extent. I watched him writhe in the flames, curiously detached. I should have been feeling something, anything—but I didn't. Reed had told me about him, and we'd gotten more from the Italian authorities—reluctantly—later. He was a monster, a beast of basest instinct and little restraint. The cage I'd put him in was too kind by half, in my opinion, for what he'd done to those around him.

And that was just the stuff we knew about.

His skin burned and sloughed off down to bone and then regrew muscle and sinew seconds later, turning angry red as it came back and burned clean again. It was like watching the tide battle the sand, and the tide—the Willie Pete—seemed like it was inevitably going to swallow him.

Anselmo fell to his knees in the fire, the smoke getting incredibly heavy in the room. His vocal chords quit, and I could hear a wet hissing over the steam. I didn't know where it was coming from.

No, scratch that. I didn't want to know where it was coming from.

"Sienna," Scott said, and I could hear the horror and awe in his voice. "Sienna," he said again, and I woke from my trance of watching this psychotic beast burn and burn again. "The prison break?"

"Right," I said, shaking myself out of it. We still had Vitalik and Natasya to go. And Simmons.

"They're on the move," J.J. said, his voice a hushed whisper. I guess he was watching on the security cameras. "Heading to the roof. The police on the perimeter just reported a chopper flyover. They're moving to extract."

"Dammit," I said, "let's get them," and started toward the stairs. I just ignored the flaming pile of Anselmo, somewhere in the white-hot fire. I could still hear him moving around in there, but it wasn't like there was a lot I could do for him either way. I mean, I could have Scott put the fire out, maybe, but assuming Anselmo was still alive, that wouldn't exactly do me a lot of good.

So I left him burning and headed for the stairs.

"NOOOOOOO!" J.J. cried out into my ear, loud enough that I almost yanked the microphone out.

"What the hell, man?" Scott asked for me. I looked back to seem him cringing from it. His hearing was meta, so it was better than Reed or mine's, at least at the moment. His expression was pained.

"Sienna," J.J. said, his tone verging on panic, "problem."

"No more problems," I said, halting, looking back at the white phosphorus fire, still doing … what it did. "Solutions, please."

"Problem, man," he said. "I was watching you guys during the Anselmo thing and I—aw, dammit! Aw, damn!"

"J.J.," Reed said. "What is the dilly-yo?" I blinked at him; he shrugged.

Weirdo, my look said.

You should talk, his said in reply. Point taken.

"The brain, man," J.J. said, "the brain was still breaking through our—they were using our network access, and I'd been blocking them, but I lost focus and—they're in! They're totally in." He just deflated, from sixty to zero like he had the best brakes in the world. "We're compromised."

I just stood there, waiting for translation. "And this matters why …? Their people are running like scared squirrels." This time, Reed gave me the look. My return look said, *Don't judge*.

"Because—oh, God, I can see what they're doing," he said, low and scared. "Because the brain—whoever they are— they're watching through the cameras, first of all, but second—and so much worse …"

"Spit it out, dude," I said, making for the stairs again. "I have zero time."

"They're working on opening the doors of every prisoner in the Cube," J.J. said. "In about two minutes, every prisoner we've got is … they're all … they're all about to get a real early release."

47.

I was so hot I felt like I was going to burst into flames like Anselmo, but from the inside. The brain opened my prison. Seriously. I was the warden of that place—still, I think? Damn Phillips. Whatever the case, I felt a sense of responsibility for it all, since I'd put those clowns there. I couldn't remember off the top of my head how many of them were left, but almost every one of them was a seriously bad dude, villains with first-rate ambitions and last-rate executions. Not high on the power scale, but right at the top of the vicious scale.

How did they get there? Power unchecked. I'd done some reading on their backgrounds in the course of the investigations that led me to them. Every one of them, without exception, started small and grew into a killer. They thought they could get away with it, and they did, their schemes and contempt for order growing larger and larger.

Until I showed up.

This was how the old gods were made, I knew. That hubris, that feeling that no one could stop them? It came from the fact that no one could. When the cops showed up to bring you in and you took down all of them, it was a rush. A sense of youthful imperviousness is common, in greater or lesser form, in most people under the age of twenty. A sense of lawlessness and a total lack of need for impulse control common to the criminal class. Want, take, have, I've heard it expressed. Because when you're a person with power, who's gonna stop you?

No one had stood up to these cowards. Every time someone had tried, they'd come out on top. They thought they were invincible, like Anselmo, although they didn't have a tenth of his power. They could put a hell of a show on for the local PD, though, that was for sure. Put a dozen cops in the hospital with their schtick.

But you put me up against any one of them on my worst day, and they're a smear on the pavement when I get irritable.

I was heading down when I should have been heading up, and I was getting angrier by the minute. This brain was a pain in my ass, and I was resolved to find him, her, or it at my earliest convenience.

Unfortunately, if they kept throwing these obstacles in my way, it was going to be later rather than sooner that I'd get to make good with my threat.

I threw open the door to the lobby and headed straight for the tunnel. I was seeing red, crimson, maroon, chartreuse, and every other color of the spectrum related to rage and fury. I had my shotgun in hand, my Glock reloaded in my holster, and I was striding with a purpose toward the security room when Reed hauled on my arm and stopped me cold.

"What the hell are you doing, Sienna?" His voice was whisper-quiet, a hush, urgent and fearful all at once. "There are like twenty people down there who would love to get their hands on you, and you've got no powers, in case you forgot."

"I haven't forgotten," I said and ripped my arm free.

"You could die!" Reed said, doing a yelling whisper. I didn't think that was possible, but he managed it. "They're not gonna go light on you just because you're chemically under the weather!"

"They're not gonna do jack to me," I said and ripped open the door. I was heading down into the tunnel with my shotgun raised and a sneer on my lips.

"What the hell makes you say that?" Reed asked, following behind me like he knew, for a fact, that I'd lost my damned mind.

"Because of what they *haven't* forgotten," I said.

I walked into the Cube to find the doors sliding open to every single cell. Men were stepping out with that cocky look on their faces, but still a little hesitantly, peeking to see what was up, how this significant change to their interminable daily routine was going to work out.

"Hey there, Lady Warden," Crow Vincent said, stepping out of the cell nearest me. He had a wicked grin on his face, and was doing this little shoulder bob walk as he stepped outside. I guess he thought it looked cool. "Looks like you're out of guards. Saw a couple of your detainees go walking out the door." He grinned. "Looks like you ain't having a great day."

"It's night, actually," I said and looked at him, hard. I saw Timothy Logan peeking out of the cell just behind him, like he wasn't sure whether he should come out or not. "You hear any of what those guys were discussing?"

Crow just laughed. "Didn't need to hear anything. School's out, baby." He swept an arm around. "Looks like a weekend pass, huh?"

"Get back in your cells," I said, raising my voice and using that hard edge voice I can summon up on command.

"I figured you were dead," Crow said, taking a step closer to me. "Figured no one would get one over on the Lady Warden." He made a hiss of a laugh. "But you're weak, girl. You must be slipping, to let them fools in here, let them walk out of here, let them open all the doors."

"It's a technical glitch," I said, staring him down. "You'll want to be getting back in your cells now." I didn't feel a need to attach a threat, because a threat at this point would probably be less effective. Let their imaginations run wild, I figured.

Crow turned his head sideways, and I remembered why they called him Crow. "I don't think I need to be—"

I raised the barrel of the shotgun and blew his head clean off. Blood and all else splattered on the wall behind him as 00 buckshot did its thing to skin and bone.

I waited for the thunder of the gunfire to clear from the air and then spoke into the shocked silence. "Thinking is not a good idea for you all. Your thinking and decision-making have carried every last one of you into these cells, and it's highly unlikely that it's going to get you out again any time soon, at least not any way but feet first." I studied my charges. "Back in the cells, or start rushing me. Maybe if you're lucky and you all come fast, you can overwhelm me." I didn't rack the shotgun, because it was an automatic, but I gave it a subtle flourish. "Who wants to go first? I don't favor your odds, but if you want to die, let's get to it. I've got other places to be, and some other people to be killing."

I saw movement across the catwalk, on the far side. Thunder Hayes, his dark eyes staring me down. He was considering it. I would have flattened him, but the shotgun's reach wasn't quite far enough for me to do to him what I'd done to Crow, not at this distance. I was bluffing all the way, but I was counting on the fact that every last one of them had a painful, fearful memory of me etched into their deepest neurons. However bad they wanted to kill me and walk free, they had to remember that the last time they'd come up against me, I'd whipped their asses and thrown them down here. For most of them, it was the first defeat of their meta lives.

Which is something they were unlikely to forget.

Months and years of solitary was a lot of time to dwell on the past. I had to guess that the specter of defeat was probably high up on their list of revisited memories. All that time to think, to plan—though most of them weren't even half-capable planners—and the number one thing they'd be thinking about was how I'd whooped them. That and how I kept bringing more and more whoopees to join the party. An unbroken succession of reminders that they were not nearly so badass as I was. All that time to think, and no chance to prove to themselves that I was anything less than a goddess of wrathful vengeance, the meanest, most vicious release of hell-on-earth that most of them had ever laid eyes on.

Not a bad atmosphere to breed fear.

"You know she'll do it," Timothy Logan said, giving the air just the right injection of piss to put out their growing campfire. I could almost hear the hiss as the enthusiasm for revolt guttered out.

"I've got control of the doors!" J.J. shouted in my ear. "I got it!"

"Man …" Thunder Hayes said, shaking his head. "It ain't worth it. We'll get you some other day, lady. When you ain't holding a shotty." He walked back into his cell, trying to keep his head high for pride. But I saw the slump of his shoulders. I saw it in every one of them as J.J. started shutting the doors as they went back inside, one by one giving up on their dream of freedom.

"NO NO NO!" J.J. shouted as I stared at the last three, already turning to go back inside. They were savoring their moment of freedom, I guess.

"I don't like it when you say that," I muttered.

"They're in the PA system! They're gonna—!"

He didn't even finish before I heard the snap hiss of the overhead speaker, followed by a female voice.

"You shouldn't give up so easily," she said low, almost breathless. "Sienna Nealon is power!—"

I blasted the speaker with my shotgun, a shot sixteen feet straight up that shattered plastic and drew sparks. "This isn't your party," I said, irritable. "So get the hell out." I covered the last three with my shotgun, stock against my shoulder. "Back inside," I said, reaffirming my control over the situation. They dawdled, but they went back in, and J.J. shut the doors with a clank. "Are we clear here?" I asked.

"I'm trying to purge it out of the system—"

"Her," I said, thinking about that voice. "The brain is a her." I looked up at the ceiling. "And she should know that I'm coming for her. I don't care if it takes an hour, a year, ten decades or a thousand years …" I hardened my voice and stared into the nearest surveillance camera with all my furious fortitude, sure she was still watching. "I am coming for you, lady."

"Wow," Reed said, "I think I just crapped myself in fear a little."

"Chopper just took off from the roof with the escapees," J.J. said.

"Get the Air National Guard on the phone," I said. "Shoot 'em down."

"That could take a while, this time of night," J.J. said, and I turned to walk back up the ramp. Reed and Scott fell in beside me, exchanging a look between them that was somewhere in the neighborhood of *So, that just happened, right?* and a *Yeah, brah,* in return.

I liked it.

The lady has brass. I heard a faint whisper in the back of my head, like someone talking outside a door. I listened closer but heard nothing more. Did that mean …?

"FBI's HRT is here," J.J. interrupted my train of thought, "and they've got a chopper of their own with a bunch of sweaty, angry guys who just had to wake up in the middle of the night and fly in from Chicago." He almost sounded like he was smiling. "They want to know if you'd like to go on an evening ride with them, maybe to the Eden Prairie airport? Because based on the flight vector, that looks like where our escapees are heading, and it sounds like these guys would like to throw a party of some sort for them there."

I felt a smile break through my look of harsh, leaden fury as I entered the stairwell, listening to the buzzing of the fluorescent lights as I ascended the steps two at a time. It sounded strangely louder than it had earlier. "Tell them I would love to attend their party," I said. "And that I'll meet them on the roof in sixty seconds."

48.

Natasya

"Whoooooo-eeeeeeeeeee!" Simmons was a child in Natasya's eyes, a baby she had to sit for, an infant who needed to be burped and taken care of. His requests were unreasonable at best, those of an adolescent at worst. She listened to the voice, now piped through her headset, though, and watched him warily.

"There's an FBI chopper that's going to be coming up behind you, and soon," the voice said. "It swung back to pick up Sienna Nealon, and it's turning around to pursue you."

Natasya tried to fill her veins with a sense of ice. This confrontation was edging ever closer to inevitable, this moment between her and Sienna Nealon. "Can we outrun it?"

"It's a military Black Hawk and you're in a civilian Huey," the voice said. "The engine specifications say no."

Natasya caught the sense of satisfaction in the answer. "But …?"

The voice was smiling on the other end of the connection, of that Natasya was sure. "Stay on course and you'll be fine."

Natasya heard that certainty and stared at Simmons, headset on, hanging out of the chopper, and watched his disposition change suddenly. It was like he'd heard something. She watched him turn, slowly, and look at her. He said nothing, just stared for a second, then said, "Yeah," like he was talking to himself.

The voice. Was she … talking to him individually now? Natasya felt her eyes narrow as she considered it. Was it a casual conversation or some form of instruction? She'd trusted the voice to deliver what had been promised, and what had been promised was a plan that sounded so slick in its execution that she was certain it would go off with only a minor hitch, like the depot heist.

Instead, she was sitting in a helicopter with two of her people lost and a trail of bodies left behind. She sniffed, and the smell of burnt flesh filled her nose.

There was no changing it, now. She knew what the voice wanted her to do, but she had no intention of being a sacrifice in the name of Eric Simmons. She stared out into the night as the helicopter swept over woods and fields, toward city lights in the distance. If all else failed, she still had her own powers to fall back on.

And those might be just what she'd need before this was all over.

49.

Sienna

"Where's Harper?" I asked as the FBI chopper blew my hair back, roaring as it came in for a landing. I should have been wearing ear protection, but I wasn't working in a training environment and I used to be able to heal from whatever happened to me, including hearing loss.

Used to. Hopefully would again, and the sooner, the better.

I swallowed that fear, saving it for later as J.J. answered. "I'm patching her in now."

"Hello?" Harper sounded sleepy. Part of me wanted to remonstrate J.J. for not calling her earlier, but it wasn't like this was something he had a ton of experience with. Plus, I could have had him call her earlier if I'd really been thinking about it.

"Harper, I need you on site now," I said, "unless you've got access to a drone control at your house?"

"At my house?" she asked with a measure of incredulity. "Oh, yeah, Nealon, I always bring highly classified military hardware to an unsecured location. Because I love the idea of a court martial, it sounds like fun."

"Doesn't the military have some kind of prohibition on insubordination and smartassery to your higher-ups?" I asked as the chopper started to settle on the pad.

"One, you're not in my chain of command," she said, still

244

sounding pretty sleepy, "and two, I've just been following your lead—sir." She snarked with a smile on that one, and I had to smile in return.

"Fair enough," I said. "We've got a situation here, and I need eyes on. How soon can you be there?"

"I live in Chanhassen," she said, and I could faintly hear her moving around. "Be there in twenty." She hung up without another word.

"She must drive like the wind," J.J. remarked. "Or else she's coming in in her PJ's."

"Maybe she sleeps naked," Scott mused, causing me to turn and look at him. He just shrugged. "What?"

I just ran for the chopper. The door was already open when I got there, and I saw two seats available. A young guy, a little older than me, was standing there with the black tactical vest on, holding the door. What a gentleman. Handsome, too, I saw from the brief look I gave him as I stepped up.

"Jeremy Hampton, ma'am," he said, with a tip of the finger from his forehead that looked like a salute. "FBI Hostage Rescue Team."

"Good thing you told me that, Hampton," I said over the roar of the helicopter rotors, "because I was sure that this was a Boy Scout party bus."

He smiled and settled back on his seat, quickly glancing from me to Scott and Reed, then back again. His eyes then shuffled to the empty seats and back to me. I got his meaning.

"Reed, you stay here and start buttoning up the campus," I said, looking back at him for only a second. "Scott, you're with me."

"Yes, ma'am," Scott said, shrugging as he stepped into the chopper and sat down next to me. I saw Reed's look of betrayal disappear as the chopper took off without him, bucking and shaking as we lifted into the air. I settled back in my seat. It was quasi-military, not built for comfort. The pilot certainly didn't take easy turns. He spun us about and headed us back in the opposite direction as soon as we were marginally clear of headquarters, and we shook as the helo started to climb.

Hampton gestured to the wall behind me, and I grabbed a set of earphones and put them on, sliding the boom mike down over my mouth. "I heard you've had a good night so far, ma'am." His smile told me that he was like me, a hunter.

"Not sure I know what you're talking about, Hampton," I said, returning his smile with one of my own. "I've had a prison break, I've had to kill about twenty mercenaries and three metas, blown up a building, and put the fear of me back into a bunch of my detainees."

He tilted his head to the side. "Sounds like fun."

"You should see what I do for an encore," I said under my breath. He smiled like he'd heard me.

The chopper rattled on, bumping with turbulence. "Eden Prairie airport is zero-five mikes out. Intercept with target is estimated at zero-four-thirty mikes," the pilot said.

"So we'll beat 'em by thirty seconds," I said, translating from military-ese. These guys. I liked them, but sometimes the way they said things was confusing.

"That's affirm, ma'am," the pilot replied, proving my thesis.

I sat there, a little antsy, wondering why I was suddenly feeling a little tickle in the back of my mind, like a faint and distance hum of chatter under the hiss of the headset, the chatter of the pilots, and the muffled roar of the helicopter.

It sounded a little like ... whispers? Again.

"RPG!" Hampton shouted, and I spun my head to look where he was pointing. He shouted some other stuff, direction and bearing, but I was too busy looking out the side of the window. A contrail zipped through the sky toward us, an unerring finger pressing toward its mark. It disappeared behind us and I heard an explosion.

The helicopter pitched, gravity gave out, and we dropped into a spin that was as sudden as a car crash. We went around three times, and I suddenly felt like I was in a washing machine, yanked in a hard circle by centrifugal force as we descended. I didn't count, but it was seconds before I felt and saw the first tree impact the side of the helo. It hit the closed door and shattered the windows on that side, showering me with glass.

The world slowed down around me, and I watched Scott close his eyes as we dropped the last fifty feet. The impact was sickening, the lurch and crash like the world ending around me. My head snapped back against the seat, all sound of whispers forgotten, and I collapsed into blackness.

50.

Natasya

"Idiot," she pronounced, staring at the empty seat where Simmons had been sitting a moment earlier. She'd looked out the side of the chopper to see the RPG take down their pursuers, and when she'd looked back Simmons had been gone, taking their other unexpected passenger with him. The two remaining mercenaries were exchanging glances as well, but her eyes were locked on Vitalik, and his on hers.

"If she was in the helicopter, perhaps the landing killed her?" he asked, sounding hopeful.

Natasya pursed her lips. "Perhaps. But would you care to gamble your life on that?"

Vitalik's eyes fell. "Perhaps not." He looked out the open door where Simmons had jumped. "Do you think the—" he looked at his headset as though it were watching him, "—the voice is done with us?"

Natasya looked at her own headset, and down at the phone. Its faceplate was black, dead, and it had not responded to an attempt to turn it on a moment ago. She tried again, getting a similar response. "I don't know how this technology works, but coupled with the absence of her presence on our headphones, yes, I would suspect betrayal." She glanced back, as though she could see the crashed helicopter miles behind them. "One last hedge, one final smokescreen to be sure her

248

beloved returns to her safely."

Vitalik pursed his lips. "We're the rabbit the dogs are to run down, then, if they live?"

Natasya felt the crude sense of being used that she hadn't felt since her training days with the KGB. "Yes." It made her want to spit. "That would appear to be us."

51.

Sienna

I awoke to screams, but they were all in my head.

Sienna!

Wake up!

"I'm awake," I muttered, feeling my shoulders against the straps. "I'm awake." I looked to my left, expecting Scott to be the one speaking to me, but his head was tilted sideways, his eyes closed. I looked around the helicopter in alarm, and found only Jeremy Hampton moving, moaning softly.

Who the hell was talking to me?

Sienna! Zack Davis shouted in my head, snapping me out of my torpor. I battled with the straps, fumbling for the buckle and slipping them off my shoulders.

Welcome back, Roberto Bastian said. *You've got a pretty FUBAR situation here.*

Nothing new about that, Eve Kappler added.

Same old story, Bjorn agreed.

"Ugh," I said, shaking my head, which was aching. "It's nice to see all of you, too." I ripped the straps from Scott's body and thrust fingers against his neck in a moment of panic.

There was a pulse.

Whew.

His eyelids fluttered and he looked up at me, dazed. "Sienna?"

I kissed him full on the mouth, relief overwhelming my good sense as I held my hands to his cheeks. I should have done this before, before my powers came back. I could have done it for longer … could have done it forever.

Uh … whoa, Zack said.

Sigh, Aleksandr Gavrikov added, a sound of mild exasperation.

I broke after counting off six seconds and looked right in Scott's eyes. He blinked again, face vacant. "What … was that for?"

I felt a well of emotion inside and capped it. "Just … glad you're okay." I looked again around the helicopter cabin, the dim gunmetal dark in the night.

But not dark enough to hide that it was a tomb, filled with the bodies of the Hostage Rescue Team.

"Ouch," Jeremy Hampton said, and I turned to see him easing out of his seat. He winced, then started checking pulses to confirm what I already knew. "Dammit." He tapped the headset he was still wearing. "This thing's out."

I fumbled for my earpiece and found it missing. I looked around and caught a hint of glowing light on the deck and swept it up in my hand, shoving it in my ear. "Anybody there?"

"Still here," J.J. said tensely. "Got Harper on the line, she's here now. And Reed. Not Scott, though. Not sure what happened to—"

"Our chopper got shot down," I said brusquely, no time for anything but business. "Harper, I need eyes on Eden Prairie airport."

"Well, this must be your lucky night, because I've got eyes on Eden Prairie airport," she said. "Clearly I'm growing psychic metahuman powers."

"If only," I muttered, banging my head on the chopper's ceiling as I stood. Scott was trying to stand, weakly. He looked disoriented, possibly concussed. "We've got wounded here."

"You're in the middle of a field at gridpoint—" Harper started.

"Just send medical," I said and stepped out into the freezing night. I was only wearing a windbreaker, and it didn't do squat to break the howling, frigid wind that swept down on me across the field I was standing in. There was a massive oak a few feet away, the one we must have hit when we came down.

"What are you gonna do?" Reed asked, tentative, in my ear as I stood there, staring at the sky. It was showing a hint of purple, somewhere on the far horizon. Was it really getting close to morning?

"What I have to, I hope," I said, then stared at the sky.

Gavrikov? I asked, inside.

Yes? came the blessed reply.

I fell my skin shiver in the cold. *Can we?*

There was a pause that lasted a night. *Yes. I think so.*

And I felt my feet lift off the ground.

"Whoa," Jeremy Hampton said, standing at the door of the chopper, Scott's arm around his shoulder. "I bet this is gonna be good."

"Not for everybody," I said with a chilling fury as I lifted up into the air, soaring into the night and arcing toward the eastern sky.

For at least a few people, it was going to be the last night of their lives.

52.

Natasya

She was out of the helicopter before it landed, dropping out the side and floating to the ground, feet landing solidly on the tarmac as she headed toward the plane. It was there, waiting, as promised, even though nothing else had seemed to go their way. Natasya felt like she was running down an empty hallway, pursued, and the thing—the person—that was dogging her was only steps behind now.

She shouldn't have felt that way; she'd watched the chopper go down. That was the sort of thing that could kill a person. Maybe had, if she was very lucky.

But after the events of this night, lucky was one thing that Natasya did not feel.

She half expected the plane to be empty, the doors closed, but the helicopter pilot hurried over as soon as he had landed, went straight to the cockpit. So they did have a pilot, after all. The plane was a newer-looking thing, far different from what she'd been used to before she'd made the fateful decision she'd made, the one that had landed her in prison for thirty years.

Times changed. Enemies changed. She sighed. They were both getting worse, and there was nothing she could do about it.

"You planning to fly yourself to Cuba?" Vitalik said with a smile as he ran up the open steps onto the plane. He was feeling the light relief, sure they were free and clear.

Natasya felt nothing of the sort. "Only if I have to." She did not smile.

The last two mercenaries boarded in a hurry. Surely they didn't care to be left behind in the United States. Which was wise, because they'd certainly be hunted by every single resource the Americans had available to them.

Natasya stared into the night, and she could feel day approaching. The chill seeped into her clothes; the chill of the air, the chill of what had happened. Thirty years in hell, and now this. It had seemed too good to be true, and it had turned out to be just that. So much promise the voice had offered; but if they made it to Cuba, the promise would at least be fulfilled to some extent. Natasya had spit in the eye of the Americans, after all, given them a firm, open-handed slap to their capitalist crotches. They'd felt it, surely. Would feel it more, soon.

Was the comeuppance worth it?

Perhaps more than what she'd done her time in the gulag for, at least.

"Come on, Natasya!" Vitalik called from the entry to the plane. The stairs were built into the door, and he looked like he wanted to get going. She could hear it starting up, the sound of mechanical things moving in the still night.

With nothing but a hint of dawn on the horizon and a feeling of foreboding in her gut, Natasya headed for the plane. Luck. That was what was needed here. It was the only thing that would carry her through. Certainly not that damned voice, because she'd gotten what she'd wanted and called it done. Now it was all down to luck, Natasya knew, luck and her own skills. And she didn't have much faith left in the latter to save her from Sienna Nealon.

53.

Sienna

The wind roared in my face like an old friend, whipping my jacket around my body as I flew. I felt reinvigorated. The pain in my shoulder from the cut had vanished like half my troubles, and now I was staring down the eastern horizon as I soared toward Eden Prairie airport.

"Harper," I said, "what's the status?"

"Got a plane taking off right now," Harper replied, terse. "Gulfstream of some type, maybe. It's in the air."

"Eden Prairie PD have the airport surrounded," J.J. threw in. "I gotta jump off to talk to law enforcement, BRB."

I stared ahead in befuddlement until I realized BRB must be code for "Be right back."

"Sienna," Reed said, "the hostages are safe, campus is clear." He sounded more than a little reluctant, and I thought it might be because I'd ... well, you know. Ditched him. It wasn't. "I've got someone here who wants to talk to you."

"Oh, goody," I said, narrowing down by his tone who it might be. I had a suspicion.

"Nealon?" came the blunt inquiry of Andrew Phillips.

I left a few possible replies in the wind before I finally came up with one suitable for the occasion. "Yo."

"What's going on?" he asked me, even as ever.

"Well, apparently your plan to invite the Russians over for

a party was a bad idea …"

"What's your current status?" he amended, not sounding too happy.

"I'm zipping through the air at about a thousand feet, heading to Eden Prairie to catch their plane." I sniffed, and felt all my nose hairs freeze. "What's up with you?"

There was a long pause. "You are cleared to do … whatever you think appropriate. Act at your discretion."

"Been doin' that all night," I said. "Shouldn't be a stretch to keep on with it."

"I noticed some of your handiwork around campus," he said.

"You rethinking that discretion thing?"

He was silent for a moment. "We'll talk about it after. Go get 'em, Tigress."

I felt my face sketch a frown. "Will do, Euphrates."

"Man," J.J. said, coming back on, "is this thing over yet? I just, like, want to go home and play some *Destiny*. I got Crucibling to do." He paused, and I smelled a set-up line. "Or Cruci-BALLIN' if you know what I mean!" He laughed, and it turned into a snort.

I just shook my head as I caught sight of a plane lifting off into the clear sky ahead. "I feel like I never know what you mean. And that's probably a good thing."

"Who is this?" Phillips asked, breaking into the conversation. "Who's on the call?"

"Is that Phillips?" J.J. asked, one step below panic. "No one, man. No one is on this call. You're … you're having post-traumatic stress hallucinations. Err … post chemical-exposure delusions. Delirium!"

"J.J., don't be an idiot," I said as I honed in on my target. They were not getting away. "You've saved a lot of lives tonight. You're not going to get in trouble for being a weirdo on an open channel." Probably. Up to Phillips, I guess.

"I hate to interrupt this," Harper said, "but Sienna … what's your plan for dealing with the plane?"

I smiled as I turned on the afterburners and went supersonic. Phillips had told me to act at my discretion …

54.

Natasya

The plane rattled as it rose, the subtle, low thunder that would shake a teacup in its saucer, would send light tremors through a body. Natasya held tight to her armrests, facing forward, watching the bulkhead, waiting. She was counting seconds, waiting for something to happen, though she didn't know exactly what. The sky to fall, the world to end.

Something.

Anything.

The plane rattled again, another subtle vibration. The pilot's chatter was barely audible, the cockpit door standing open because no one had bothered to shut it before takeoff. The mood had been tense, but now it seemed ten thousand kilos lighter, and Vitalik was actually joking with one of the mercenaries. They were chortling among themselves because the plane was off the ground now, because they would be in Cuba in a little over three hours, and they'd be flying low to avoid radar most of the way.

It should be clear sailing. A little more stressful if the authorities were after them, but hardly a deal-breaker. The hard part was behind them, in theory.

The plane rattled again, and Natasya squeezed her hand rest a little harder.

"Hey," Vitalik said, low, staring across at her. "It's okay.

We made it."

"This isn't Cuba yet," she cautioned him.

"It's not far," he replied. He was smiling at her. He did that sometimes, thinking he could charm her like he did other women. It hadn't worked so far; she was wise to his type before she'd ever even met him. "Relax."

"I'll relax when I'm on the tarmac in Havana and been welcomed with open arms by our comrades," she said, but the moment after she said it, she knew it wasn't true.

She'd be looking over her shoulder for the rest of her life.

She was about to voice one of these thoughts to Vitalik when the pilot spoke loud enough she could hear him even in the cabin.

"What the hell is that?"

And then the world exploded around her.

55.

Sienna

Bringing a plane out of the sky isn't very hard, especially a small, two-engine plane like the one my targets were riding in. All I'd have had to do was rip the engines off, or drop something in there to blow them up, then let Sir Isaac Newton's most famous discovery work its magic.

But it lacked style. It lacked pizzazz.

It's not good enough, Sienna, Wolfe said. *Not … ruthless enough.*

Sadly, on this point, Sir Devious Evil Serial Killer and I agreed.

So, instead, I flew at them and smashed into the plane at supersonic speed, feet first.

As far as brilliant ideas went, it was not among my best. It was actually cavalier and reckless and daft and—you get the point, insert various other synonyms for "stupid" here.

But after a night of feeling like these people were hounding my every step, running me to ground, it felt damned good to just unleash some good old-fashioned havoc into their annoying little lives.

I used Wolfe's power to heal as I was smashing into the plane. The whole thing seemed to happen in slow motion now that my metahuman reflexes had returned. I crashed into the cockpit, kept going through the door to the passenger cabin, and then hit the back wall hard enough to rip the plane in half with the concussive force that I'd brought with me, like a meteor hitting the earth.

My clothes ripped and tore, my skin shredded and reformed, my bones shattered and regrew, and when it was over, I hovered in mid-air, a little dazed, and watched the wreckage of a Gulfstream jet spiral down to the empty farmland below in about ten thousand pieces.

Well, nine thousand and ninety-nine pieces, anyway. One of them wasn't falling.

"Hello, Natasya," I said, and she slowly moved up to hover in front of me. Her lip was bleeding, her ears had blood dripping out of both canals. She had a lot of lacerations, and she held her arm at a funny angle, like it hurt to straighten it. "So … your power is that you can fly?"

"Yes," she said, still in that flawless English.

"Kinda useful, isn't it?" There was no reason not to be polite now. She had the look that told me she was about a half-inch from passing out.

"It has its purposes," she replied.

"If you got to be the unit-commanding badass you are with nothing but flying as a power," I said, looking at her evenly, "you must have developed quite the reputation in the Soviet Army."

She stared back at me. "I suspect mine mirrors your own," she said, sounding … weary. I wondered why she hadn't run, hadn't tried to hide in the wreckage and pretend to die. It would have been a smart move.

Then I saw her eyes. They were … empty. Haunted. She'd been pursued all night, too, I realized. Every time I'd crammed one of her plans to kill me back in her face, the screws must have tightened somehow.

Now she was as afraid of me any one of those prisoners I'd bluffed back into their cells earlier in the night. Three decades in a prison of her own, and now she was looking at me with that same fear I'd seen from them. She couldn't beat me. She knew it. She hadn't stood a chance even when I was depowered; she didn't have a hope now that I was staring her down with everything at my disposal.

She'd built her reputation on unrelenting viciousness, on doing whatever it took to get the job done. And tonight she'd finally met someone just like her, but maybe a few degrees meaner.

"How do you want this to go?" I asked.

She looked at me with bare misery. "I want to go to Cuba." There wasn't a note of hope in her voice that told me she believed it was even possible.

I just stared back at her. "How do you want this to go down?" I asked again, with a little more emphasis this time. "A cell? Or …"

Now she just looked pained. "No. No more imprisonment. Please."

I stared at her, and I felt … pity. She saw the look in my eyes, and she knew. There was a hint of a plea in there. She knew she was at my mercy, that I could drag her back to the Cube and stick her in the ground forever if I wanted to. She'd be another part of my collection, another unwilling soul serving out a sentence for her crimes that she could never outrun.

She didn't want it, of course, but she'd committed the crime, and she should have to serve the time, right?

I let out a deep sigh, and stared at her pleading eyes again, and I knew what she was asking of me. And it was well within my power to give it. "Who's the brain?" I asked.

She shook her head. "I don't know who she is. She contacted us by phone, by computer. She presented a plan. Made an offer. We never met face to face, never exchanged a name. She wanted Simmons, though. He's important to her." I could tell by the way she said it that this was her plea bargain.

"Okay," I said, resigned, and I floated toward her. She didn't run, and when I got close enough, she turned away from me.

"I've fought your government for most of my life," she

said, into the quiet night. "It was always ideological, never personal. Do me a professional courtesy … and make it quick."

So I punched her in the back of the head hard enough to stun a bull.

I could have shot her, I guess, but I didn't feel that merciful. She'd been part of a conspiracy to commit terrorist acts on my agency, and her actions had contributed to the deaths of several members of the FBI's Hostage Rescue Team. She'd let Anselmo Serafini out of my jail, sent people to kill me. My mercy has limits.

I watched her fall out of the sky without a bit of remorse.

56.

I floated to the earth to do my duty, to confirm the kill. I found her impaled on a pine tree in a small wood, head and neck askew in a way that told me she was finished. I floated to the ground and felt my feet sink into the snow as I looked out across the wreckage of the plane.

Vitalik was nearby, already dead. It wasn't a pretty sight, because these sorts of things never are. It looked like he'd tried to save himself by shooting frost at the ground, but it hadn't slowed his impact enough to keep him alive. A couple other guys wearing tac vests were also dead. I searched and searched, my fingers numb from the cold, my nose frozen, but I could not—for the life of me—find Eric Simmons's body anywhere.

"Sienna?" Reed asked over the earpiece. "Are you coming back?"

I stood in the middle of a clearing, the sun rising over the rolling hills behind some trees, turning the sky a fiery shade of orange. The little twigs and branches of dead saplings poked out of the snow as I stood there, the wind rolling over me. Snow stirred and drifted, a little cloud like dust caught on the breeze. "Yeah," I said, satisfied with the view but not the final conclusion I'd come to. "I'll be right there."

Simmons had gotten away.

57.

I set down outside headquarters in the middle of a sea of blue and red police lights that were warring with the orange of the dawn. Reed was standing there waiting, along with Andrew Phillips, who had his arms folded over his massive chest, surveying everything with a disinterested eye. Also, his lips were puckered in displeasure, which I assume was related to his first week on the job being a massive screw-up. Try and keep that one under the radar, dick.

"Glad you made it back," Reed said before my feet even touched the ground. He looked a little worried. "And that you got your powers back."

"Yeah," I said, and turned my attention rather darkly to Phillips. "Did you know what got stolen from that chemical weapons depot?"

"No," Phillips replied, staring back at me evenly.

I didn't like that answer, so I tried for another one. "Did you know that the government had a chemical weapon for suppressing metahuman powers?"

Not an inch of movement in that face. "Yes." He must have seen the surprise on mine, because he went on. "You shouldn't be all that surprised; the government's known about metas since the days when they held a convention in Philadelphia to decide how to run this country. Now that modern chemistry has brought us to the point where we can kill our fellow humans by the millions if need be, why wouldn't someone have turned that expertise toward something less lethal and more useful?"

"Useful?" Reed snapped. "Might have been useful when we were in the fight for our lives against Sovereign."

Phillips didn't even blink. "It didn't exist then. It was created specifically to stop Sovereign, but it wasn't ready until after you'd already killed him."

"And now they're keeping it around, I assume?" I asked without surprise. Phillips had made a few annoyingly good points.

"Fair assumption," he said.

"Why?" Reed asked. I could tell he was a lot more exercised about this whole thing than I was.

Phillips looked straight at me, and I could tell what he was thinking, so I took the words right out of his mouth. "In case we quit," I said. Phillips gave me a subtle nod; on anyone else, it might have been approval.

"I'll expect your report later today," Phillips said, turning away from me. I guess we were done with having a conversation.

"What?" I asked.

"You've got a senator and two members of congress who want an explanation for what happened to them tonight," Phillips said, turning back. "Something they can share with the press, something that makes the situation seem under control."

"Most of the perpetrators are dead," I replied. "Report over."

"Give me something written," he said, starting to walk away, "Directions to take the investigation from here, an accounting of what happened as best you remember. Try to keep it to five thousand words or less. Also, you'll have to meet with Jackie to prep for at least one interview, maybe more." He disappeared into a crowd of police, back into headquarters.

"What the hell, I've got homework?" I asked. "What is this, high school?"

"If it was, you'd be having the time of your life, wouldn't you?" Reed cracked. I turned to face him, but I could see that not all was quite right with him. He had that look on his face that said we were going to have a discussion at some point. Sooner rather than later, I suspected.

I heard a car come to a stop and turned to see Scott easing out of a local PD patrol car, Jeremy Hampton stepping out of the other side. They both took in the scene with a quick look and headed over to me. Scott was taking his time, but Hampton looked like he was back to normal, not a hint of injury.

"Ms. Nealon," Hampton said, doing that finger to the forehead, tip of the hat salute again. "I'm pleased to see you made it through everything all right." His lips were tightly pursed, and I remembered again the helicopter.

"I'm sorry about your men, Mr. Hampton," and I watched him wince. "You have my condolences."

"I'm just glad you got the ones responsible," Hampton said. "I hope we get a chance to work together in the future, under better circumstances." He did that same non-regulation salute again before walking off toward some unmarked cars in the distance. I assumed they were FBI, then I caught a glimpse of Agent Li in the midst of them and knew it for a fact.

"You still know how to throw a party, Sienna," Scott said, and I turned back to him. He was holding himself at a little bit of an angle, like he was hurting, and I kept myself from hugging him.

I laughed, faintly, though it was mostly to humor him. "Thank you for coming, Scott."

His face clouded slightly, like he was trying to remember something. "Why wouldn't I? I couldn't leave a couple friends in danger, not on something like this."

"You are the man," Reed said, and took his hand in a bro-shake-turned-fistbump. It was very masculine.

"I should get home," Scott said, cringing as he turned his body maybe a little too fast. "Get a shower, go to bed. Maybe

266

if I get back soon, I won't have to explain why I look like I've been out all night fighting to my parents."

"Dude, you live with your mom and dad?" Reed asked.

Scott smiled, a little embarrassed. "What? They've got a guest wing."

I shook my head at him. "Hide your shame, fellow millennial. Don't wear it on your sleeve for all to see."

His smile crinkled his eyes in a way that I hadn't seen from him in … longer than I can remember. "Take care, Sienna." He shifted his gaze to my brother. "Reed, you too." With that, I saw him head toward a cop car, presumably to get a ride back to wherever he'd parked when he came to save my sorry bacon.

Reed and I watched him go. "That was interesting," my brother said after he was out of earshot. Which, for a meta, takes a while.

"What?" I asked, my gaze falling on Ariadne, who was sitting just inside the lobby with some of the other hostages, a blanket wrapped around her shoulders. Based on the look on her face, part of me thought I should go talk to her. She'd killed someone tonight, after all. That was a heady feeling.

I decided against it. My first kill was so long ago I could barely remember it at this point, and there had been so very many between then and now that part of me felt like I had absolutely nothing to share with her that would be of interest.

"Scott," Reed said, drawing my attention back to the question he posed. "And you. I would have thought, after the breakup you had, things would be … I don't know … a little more … emotional … between the two of you."

I felt my face freeze, and it had nothing to do with being exposed to frigid air all night. "We're all grown-ups here," I said and turned to walk away, back toward the dormitory building. He followed and said nothing, but I could tell by the silence that he didn't quite believe me.

58.

I opened the door to my quarters, and my faithful dog greeted me with a wagging tail and a little mewl. I fell into a chair and patted his head, only then realizing that my brother had followed me in and was now standing by the door, frowning.

"What?" I asked, craning my neck to look at him. Sleep would be a mercy for me at this point, not that he was inclined to grant it. A flash of what I'd done to Natasya Sokolov came back to me, and I found myself strangely untroubled.

"Where was your dog when we were here earlier?" he asked, staring at my mutt.

"Hiding, probably," I said, letting my head roll back onto the back of the couch. "Gunfire, explosions going on, strangers all up in this area … not the sort of things dogs like to be around for, you know."

"Huh," Reed said, and shrugged. "Those Russians … did you ever get the background on them?"

"Just the basics in the files," I said, "woefully incomplete. Why?"

"At the bottom of what I read was kind of a footnote," he said, still standing at the entry, "sort of half supposition, half backchannel intel, maybe. Something about how the four of them had gotten sent to that prison in the first place, the one in Siberia."

"Interesting," I said. "Go on."

"They rebelled against the Soviet government for some

reason," Reed said, shuffling between his feet. This wasn't the conversation he wanted to have. This was the conversation he was killing time with until he got his courage up. "But the thing I want to know … is if these guys were the ones who rebelled against the government … who do you suppose stopped them? And where do you think those people … or person … are now, whoever they are?"

"That's a chilling thought," I said. It wasn't something I wanted to contemplate the repercussions of. I stared at him, shuffling, and just asked. "What's on your mind?"

He didn't answer at first, and it gave me time to wonder if this was going to be one of those conversations where I just let him think he was right to shut him up for a while. I saw him mentally shift gears, and then we were off to the races. "There's a part of you that really thrives on the righteous kill, doesn't it?"

I stared at him, then blinked. Twice. "I do what I have to," I said.

"No," he said and wandered past the painting I had on the wall outside the kitchen. He acted like he was going to inspect it, like he hadn't seen it a million times. "You like the fury that comes when someone deserves it. That fills you up, doesn't it?"

"Are you asking me if I like killing people?" I asked, still feeling tired. "Are you asking me if I'm a psychopath or—"

"No," he said, and his eyes fell on me. "But I am asking you why you don't seem to have a problem with it."

"Why I don't have a problem with … what?" I asked, staring back at him dully. I was so tired. "Doing … what I just did tonight?"

"What you just did tonight …" He chuckled, but it was mirthless, more of an expression of astonishment than humor. "Sienna, you killed twenty? Thirty? I don't even know how many people you killed tonight. I killed one, and I feel like I'm about to shake apart. Ariadne killed someone tonight and she looked like she was ready to break down and cry." He looked me up and down. "You look like you're ready for a nap, one that'll be filled with peaceful dreams instead of the screams of the dead."

I just stared back at him. "Fun fact: the dead don't scream. Only the living can do that."

"Jesus," he breathed.

"Let me spin a little story for you," I said, getting to my feet, slowly. "You walk into that prison tonight. Warden Reed. Man in charge." I head for the fridge, but I swivel my head to look at him the whole time. "You're out front, you're the big man on campus, and you have to get those assholes back in their cells without a gust of wind at your command." I opened the fridge and found it pretty much empty, apparently still lacking the ability to spontaneously fill itself. Thwarted again. Where could I get a miniature quiche at this hour, I wondered? I shut it and stared back at him. "Can you do it?"

I saw the resistance, the desire to change the subject, the urge to lie, all pass across his face in a second. "No," he finally said.

"No," I said quietly. "You can't. They'd have charged you. They'd have killed you. Torn you up like a wet tissue in the wind." I opened a cabinet, even though I knew already what I'd find. Empty. "I'm a hard person because I have to be. Anyone else couldn't have walked into that prison and bluffed those guys back into their cells."

Reed stared at me flatly. "I doubt Crow Vincent considered you blowing his head off a bluff."

"It was a promise," I said. "One I couldn't keep." *But not for lack of wanting,* I didn't say. I didn't need to. It was implied, because I'm me. "These prisoners ... they're animals. Animals who prey on a system that's not equipped to deal with them. They deserve to live in the jungle, not in civilization with the rest of humanity."

I could see the questions brewing behind his eyes. "How does that ... what you do ... make you any better than them? Any more deserving of ... living with humanity?"

I felt a cold chill run over me. "Reed … I don't." I felt the gulf between us. "I don't live with humanity." I felt my eyes settle lower, on the floor. "I wasn't raised to live with humanity. I was raised apart. And I'll always be apart."

I don't know how he would have reacted to that, and as it happened, I didn't get the chance to find out because the phone rang. Long, urgent tones, filling the air with that irritating sound. I needed an excuse to stop talking anyway, so I answered it. "Hel—"

I didn't even get it out before J.J. started talking. "So, uhm, yeah, there's a problem. Again."

I stared at Reed, newly emboldened by the interruption to make eye contact again. "Of course there is. What, specifically, is this particular problem?"

"We've got all these emergency crews wandering around here, and they're picking things over," J.J. said. "They got to the hostage place on the fourth floor, trying to figure out what happened there to reconstruct it for forensics and all that fun stuff—"

I put him on speakerphone so Reed could share the verbal diarrhea. He gave me a pitying look.

"—so anyway, I came out of the closet to walk them through it all—literally, no jokes here, guys, I'm not—you know, not that there's anything wrong with, you know, what with Ariadne and all—"

"J.J.," I said. I would liked to have been sleeping already.

"Anyhoo," he got back to it, "I came up to the fourth floor to look it over with them, and you remember that melted heap of slag where you set infinite fire to Anselmo?"

I stared at Reed. He stared at me, brow puckered with curiosity. "Vaguely," I said, prompting my brother to give me a disappointed look.

"Yeah, well," J.J. said, "there's nothing left."

"Of Anselmo?" I asked. "Good. I'm sure he'll be mourned by—oh, right, not a damned soul on the planet."

"No, I'm saying there's not much left," J.J. said. "Like, if he had melted to slag, there should have been tons of organic material, but as it is—"

"J.J.! The point, please. Before I fall asleep right here on the phone." I hoped this story had a happy ending, but my stomach was warning me it might not.

"I rewound the security footage," J.J. said, "to when he got burned, and, uh … well, guys … it looks like Eric Simmons came and carried him to the helicopter. Took him along on their flight into adventure."

Reed looked at me, and he was cool on the outside. I could tell he was in low-grade panic on the inside, though. "Did you see anything at the crash site that could be—"

"No," I said, playing it back in my mind. "No. I didn't." I looked Reed straight in the eye. "He wasn't there."

And I felt my empty, acid-riddled stomach drop.

That meant Anselmo Serafini and Eric Simmons were *both* still out there, along with the brains of this whole operation … and probably mad as hell at *me*.

59.

Simmons

The trip from Minneapolis to Omaha took the better part of the day, because the driver stuck to back roads and avoided the interstates. "Better to avoid the government eye," he said, in an accent right out of Simmons's vision of every hillbilly movie ever. But he kept the pickup moving fast over those back roads, all the way to the farm outside of town.

They pulled up as the sun was setting, Simmons feeling like his ass was gonna fall off and not sorry to have seen the last of that drive. He'd stuck his head out the window every now and again, to make sure someone wasn't flying over him. He'd talked to Cassidy on the way. She was keeping an eye on them, mostly. Whenever the satellites she had a backdoor into passed overhead, anyway. She said it was clear.

Twelve hours and hell if he knew how many miles later, they were there. It wasn't so bad on him; he was just glad to get out of the prison. It had to be hell on Anselmo, though. That poor guy.

The driver threw the pickup into park and just got out. Left Simmons sitting there, Anselmo leaning over on his shoulder. Anselmo had been leaning on his shoulder the whole trip. It felt a little gross, given how the dude looked at this point, but when Eric lifted the Italian's face off his shirt at that first diner where they'd stopped for lunch, it hadn't left anything liquid behind, so it was all good.

"Dude," Eric said as the driver walked away, "a little help here?" The driver just kept on walking, heading for the main house, pulled open an old, wooden screen door and stepped inside, letting it shut behind him with a clatter. He'd kinda given the impression throughout the ride that he was a dick. His name was even Richard, though he didn't go by it or Dick. He'd shown up when Eric and Anselmo had fallen out of the helicopter, driving the pickup with an RPG tube still smoking in the back, and he'd introduced himself as Clyde, Jr.

"Damn, Anselmo," Eric said, and the Italian stirred a little at his side. He still smelled like burned pizza or something, just awful. They'd bought him some cheap clothes at a gas station, but they were sticking to him. He had no hair, either, but that was the least of his problems. "I guess we're gonna have to do this ourselves."

Anselmo made a weak, gurgling noise. That was about all he'd been capable of the whole trip.

Eric opened the passenger door of the pickup and stepped out, propping Anselmo against the seat, holding him up with one hand. The air was filled with a dry, dusty aroma. There was no snow on the ground here, which felt weird after driving through the blizzard-drenched states of Minnesota and then Iowa. Nice change, though.

"Dude, Anselmo," Eric said, looking in at him, "can you walk?" He looked at the man, and faint slits of eyelids opened enough for him to see someone staring back at him. "Can you hear me, man?"

"I ... can hear you," Anselmo said. Those were the first words he'd spoken all day.

"Whew," Eric said, and made a show of mopping his brow. He looked out across the flat horizon at the empty fields and took it all in. It damned sure wasn't L.A. "We're here, man. We gotta go inside. Do a meet and greet with our new friends."

Anselmo barely registered that. "Friends …?"

"Yeah, man, Cassidy found us some …" Eric waved his hands at him. "Forget it, just—let's go in. I'll explain when we get there."

"All right," Anselmo said, and he spoke with a rasp of his own. Sounded a little like Cassidy that way, actually. Weird. Probably inhaled some of that fire stuff that bitch had used on him, burned his airways. Eric took him in hand and started carrying him, helping him walk. His skin felt funny, all ridged and knobby, scarred all over.

"Hello?" Eric asked as he opened the screen door. The inner door was open and something smelled like it was frying inside. Kinda made Eric feel a little sick, that smell. He didn't do fried stuff; it messed with his stomach. "Anybody here?"

A woman appeared at the edge of the porch. She was a pretty big lady, apron hanging off her neck and covering her front as best it could. It missed a lot of ground, but he could see a polka-dotted shirt beneath it, and she wore a pair of brown pants that looked ill-fitting to say the least. "Well, come on in," she said. Her face was dowdy, with a pinched line for a mouth. She looked at him, half-carrying Anselmo, and disapproval showed instantly. "Gawd, he looks like the devil himself did a number on him."

"He kinda got burned," Eric said, dragging Anselmo in past her. She moved to let him through, but she didn't offer any help.

"Well, that much is obvious even to the unpracticed eye," she said with a drawling accent. "Is he pussing?"

Simmons blinked. "What?"

"Is he dripping puss?" she asked again, taking him for a moron. "Clearly he's had some injuries. I just don't want him dripping anything foul on my upholstery."

Now that he was inside, he got a look at her living room and wasn't sure why she was worrying. The couch was ripped in at least twenty places and looked like it might have been old when the seventies were just starting. "Ummm … just set him over here?"

She chewed on that for a minute. "All right," she finally conceded, like it was a major imposition.

Eric set him down carefully. There wasn't an inch of Anselmo that wasn't scarred. It was like nothing he'd ever seen before on a meta, like his skin had tried to regrow itself where it had been lost, but stretched over boiling metal or something. He had ripples everywhere, like stuff was still under his skin, and none of it was smooth. The man was a freak-show attraction, and if his body hadn't healed it by now, Simmons kinda doubted it would ever heal.

Simmons looked back at the dowdy woman, but she was already on her way back to the kitchen. "Can I ... get something to drink?"

"There's beer in the fridge," the woman answered, disappearing into a side room. He stood there in the room for a moment, looking around at ratty decorations—a couple of dusty deer heads on the wall, a mirror with a beer brand on it, an old box TV, not a flatscreen, and decaying furniture.

What the hell was Cassidy thinking, dragging him to a place like this?

He heard talk coming from where the woman had gone, so he followed. Nothing to do here but listen to Anselmo moan in his state of semi-consciousness anyway.

Eric passed into a goldenrod kitchen that hadn't been painted in a few decades. He was starting to see a theme in this place. There was another woman waiting in there, features similar enough to the woman he'd met before to mark her as a daughter. Had to be a daughter. "Hi," Eric said, smiling tightly at his hosts.

There had been some talk going on, but it shushed the minute he entered the kitchen. The daughter was sitting in a chair at the table and stared at him, taking stock. She finally just nodded her head toward an archway over her shoulder. "She's through there, in the parlor." Like there was no other reason he was talking to her. He had to admit, if he hadn't been in her home … he wouldn't have.

Her blessing given, Eric went on through. The room beyond had old floorboards darkened with age, no carpet to hide them. Here he was greeted with furniture that was maybe a little newer. Leatherbound sofas sat side by side, and the driver was on one of them, attention transfixed on a TV in front of him. This was a flatscreen. The place looked like a den, whereas the other room beyond the kitchen looked like someone's grandma's sitting room, from the days when they had sitting rooms.

"GO GO GO GO!" the driver shouted, so loudly and suddenly that Eric jumped back. The driver—Clyde Jr.—had his attention focused on the screen in front of him, hadn't even noticed Eric in the room.

Eric watched for a minute; it was a football game on. "Who's playing?"

"OSU, of course," the driver said, like he was stupid for even asking.

Eric did feel stupid. Felt stupid for coming here, stupid for staying. But he had business to attend to. He needed to find Cassidy. Couldn't leave without her. "Where's—" he started to ask.

"GO GO GO, you stupid bastard, RUN!" Clyde Jr. yelled, like that would somehow influence the events unfolding before him. Hell of a cheerleader, that guy.

Eric started to leave, caught a whiff of something familiar—maybe a little pot in the air, maybe a little something else—and stayed a second longer. He couldn't smoke around Cassidy. This smelled like it had been in the air a while, just traces, something that had happened a long time ago and was still lingering.

"She's over there, man," Clyde Jr. said, pointing to the corner. The place was so overstuffed with crap that Eric hadn't even noticed it there, hiding behind a quilt rack. He'd just taken it as part of the decor.

The chamber.

He walked over and tapped on the lid with one finger, a little message in Morse code. She liked it when he played cool, acted a little smart, did the slightly unexpected. It was all she could hope for, really. She had a brain unlike any other person on the planet, and surprising her was … well, on the big things, it was nearly impossible.

Sometimes, on the small things, though … it was all the fun in the world.

The lid cracked immediately, and smell of salty water from inside the chamber came rushing out. It was pretty reasonably sized, the sensory deprivation tank. The lid lifted end up, and the three different computer screens Cassidy had in front of her swung with the lid, safely clutched by their reticulating arms from falling into the saltwater solution that kept her afloat when she was inside. He caught the first glimpse of her pale face, heard the first gasp and wheeze as she tried to sit up. She fumbled for the inhaler that she kept in a waterproof pocket near the lid and forced it into her mouth, forming her lips from the smile of greeting into a closed O as she inhaled. Her eyes fluttered, and then she slipped the inhaler away and started to get up, reaching for him.

He pulled her out of the chamber and hugged her tight. It had been days, a week—he didn't even know. "Oh, baby," he lied, "I missed you so much."

"I missed you too," she said, slow and breathy. Her wet hair fell across his shoulder, she planted her cold lips to his neck and he shuddered. He hated the feel of her when she was just getting out of the tank. Her body was thin, skeletal; it felt weird compared to the other girls he'd been with. Being with Cassidy had pushed him in the opposite direction; when he was away from her now, he automatically went for the bigger girls. Like a reaction.

She pulled herself off of him, leaning against the chamber. He felt his wet clothes and ignored it; he'd had to make a lot of compromises to keep Cassidy in his life. But it was all worth it, having the biggest brain on the planet at your disposal. "You don't like our new hideout," she said, like it took all her genius to figure that out.

He took the den in with a sweeping look once more, and saw the older woman, the mother, standing in the archway to the kitchen. Just watching. "I, uh …" Eric started, trying to be diplomatic, "… I'm just trying to figure out why we're in Nebraska, baby."

"There's a real good reason," Cassidy said. "Because we needed help."

Eric looked it over again, expecting the place to change somehow. It didn't. "Well, now we have had the help, and we can go to … L.A., maybe? San Fran?" Even Denver would be a nice change from this. Or Aspen. He could do some snowboarding. It was close, wasn't it?

"Y'all gonna stay right here until I get what I was promised," the woman said from the archway. Eric turned to see her, arms folded over her apron.

"Eric," Cassidy said gently, "this is Ma. You already met her daughter, Denise, and her son. She's a … friend. We have something in common."

"Oh, yeah?" Eric asked, not taking his eyes off "Ma." Probably not her given name, he decided. "What's that?"

"Sienna Nealon killed my boy," Ma said, and she put her head down like a bull ready to charge as she said it. "My little Clyde. Left his two youngins behind without no daddy." She nodded to the driver, Clyde Jr. on the couch. "She needs to pay for that."

"We have a man on the inside of her agency," Cassidy said as Eric turned back to her. "He confirmed for the Clarys here what they'd already suspected. Heard it straight from her own lips that she killed him. They're …" Cassidy smiled, "… not the forgiving sorts." She leaned in a little closer to him, and he felt her wet hair against his neck again. Cold. "Like your friend Anselmo, I think." She nuzzled into him. "Like you … maybe?"

Eric stared straight ahead, at a faux wood-paneled wall that looked like it had been shit out of the dirtiest forest known to man.

Nebraska, huh?

Couldn't be all that bad.

"Maybe we could stay for a little while," Eric said, putting a hand against her head, feeling her cold, clammy skin against his. What was that old saying, about revenge and how it ought to be served? He'd prefer it hot, but Cassidy, she knew how to do it right. He looked around the room, saw Ma's face, and knew she was in for a helping of it exactly the same. "Have ourselves a little ... fun."

Sienna Nealon Will Return in

GROUNDED

Out of the Box
Book Four

Coming June 1, 2015!

Note From the Author

I had a world of fun with that one. Maybe you'd think after eleven books of Sienna as a main character, number twelve would start to feel boring for me, but NOPE. That one may have been the most fun one I've ever written. I love letting Sienna be Sienna, pitting her against some really bad people while I sit back and watch her do her thing. The other fun part of this one was gearing up the next big story arc, which will run from now until book six of the series. I call it the "Vengeful" arc, and I think you've probably gotten a taste of who we'll be dealing with in this storyline. But how it all unfolds? BWAHAHAHAH! That should be…surprising. These smaller stories are how I plan to handle things in Out of the Box; that way you'll see the end of this story arc by the end of 2015, and there'll be another for 2016, 2017, etc. for however long the series runs (still plotted at 25 books with an overarching storyline that is looser than Girl in the Box and won't fully pay off until then.

I've set a release date for book four. I make no promises about doing this for future installments. If you want to know when future books become available, take sixty seconds and sign up for my NEW RELEASE EMAIL ALERTS by visiting my website at www.robertjcrane.com. Don't let the caps lock scare you; I don't sell your information and I only send out emails when I have a new book out. The reason you should sign up for this is because I don't like to set release dates (it's this whole thing, you can find an answer on my website in the FAQ section), and even if you're following me on Facebook (robertJcrane (Author)) or Twitter (@robertJcrane), it's easy to miss my book announcements because…well, because social media is an imprecise thing.

Come join the Girl in the Box discussion on my website: http://www.robertjcrane.com !

Cheers,
Robert J. Crane

ACKNOWLEDGMENTS

Okay, I'll admit it. I've run out of new ways to thank people and make it interesting. I'll try again next book.

My thanks to these fine folks, without whom this book would not be possible:

Sarah Barbour, Jeff Bryan and Jo Evans – Editorial clean-up crew.

Nicolette Solomita – First reader.

Karri Klawiter – Cover by.

Polgarus Studios – Formatting.

The fans – For reading.

My parents, my kids, my wife – For all their help.

About the Author

Robert J. Crane is kind of an a-hole. Still, if you want to contact him:

Website: http://www.robertJcrane.com
Facebook: robertJcrane (Author)
Twitter: @robertJcrane
Email: cyrusdavidon@gmail.com

Other Works by Robert J. Crane

The Sanctuary Series
Epic Fantasy

Defender: The Sanctuary Series, Volume One
Avenger: The Sanctuary Series, Volume Two
Champion: The Sanctuary Series, Volume Three
Crusader: The Sanctuary Series, Volume Four
Sanctuary Tales, Volume One - A Short Story Collection
Thy Father's Shadow: The Sanctuary Series, Volume 4.5
Master: The Sanctuary Series, Volume Five
Fated in Darkness: The Sanctuary Series, Volume 5.5*
    (Coming in 2015!)
Warlord: The Sanctuary Series, Volume Six* (Coming in late
    2015!)

The Girl in the Box
and
Out of the Box
Contemporary Urban Fantasy

Alone: The Girl in the Box, Book 1
Untouched: The Girl in the Box, Book 2
Soulless: The Girl in the Box, Book 3
Family: The Girl in the Box, Book 4
Omega: The Girl in the Box, Book 5
Broken: The Girl in the Box, Book 6
Enemies: The Girl in the Box, Book 7
Legacy: The Girl in the Box, Book 8
Destiny: The Girl in the Box, Book 9
Power: The Girl in the Box, Book 10

Limitless: Out of the Box, Book 1
In the Wind: Out of the Box, Book 2
Ruthless: Out of the Box, Book 3)
Grounded: Out of the Box, Book 4* (Coming June 1, 2015!)
Tormented: Out of the Box, Book 5* (Coming September
    2015!)
Vengeful: Out of the Box, Book 6* (Coming December
    2015!)

Southern Watch
Contemporary Urban Fantasy

Called: Southern Watch, Book 1
Depths: Southern Watch, Book 2
Corrupted: Southern Watch, Book 3
Unearthed: Southern Watch, Book 4* (Coming Early 2015!)

* Forthcoming and subject to change

CPSIA information can be obtained
at www.ICGtesting.com
Printed in the USA
LVOW13s1511140317
527180LV00009B/604/P